Bello:

hidden talent rediscovered!

Bello is a digital only imprint of Pan Macmillan, established to breathe new life into previously published, classic books.

At Bello we believe in the timeless power of the imagination, of good story, narrative and entertainment and we want to use digital technology to ensure that many more readers can enjoy these books into the future.

We publish in ebook and Print on Demand formats to bring these wonderful books to new audiences.

About Bello:

www.panmacmillan.com/imprints/bello

About the author:

www.panmacmillan.com/author/andrewgarve

Andrew Garve

Andrew Garve is the pen name of Paul Winterton (1908–2001). He was born in Leicester and educated at the Hulme Grammar School, Manchester and Purley County School, Surrey, after which he took a degree in Economics at London University. He was on the staff of *The Economist* for four years, and then worked for fourteen years for the *London News Chronicle* as reporter, leader writer and foreign correspondent. He was assigned to Moscow from 1942–5, where he was also the correspondent of the BBC's Overseas Service.

After the war he turned to full-time writing of detective and adventure novels and produced more than forty-five books. His work was serialized, televised, broadcast, filmed and translated into some twenty languages. He is noted for his varied and unusual backgrounds – which have included Russia, newspaper offices, the West Indies, ocean sailing, the Australian outback, politics, mountaineering and forestry – and for never repeating a plot.

Andrew Garve was a founder member and first joint secretary of the Crime Writers' Association.

Andrew Garve

A PRESS OF SUSPECTS

First published in 1951 by Collins

This edition published 2012 by Bello
an imprint of Pan Macmillan, a division of Macmillan Publishers Limited
Pan Macmillan, 20 New Wharf Road, London N1 9RR
Basingstoke and Oxford
Associated companies throughout the world

www.panmacmillan.co.uk/bello

ISBN 978-1-4472-1532-5 EPUB
ISBN 978-1-4472-1531-8 POD

A CIP catalogue record for this book is available from the British Library.

Chapter One

At the wetter end of Fleet Street, close by the Crown Inn and not far from the famous Cheshire Cheese, there is a five-storey red brick building which houses the London *Morning Call*, a national newspaper with a certified daily net sale of nearly two million copies. Though the paper is popular, no one has ever been known to say a good word for the building in which it is produced—a late-Victorian monstrosity of classic ugliness with an incongruous flesh-pink filling where a hole blown in the structure by a delayed-action bomb in 1941 has been repaired.

In addition to being unsightly, the building is inconvenient for its purpose. Its interior may have been functional enough in the leisurely days when reporters travelled to work in top hats and morning coats, and leader-writers fulminated with a bottle of port at the elbow, but its dark narrow passages, steep stone stairs, antiquated lifts and multitude of small rooms with heavy mahogany doors are quite unsuited to the production of a modern newspaper. The directors have long intended to pull the whole place down and build on its site a worthy neighbour to the black-and-shiny *Daily Express* and the dignified *Daily Telegraph*, but having missed their chance before the war they now face insuperable problems of temporary accommodation and building licences. They have therefore had to content themselves with such interior improvements as the modernisation of the plumbing and the provision of additional amenities for the higher-placed executives.

On a hot Monday evening in late July, 1949, there was the usual lull in office activity as seven o'clock approached. The work of the day staff was almost done and the work of the night staff had barely started. It was the hour of editorial slack water, when those who were going to see the paper through the presses took over from those who had planned it in outline.

The specialists had already begun to trickle out past the green-uniformed commissionaire at the front box; the Literary Editor first, with an armful of review copies; the Sports Editor, who had a darts match to play off at his "local"; the Agricultural Correspondent, who owned a farm and made a useful profit writing about his losses; and the Columnist, who did very much as he liked. The Open Air Correspondent, whose accounts of arduous hikes personally undertaken were at once an example and stimulus to the rising generation, was starting up his car in the office garage preparatory to the effortless exploration of yet another route. Upstairs, other privileged experts with rooms of their own and names on their doors were jingling their keys and reaching for their hats. The Leader Writer had just been handed a damp galley proof by a white-aproned printer and was concentrating on the last and most trying stage of his normally unexacting job—the excision of three superfluous inches from a column that could spare almost any three inches without irreparable harm. In a few minutes, he too would be gone.

In the News Room, pressure had cased. The News Editor had handed over most of his problems to the Night News Editor, and in spirit was already having a drink with his pretty new girl reporter. One or two people drifted in and out on final missions—to get an expense account signed, or a draft letter approved, or just to say "Good-night" before departing. The Diplomatic Correspondent strolled in to tell the Night News Editor that he would be at the Savoy if wanted. The Night News Editor was studying the night rota, reflecting on the dullness of the news, and privately hoping for a big fire or explosion with heavy loss of life. The undersized youth whose job it was to tear off the ticker tape had sensed the temporary preoccupation of authority and was buried in a lurid "Western".

The Reporters' Room, separated from the News Room by a glass door, was as untidy as a battlefield. Despite the dearth of big stories—or perhaps because of it—a busy day had evidently been had by all. Old newspapers, clippings from the Library, reference books, telephone directories and mounds of copy paper were piled in disorder on the desks between the typewriters—a cleaner's nightmare. Huge waste-paper baskets overflowed like horns of plenty. On the floor beside one of the chairs a dozen sheets of discarded copy paper were scattered, each with the single unfinished sentence, "An unparalleled nation-wide scheme . . ." or as a variant, "A nationwide scheme which will revolutionise . . ." Someone had evidently been in creative travail here. On the Chief Reporter's desk, a printed card in a holder read "You don't have to be mad to work here, but if you are it helps." In one of the many telephone boxes which lined the walls, a shorthand-writer was taking a story from Rome. Two day-staff reporters, about to go off duty, were playing cricket with a paper ball and a broken chair leg. The pretty girl reporter was keeping an eye on the glass door and polishing her nails. By the window, where a million specks of dust floated in a shaft of evening sunlight, one of the night men who had just come on duty was unaccountably cleaning his shoes. Presently the door opened, a colleague from another department gave a peremptory, intimate jerk of the head to the two cricketers, and the three of them departed for the Crown.

Across the passage, the Sub-editors were sorting and savouring bits of copy in a desultory way, exchanging pleasantries while they still had the leisure to do so, and chaffing a waitress who had come down from the office restaurant with the supper menu. Some of them were quiet, respectable family men; men with neat houses at Streatham and Penge; pale men who rode on night trams and had almost forgotten what a beauty sleep felt like; amiable, worthy men, who drank a great deal of tea and whose thoughts dwelt much on pensions. Others stoked secret fires and contemplated personal or professional adventures. The view widely held among the reporters that the Subs were smug, stodgy and dim-witted almost to a man was the result of prejudice rather than of dispassionate observation.

Along the corridor, the deep peace of the Foreign Room was

broken only by the sound of the tape machine ticking out the "cold war" round by round. The inevitable boy crouched by the machine. The Assistant Foreign Editor sat in watchful contemplation of the clock, for he had an appointment with the Editor in five minutes' time. The Features Department—the mahogany door a few yards along the corridor—had temporarily closed down, and a note pencilled on a pad beside a wet page proof said "Gone to CEN 43029"—in short, to the Crown.

At the end of the passage, the hard-working Assistant Editor was discussing the "make-up" of the paper with the Night Editor. They were not aware of any lull. The Editor, a couple of doors away, was winding up the administrative work of the day. As was his custom at this hour, he was seeing members of the staff whose problems had been crowded out by the day's rush. In the adjoining room, his secretary worked on as steadily and imperturbably as though she had just come on duty.

Chapter Two

Precisely at a quarter to seven, Edgar Jessop, the Assistant Foreign Editor, put on his jacket and prepared to keep his appointment. He was a neat, spare man of less than average height. From his general appearance his age might have been anything from forty-five to fifty-five, but in fact he was an embittered forty-two. People who had known him in his youth would scarcely have recognised him now. Then he had been pleasant-looking in an unobtrusive, dapper sort of way, with thick dark hair, mild hazel eyes, and a smile that gained him all the friends he needed. Now his hair, meticulously parted in the middle, was uniformly grey, and so scanty as hardly to warrant the repeated gesture with which his right hand smoothed it back. His face had a drained look, a bleached papyrus-quality under its light tan, like that of an English child brought up in a hot country. His eyes, unless their interest was directly challenged, were for long periods expressionless, as though all his thoughts turned inwards. Only the sardonic droop of his mouth below the long clean-shaven upper lip gave any clue to the nature of those thoughts. In his rather timid manner there was certainly no hint of the nervous vitality that made him as potentially dangerous as a high-tension cable. Outwardly he was just an insignificant little man who looked as though worry and premature middle-age had got him down a bit.

He gave a short instruction to the boy in charge of the tape and walked quickly along the corridor. He felt anxious, and was uncomfortably aware of a pounding pulse. This interview mattered a great deal to him. The Foreign Editor of the *Morning Call*, a man named Lambert, had just left to join another paper, and Jessop hoped to move into his vacant post. He was, he had told himself a score of times, fully entitled to it; if he didn't get it, it would be grossly unfair. But he had been passed over so often already that he couldn't help feeling apprehensive. Luck had always been dead against him, and the high-ups had been slow to recognise his abilities.

He turned the knob of the secretary's door and saw with relief that Miss Timmins was alone. Sometimes at this hour she had to control an unruly mob, like the janitor at a stage-door; and he wanted to get his ordeal over quickly. He directed an inquiring glance at the inner room. "Is he free?" His voice was thin, his enunciation precise.

"He's got Mr. Iredale with him," said Miss Timmins, "but I shouldn't think they'll be long—they've been talking quite a while already." She gave him an encouraging smile. "I should wait if I were you." She was a bright little woman in her early forties with a darting, observant glance, a kind heart and an unshakably cheerful disposition. She was slightly over-rouged and her black hair was definitely over-dyed, but her dark dress was the last word in neatness and her collar was startlingly white. Miss Timmins looked her own idea of the perfect secretary.

Jessop sat down on a hard-backed chair and stared glumly at the floor. Miss Timmins put another sheet of paper in her typewriter. "I'll have to get a move on with these letters. Mr. Ede will want to sign them directly he's seen you."

"You work too hard," said Jessop. "You'll get no thanks for it in this place."

Miss Timmins chuckled, and her agile fingers began to clatter over the keys. "No good looking on the gloomy side, Mr. Jessop. Do things cheerfully and they don't come so hard, that's what I say."

The office was in fact Miss Timmins's life. She had sat in that ante-room for more than twenty years; she had served several editors, though none, in her view, more pleasant than Mr. Ede; she knew everything that went on in the office and enjoyed the confidences of half the staff. By normal standards she was grossly overworked, but apart from a regular Friday practice with the

Brondesbury Female Choir and an occasional visit to her married sister at Wembley she had nothing particular to do with her evenings and she flourished on overtime and the sense of being needed. The Editor had only to say that he really couldn't let her take on anything more and she would shoulder the new load happily.

Above the clicking of her machine the sound of raised voices came suddenly from the inner room. Miss Timmins stopped typing and looked slightly incredulous. It was rare for the Editor to get heated with any members of his staff, but foreign correspondents were notoriously temperamental. They got spoilt living abroad and became too independent. "Mr. Iredale seems to be giving trouble," she said. "It's very naughty of him."

Jessop listened, conscious of a vicarious excitement as the exchanges grew sharper. He couldn't make out what was being said, but he could hear Iredale's tone of angry protest and something very like the sound of a heavy fist being brought down on a desk-top. It was good to hear someone answering back and insisting on his rights.

"Bill said he was going to have a show-down," he remarked. "I don't blame him, either, considering the way he's been treated." It was as though he were expressing his own feeling of resentment. "After all, what was the point of sending an experienced man like him to the Outward Islands in the first place if we weren't going to trust his judgment? And then getting a chit of a girl to write up the story from office clippings—just because he sent something out of line with policy! It makes me sick."

"Oh, you're prejudiced against Katharine," said Miss Timmins. "I don't know much about the subject but I read her article and I must say it seemed to make everything nice and clear."

"It's easy to make things clear when you put in only half the facts," said Jessop sourly. He knew that he was coming to Iredale's defence when the battle was over, and that he was protesting in the wrong quarter; it gave an added bitterness to his complaint.

Miss Timmins made a non-committal sound and went on with her typing: She had long ago learned the wisdom of keeping neutral in these recurrent office disputes, though she was quite willing to bandage the wounds. "Anyway," she said after a few moments, "I expect Mr. Ede knows what he's doing."

"Don't you believe it," said Jessop. "He's still an amateur at this business. So's Katharine Camden. So are a lot of other people on this paper. Too many damned intellectuals altogether, if you ask me." Jessop had started his career on the *Morning Call* as a messenger boy at the age of fourteen, and had learned his job the hard way. He didn't approve of people who took short-cuts—particularly graduates from Oxford.

"Look how they stick together, too," he went on "Why do you suppose the Editor took Munro's view of the riots rather than Bill's? Do you think it's because Munro is Governor of the Outward Islands and so ought to know all about them? Not on your life. It's because Munro was once a leader-writer on this paper and has a couple of degrees and wears the same tie as Ede and they both know a bit of Greek. Whereas Bill, after all, is just a glorified reporter—and a reporter, in Ede's view, is no better than a literary barrow boy." Jessop's eyes had lost their inward look and his mouth twisted contemptuously.

"That's right, get it off your chest," said Miss Timmins cheerfully. "Don't mind me—I can take it." She typed a few more lines. "Did you know Mr. Munro was coming to lunch here to-morrow?"

Jessop's sardonic expression was momentarily replaced by one of curiosity.

"Is he?"

Miss Timmins nodded. "One of the usual office lunches—he's the guest of honour. It'll be queer seeing him back here after all this time, won't it? It seems ages ago that he used to sit in that easy-chair over there, waiting to show his leaders to the Editor."

"*He* didn't stick it for long, did he?" said Jessop morosely. "He knew which side his bread was buttered. I never could stand the fellow—interfering busy-body!"

Miss Timmins looked rather disapproving. Mr. Jessop was really being very difficult this evening. She remembered now, though—there had been some trouble between him and Munro long ago. "I suppose that's why your name's not down on the list for the luncheon this time, Mr. Jessop," she remarked.

Jessop shrugged. "I don't know about that—someone's got to bring out the paper. We can't all sit over liqueurs and cigars until three in the afternoon." His tone was offhand, but he knew that he hadn't deceived Miss Timmins. "Who'll be there, anyway?"

"Oh, it's only a small affair. Mr. Ede, Mr. Munro, Mr. Cardew and Mr. Hind."

Jessop's gloom deepened. To ask Cardew and not him was a deliberate snub. Cardew was only the Diplomatic Correspondent. Surely, in the absence of a Foreign Editor . . . He sensed a conspiracy.

The inner door suddenly opened and Nicholas Ede appeared, beckoning Jessop with a crooked forefinger. He looked very cool in a semi-tropical cream suit and seemed unruffled by his stormy interview with Iredale.

"Oh, Miss Timmins," he said, "you might ring my wife, will you, and tell her I'll be about half an hour late. Break it to her nicely!"

"Of course," said Miss Timmins, resisting an impulse to shake her head at the way he always got behindhand with his engagements.

"Now then, Jessop," said Ede, switching on an attractive smile and immediately switching it off again, as though it were current not to be wasted. "Come in, will you?" His voice was rich and fruity. He held the door with an expensively-shod foot and then let it close on its spring.

Jessop preceded him into the empty room—Iredale had evidently left by the other door. Ede walked quickly past him to his private shower room—one of the directors' post-war installations—and turned off a dripping tap. It was his only sign of irritation. Then he sat down behind his outsize desk, adjusted the framed photograph of his wife as a reminder that he must keep this interview short, and lit a cigarette. "Have a chair, my dear fellow," he urged, surprised to see that Jessop was still standing. He waved the Assistant Foreign Editor to a soft capacious seat and scrutinised him for a moment in silence.

Nicholas Ede was younger than Jessop; actually he was not quite forty, but his short pear-shaped figure and heavy shoulders suggested a much older man. Massive horn-rimmed spectacles half concealed the alertness of his eyes, and only when one was close enough to observe the smoothness of the skin above an unusually dark jowl did his comparative youth become obvious. He had been precocious in childhood and brilliant in his academic generation, and so far in his life had had no reason to suppose that he could not succeed in whatever he attempted. His whole manner and bearing gave an impression of self-confidence and strength. Yet he was genuinely kind-hearted, and the charm of manner that the envious derided in him was not entirely the cultivated attribute they suggested. He was sincerely interested in almost everyone he met—for a short time. Like Lord Melbourne, he preferred the company of any new person, for half an hour, to that of the dearest old friend. He was often strongly attracted to people, but he rarely allowed himself thoroughly to dislike anyone. The nearest he got to it was being bored. This was the feeling he tried to throw off as he looked at the man before him.

"Well, now," he began, "let's get to business. I asked you to come and see me because I thought it was time we had a discussion about your future on the paper."

"Oh, yes?" murmured Jessop. Now that he was actually in the presence of authority his resentment had ceased to be articulate. He felt insignificant, buried in that vast chair before the genial, self-assured Ede. He massaged the palms of his hands with the tips of his fingers, nervously restless. His mouth felt dry. Ede knew him as a conscientious worker and a first-rate technician, but at that moment he looked definitely unimpressive.

"Yes," Ede went on smoothly, "I've been giving a good deal of thought to the matter. Of course, now Lambert's gone one obvious possibility is to appoint you Foreign Editor." He saw Jessop wince at the implication of the sentence and hurried on. "Perhaps you ought to know that Lambert strongly urged your claim before he left. He was certain you'd do the job very well, and I think you would. All the same . . ." He paused, searching for the right words.

Rage welled up inside Jessop, till he felt he would choke. He was going to be passed over again. He wanted to protest, to urge his title, to recall his lifetime of devoted efforts for the paper, to bang the desk as Iredale had done—but no sound came.

"Let me put it like this," said Ede. "You've certain obvious recommendations for the post. You've shown yourself an excellent administrator and desk man. You've managed to keep on good terms with all your foreign correspondents . . ." he switched on a rueful smile, ". . . which is more than I seem able to do!" The smile took Jessop into his confidence, the confession sought to put him at his ease. "You know your stuff: I don't suppose there's anyone in Fleet Street with a better theoretical grasp of the international situation than you have." He paused. "All the same, I think a Foreign Editor should have something more than an academic knowledge of affairs. He ought to know something at first hand of the countries he's dealing with. Don't you agree?"

"I suppose so," said Jessop dully.

"Good. That's my view, too. So for the time being—nothing is ever permanent, of course, particularly in Fleet Street—for the time being, as I say, I'm going to put Cardew in charge of the Foreign Room. He's knocked about quite a bit at conferences, and it won't hurt him to sit on his backside and sort copy for a while. In fact, it'll steady him up a bit. And we'll take you off the leash. How would you like a foreign assignment, just for a year or so? A roving commission, if you like."

Jessop moistened his dry lips. So that was the plan: to brush him aside, to send him off somewhere where he'd be forgotten. "The idea had never occurred to me," he said slowly. "I—I think perhaps I'm a bit too old to start foreign reporting."

"Old?" Ede shook his head vigorously. "Not a bit of it! On the contrary, your experience should be a great advantage—it will give balance to your dispatches, and you won't be so likely to go off the deep end as some of your colleagues." The memory of his talk with Iredale evidently still rankled. "What I suggest is that you make a start by flying to Malaya for a couple of months. As you know, we've been without proper coverage there since poor old Eversley was ambushed, and the situation's boiling up into something pretty big. After that, you could spend a few months in Indo-China and Burma on your way home." He smiled. "A tour of the trouble-centres—the dream of every newspaperman. It should be most interesting for you. What do you say?"

Jessop's face had become more like parchment than ever, and he seemed to be having difficulty in swallowing. "Is this an instruction, sir?"

"Good heavens, no, my dear fellow." Ede was all charm. "It's an offer—an opportunity. Most men in the office would give their ears for it. It'll widen your horizon, give you self-confidence, and probably equip you to do a first-class job in the office later on. Frankly, Jessop, I think it'll be the making of you. Of course, if you feel the whole thing's too much for you to undertake . . ." his full lips pouted in reflection, ". . . well, I suppose there's no alternative but for you to carry on with your present job, under Cardew. It's up to you entirely."

"Eversley . . ." began Jessop, and stopped, uncomfortably aware of Ede's piercing look. "Eversley . . ."

"Eversley had bad luck. That's not likely to happen again. Still, there's no point in going out if you feel nervous about the job." Ede glanced up at the clock on the wall. "Anyway, think it over. And let me know by the end of the week what you decide, will you?"

He got up—the interview was over. He walked with Jessop to the outer door, his plump hand resting lightly on the older man's shoulder. "I can tell you this—I wouldn't mind the chance of going myself!" He gave Jessop a smile of dismissal. "Good-night."

"Good-night," muttered Jessop, closing the door behind him with unintentional violence and almost putting his head in again to apologise. Ede returned to his desk, frowning a little, and rang the bell for Miss Timmins.

Chapter Three

The Saloon Bar of the Crown was large enough to accommodate a considerable part of the *Morning Call*'s editorial staff, and this evening it appeared to be doing so. Bill Iredale, still fuming after his interview with Ede, decided that the crowd at the far end of the long curving counter was excessive and selected a quiet spot near the door for his cooling-off process.

Iredale was a big man in his middle thirties, with strong irregular features that had a rugged East Anglian glower when in repose. He had been born in Great Yarmouth the day World War I started. His father, skipper and part-owner of a North Sea trawler, had wanted him to grow up tough; his mother, a school-teacher until her marriage, had wanted him to grow up educated. Always independent, and eager to find adventure in his own way, he had compromised by going to London at eighteen and getting himself a job as a cub reporter on a suburban newspaper. At twenty-one he had chanced to meet Edgar Jessop, then reporting for the *Morning Call*, at an exhumation, and the contact had brought him an opportunity on the same paper. Reporting had given him all he asked of life until World War II broke out, and then he had been accredited as a war correspondent at his own urgent request. He had covered the early campaigns in Africa, been transferred to Russia during the middle years, and towards the end of the war had been switched to the Far East. Since then he had been constantly on the move, building up a sound reputation in a Fleet Street that he rarely saw.

He still liked the life. Nothing gave him more satisfaction than to fly to a country that was new to him and start from scratch to find out all he could about it. He did any job that came his way, and if hot news were wanted he gathered it up and sent it, but the superficial never attracted him. What he liked best was to spend time in a place, to soak himself in atmosphere, to master the background, to mix with the people and get all angles on the problem. The more complex and controversial the local situation, the more he enjoyed probing it. When he had got his facts, nothing would stop him reporting them. He had no sense of mission, but he was proud of his craft. He was realistic, obstinate, human and remarkably honest, and he did his job without fuss, unless fuss were necessary.

He had just taken his first long pull at the soothing pint when Katharine Camden walked into the saloon. He had never seen her before, but from Edgar Jessop's description he felt pretty sure it was she. As she passed him he called out "Hi!" on a sudden impulse. She looked back, and he pushed forward a stool in a gesture of invitation. "I'm Bill Iredale. Will you join me in a drink?"

Katharine hesitated for a moment, and though she would have preferred to plunge into the anonymous din at the far end of the bar; then, with a smile, she accepted. She was a tall, good-looking girl of about twenty-six, pale-skinned, with soft dark hair drawn into a large knot at the nape of her neck. A little black hat was set jauntily on the back of her head, but her light grey suit was almost Quakerish in its simplicity. Taking her in with a practised eye, Iredale saw that she had a superb figure, wide-shouldered and slim-hipped, with long legs and neat ankles. Just the kind of figure that appealed to him. He liked her face, too, with its small straight nose and large grey-green eyes. All the same, he wasn't in the mood to make concessions on that account. The world was full of attractive women, and the others hadn't messed about with his dispatches. He said "What'll you have?" in a curt voice, as though he were offering her a choice of weapons.

Katharine sensed trouble. She accepted a cigarette from the rather battered packet he extended to her, and fitted it carefully into an onyx holder. "Gin and something, please. French, I think." She perched gracefully on the stool, blew out a cloud of smoke, and prepared to resist aggression. "Why am I singled out for this honour?"

"I thought you might put me wise about the Outward Islands," said Iredale, handing her her drink. "It seems you are an authority."

She surveyed him coolly. She'd heard a lot about him, and people who knew him seemed to like him, but at the moment she couldn't think why. Certainly he wasn't bad to look at. His eyes were a little too old and wise for a man of his years, as though they had seen things that weren't good to see, but they were the deepest blue. White crowsfeet fanned from their corners where the sun of the Outward Islands had failed to penetrate. There was a glow of health about his brown skin and his thick brown hair.

"Aren't you being rather childish?" she said coldly. "I can understand your feeling annoyed about those articles, but why take it out on me? I was given a job to do, and I did it."

"I'll say you did. You really threw yourself into it, didn't you? That piece of yours positively bubbled with righteous indignation. What did you write it with—boiling pitch?"

"Is there anything wrong with having feelings?" The grey-green eyes flashed. "It's obvious *you* haven't any. 'Shoot the so-and-so's down'—that seems to be your attitude to the problem. Not exactly constructive, is it? I thought we were supposed to be progressive on this paper."

"We're supposed to be reporters," said Iredale shortly, "and that means sizing up a situation as it is, not dreaming it up from old clippings in a sentimental haze."

"Is it sentimental to suggest that negro sugar workers are being exploited when it's obvious that they hardly earn enough to keep body and soul in close proximity, let alone together?" Katharine was indignant. She had done some lengthy research into labour conditions in the Outward Islands, helped by a Royal Commission report.

"The time to dwell on that," said Iredale, "was before the riots began or after they were over, not in the middle of them."

"Jam yesterday, jam to-morrow?"

Iredale gave an exclamation of impatience. He hadn't meant to get into this squabble with a girl he'd never seen before, and he had an uncomfortable feeling that she was making him sound pompous and overbearing. "How long have you been a reporter?" he asked more amiably.

"Five years."

"The cushty jobs—or as it came?"

"The whole works," she said, with a touch of pride.

"Then you ought to know by now that the world's a pretty rough place. When I got out to Port Sargasso, the rioters had just burned a native policeman alive and fired about ten thousand acres of sugar-cane. They were led by a Bible-punching fanatic in an advanced stage of V.D. and it was as plain as daylight that the situation would soon be out of hand. Dawson Munro should have ordered extra police to the trouble spots and given instructions that they were to shoot to kill. I know that doesn't solve the economic problem, but once you let a murderous mob get on the rampage there's no other way."

Katharine seemed unconvinced. "Surely there's such a thing as meeting them half-way?"

"If you meet them half-way when they're in that mood they knock you on the head. And that's exactly what happened. Munro left things too late because he's a sloppy wishful thinker who believes you can make the world behave itself by kindness. Result—a planter's family was murdered; and then, of course, there was far more shooting than there need have been. If my first dispatch had been published when it was sent, and *as* it was sent, it's just possible that someone might have prodded Munro into action while there was still time. Instead, the story was passed to you with a lot of namby-pamby instructions and you turned it inside out, and the very morning our readers were having a good cry about the poor downtrodden natives old Clinton's household was wiped out with cutlasses."

Katharine weighed that up. "Is it because his family was wiped out or because I altered your story that you're so riled?"

Iredale looked at her, and a slow smile spread across his dark face like the coming of daybreak. "I have my pride," he said.

Katharine was disarmed. "They ought to have trusted you," she admitted. "You were on the spot. All the same, what should I have done? Ede gave me instructions himself, and there was plenty of material to support his line. I could hardly have refused to write the article, and it seemed rather a break at the time."

"Sure," said Iredale. "Let's forget it. What about another drink?"

"My round," said Katharine, tapping on the counter. "Anyhow, you're not going to resign over it?"

Iredale grinned, and the white crowsfeet disappeared. "If a foreign correspondent resigned every time he thought he'd had a raw deal he'd soon get St. Vitus's dance. I've had a thundering good row with Ede and now I suppose it'll blow over. I've just been bidden to lunch with Munro to-morrow, anyway, so he obviously believes that relations will be patched up. Now let's talk about something else. How did you get into this racket? Fleet Street's no place for a nice girl like you."

"My God, aren't you patronising! Do I look as though I've taken any harm?"

Iredale contemplated her with critical detachment. "No, but you will." He glanced across the saloon to where Joe Hind, the News Editor, was drinking with the crowd. Hind's tones of loud good-fellowship carried easily across the bar. One of his flabby white hands rested possessively on the shoulder of a pretty girl. Iredale frowned as he looked. "Seriously," he said, concentrating again on Katharine, "it's a bad life for a woman. Too little sleep, too much gin, too long on your feet. In a few more years your skin will get coarse and your eyes bleary and you'll suffer so much from indigestion that you'll have to live on peppermint and bismuth. I've seen it happen again and again."

She laughed. "What a dreary prognosis!"

"You'll see! Anyway, how did you come to join the paper?"

"It was during the war," Katharine told him. "You were in Russia at the time. I used to read your dispatches and envy you like hell. I was studying law at Oxford, but one evening I happened to be in town—it was during the Christmas vacation—and there was a rather bad raid. I took shelter in a basement. There were several people down there and of course we started talking. One of the men turned out to be a very important fellow on the *Morning Call*—our own Joe Hind, no less. He was short of reporters and he offered me a job, there and then. I accepted there and then—and Oxford knew me no more. It was rather a blow for the family. My father's a K.C., and he had ambitions for me."

"Called to the wrong bar, eh?" Iredale shook his head. "Hind's certainly a fast worker—he always did fancy himself as a talent scout. As a matter of interest, did he make a pass at you while you were actually *in* the shelter, or did he wait till later?"

Again her laugh rang out. "He's still waiting. What a man!"

Iredale nodded. He couldn't imagine Hind having much success with Katharine, who struck him as being a fastidious type. "Who's the girl he's got in tow now, do you know?"

She glanced across the saloon. "That's Sheila Brooks—she's just started as a reporter."

"Is she any good?"

Katharine hesitated. "She's very young. She's always wanted to work on a newspaper and she thinks this is the Street of Adventure. I think she could be a nice kid, but Joe's spoiling her. He gives her the plum jobs and takes her out a lot, and she thinks he's wonderful and drinks far too much with him because she's under the impression that it's the proper thing to do. I'm not just being bitchy. It really is too bad of him."

"Somebody ought to keep an eye on her."

"Well, *I* try, but good advice isn't very palatable, you know."

"Damned little fool!" said Iredale, with surprising warmth.

At that moment, Hind and the girl detached themselves from the crowd and approached a trifle unsteadily across the saloon. Hind was a big man, as big as Iredale, but gross and flabby, with a false-hearty manner and a face like a degenerate Roman emperor. He was laughing, with an exaggerated heaving of his shoulders, at something the flushed girl had said. Sheila had a pretty rounded figure and eyes like bluebells. Just about one good meal, Iredale thought, for a womaniser like Hind.

The News Editor cast a sidelong look at Katharine as he passed and gave her a half-embarrassed, half-defiant grin. Iredale said quietly, "Still up to your old tricks, Hind?"

Hind stopped, and lowered his head like a bull. "Any business of yours, Iredale?"

Iredale looked beyond him to the girl. "If you've got any sense, honey child, you'll watch your step with Mr. Hind—and I'm not joking."

Sheila went scarlet. "Well . . ." she began indignantly. Hind let go her arm and thrust his chin in Iredale's face. "Why don't you get back to where you came from, Mr. Know-all?"

"Why don't you leave these kids alone?" retorted Iredale, pale with anger. They faced each other, hatred leaping between them.

"Break it up, you two," said Katharine urgently. "It's not exactly private here."

Iredale took a reluctant step back to the bar and picked up his beer. Hind, looking venomous, muttered something and steered Sheila to the door.

Katharine heaved a sigh. "You lack finesse, Sir Galahad."

"One of these days," said Iredale, "someone'll break that fellow's neck."

Chapter Four

Edgar Jessop rarely went to the Crown these days unless some congenial colleague practically dragged him there. For one thing, he knew that alcohol made him boastful and truculent; he was not at his best in his cups. For another, he was always afraid of running into someone he particularly disliked. This evening, in any case, his interview with the Editor had left him in no mood for conviviality. Just before eight o'clock he went up alone to the restaurant, choosing the quietest table and deliberately turning his back on the few people eating there.

It was his custom, when he had a meal by himself in the evening, to place a folded copy of *The Times* beside his plate and see how much he could do of the crossword. Usually he found the occupation restful and comforting to his ego, for he had an allusive, well-stocked memory and made good progress. To-night, however, concentration was impossible. He could think of nothing but the injustice and humiliation that he had suffered. He ate mechanically and without appetite, staring down at his plate for minutes at a time, and seeing nothing but his grievances. He felt resentment as a physical sensation—a constriction of the chest and a pounding of the blood.

He had never been given a decent chance, he told himself—and now, of course, he never would be. It was damnably unfair. No one could have worked harder or more conscientiously than he had to achieve the position to which his talents entitled him. Even as a lad, when other youths of his age had concentrated on having a good time, he had been earnest and diligent and ambitious. He had persuaded old Mr. Lyons, who had been in charge of the office-boys at that time, to arrange his duties so that he could attend night-school. He had learned shorthand and typewriting and French. He had been a regular borrower at the public library. No one could have sought knowledge and self-improvement more assiduously.

At first he had done well. He had started to climb the ladder, rung by rung, overcoming by sheer doggedness the handicaps of shyness and small stature. From being a mere "boy"—a tearer-off of tapes, a bearer of tea, a universal messenger and anonymous dogsbody—he had through solid worth become in time a skilled telephonist, taking down reporters' stories. Then the political columnist had picked him out, and he had graduated to the position of personal secretary. Finally, with the help of the columnist's good-natured patronage, he had made the difficult leap across the chasm that divided the secretarial from the editorial staff, and had become a reporter at the princely wage of nine guineas a week. On the evening of his first pay-day, he remembered, he had taken his widowed mother to dinner at the Trocadero. Looking back now, he thought that that had been the happiest day of his life. As soon as it had become clear that he would be able to hold the job down, they had moved from the mean street in North London, where he had been brought up, to a small semi-detached villa near Beckenham with some trees and a pleasant garden. Life had suddenly become gracious. His interests had quickly widened and exciting new vistas had opened. He had taken his mother to Italy for a holiday in a glow of pride. He had started to write—for her eye alone—verse that had shown a reflective sensitiveness. He had trained his ear to appreciate good music, and had learned to play the piano for their joint pleasure. The world had seemed a good place then. It had a seamy side, but he was young and an idealist, and in his day-dreams it was pleasant to think how he could help to make it better.

He had proved a competent but not a brilliant reporter. Assignments with a political flavour, interviews with the great, or stories that gave him a chance to write descriptively—these were what he had liked. He had managed to get through the other things too—the fires, the accidents, the suicides and murders and sordid court cases—but not with the tough nonchalance of his colleagues. When an opportunity occurred, he had switched over to the sub-editors' table—at ten guineas a week—and had applied himself with his customary eagerness to the acquisition of a new skill. He had been a good sub-editor—knowledgeable, careful, and with a flair for the apt headline.

The war had brought rapid, bewildering changes. For a short time he had been Assistant Features Editor. In a subsequent re-shuffle he had been made Assistant News Editor. Then the bomb in 1941 had made a big hole in the staff as well as in the building, and he had taken over the post of the deceased Assistant Foreign Editor. In that position he had stayed, marking time, for the greater part of a decade.

Jessop crumbled a piece of bread between his sensitive, fidgety, nicotine-stained fingers and reflected bitterly on the unfulfilled promise of those years. It certainly hadn't been through any fault of his own that his career had withered. He had continued to do his work efficiently, and with all the versatility required of him. He had been far more reliable, far less addicted to spectacular and costly errors of judgment, than the young men who had since come bouncing in from Oxford or the BBC, throwing their weight about and explaining in loud, cultured voices just what was wrong with the paper. Why, if it had been necessary he could have produced the *Morning Call* almost single-handed. Yet *they* had gone ahead, *they* had become the lieutenants and cronies of the Editor, *they* had been given the big jobs and the four-figure salaries—and he had remained an assistant. Always an assistant! Always the man who did the real work and never got the kudos. And why? Because he hadn't the right social background, of course; because he'd educated himself instead of going to a prep school and on to a public school and university; because he'd started work early in life instead of having everything made easy for him; because he'd never learned how to treat his superiors as equals and get away with it. Because they were all a bloody lot of snobs. When he thought of it, hatred consumed him.

He ought to have gone to another paper, of course, once it

became clear that he had got into a rut. He would have done, too, if it hadn't been for that insufferable busybody, Munro. A post with the *Courier* had been almost in the bag when Munro, then a rising Member of Parliament, had chanced to dine with the *Courier*'s editor. Munro had said something that night—the Fleet Street grapevine had never been precise about just what he *had* said, but knowing Munro from the old days Jessop could imagine only too well. "Jessop? . . ."—with a pursing of the lips and a heavy judicial frown. "I'd hardly have thought *he* was up to it, my dear fellow. A good second-rater, perhaps." Something like that, anyway—enough to wreck his chances. The odious, interfering swine!

Anyhow, the opportunity had been missed, and at the *Morning Call* the drift downhill had started. There hadn't been any demotion, of course—not even any spoken criticism. It had been much more subtle than that. His prestige and status in the office had declined imperceptibly, and along with it such self-assurance as he had. It had been a gradual slope, with no fatal falls but many shocks to his self-esteem. Little things had marked the change—the occasional hint of impatience in Ede's tone, for instance, and—more wounding still—the way in which some of his colleagues had ceased to pay attention to his words when he was talking, as though he didn't matter any more. How many times he had ventured an observation, only to have it drowned by more emphatic voices! They had begun to treat him with a sort of kindly contempt, as a man who was all right, of course, but had just not made the grade. And not all of them had been kindly. Hind, for instance, had often been deliberately brutal in public, humiliating him, inviting the world to snigger at his diffidences and his shortcomings. Editorial conferences with Hind present had become an agonising ordeal. Latterly, the decline had become swifter. There had been official slights, like this failure to invite him to the Munro lunch. Not so long ago he would have been asked automatically in the absence of the Foreign Editor—in those days he had been considered an asset. All this had driven him farther and farther into his shell, had made him more nervous, more gauche, more resentful. A vicious spiral of descent.

Well, his last hope of a come-back had definitely vanished now, thanks to Ede and Cardew. He'd been passed over finally and for good, after a quarter of a century of devoted service. His abilities, of which he was so desperately aware, were to be allowed to run to waste. He was a middle-aged failure, unappreciated, despised. The years ahead would be hard for his pride to bear. He knew just how barren they would be, for he had watched other men grow old in the office. Brilliant men, some of them, headline names in their heyday, but in the end so apprehensive and dependent, so sapped of fighting spirit, that they would accept the most menial professional jobs with barely a murmur of protest. That would happen to him. And the Edes and the Cardews, the Munros and the Hinds would flourish.

He could picture them at that lunch to-morrow—the buoyant Ede, the patronising Munro, the debonair Cardew, the gross, coarse Hind. He could see them standing by the window, smiling and joking, sipping their drinks and nibbling their olives and being such good fellows together. He could see them lolling at the table over their brandy, self-confident, socially at ease, buttering each other up—thankful, no doubt, that there was no Jessop there to cause them embarrassment. He hated them all: he hardly knew which of them he hated most.

He rose dejectedly from his seat, pushed threepence under his plate for the waitress, and walked slowly past the Directors' Dining Room where he wouldn't be lunching to-morrow, sunk in self-pity. He went down by the back stairs to avoid meeting anyone and turned into the Foreign Room with relief. It seemed like a sanctuary, with its almost sound-proof walls cutting off the outside world, its solid homely furniture, its familiar threadbare carpet, its companionable tape machine, its ancient maps stabbed with the flag-pins of two wars. Here he could brood in peace. The pleasant aroma of Bill Iredale's strong tobacco—for this was Iredale's temporary base in the office—reminded him that he still had one pal in the world. If only Cardew weren't taking over here to-morrow or the next day!—for after that, the room would seem no longer a refuge, but a prison.

He dismissed the tape-machine boy with an amiable word or two, for the youth was inoffensive. He glanced through the accumulated pile of copy, but there was nothing to warrant his attention. Indeed, he rarely had much to see to at this time of day, for Oldfield, the Foreign Sub., was kept supplied with tape from another machine and had his own ideas about what to do with the news. Somebody had to sit at the Foreign Desk, that was all—sit there till eleven o'clock to answer the telephone and be available in case a big foreign story broke. The "somebody", naturally, was Jessop. He had done the night turn in Lambert's day and he would no doubt have to go on doing it now. Cardew wouldn't expect to do it—*he* preferred entertaining at his club or drinking with the Edes or dining out with foreign diplomats. The night turn was the lot of assistants. Almost all his working life Jessop had been on late shifts, serving the convenience of others. The universal accommodator—Edgar Jessop. That's how they looked on him. The man who could be pushed around, because there was no more spirit in him. Well, they were wrong. There was still a kick in him yet.

He reached for his dispatch case and lovingly extracted the *magnum opus* on which he had been secretly working for many months—the child of his bitter discontent. It was a plan for establishing world standards of Press behaviour under the supervision of the United Nations. He had been interested in world organisation since his youth, and now he had moved into the creative stage. No one, he felt certain, was so uniquely fitted as he to make this contribution. He knew the Press from hard personal experience, he had been through the mill, he had suffered from its abuse of power, its criminal irresponsibility. He had no doubt that his scheme went unerringly to all the roots of all the evils. To its earlier pages; indeed, little exception would have been taken anywhere, for they were sober, factual, and technical. It was only in the later sections that the tone became hysterical and the language violent.

Jessop himself was unaware of the change. To him the document was a consistent indictment, and he was proud of it. Indeed, now that he was approaching the end, the grand summing-up, he saw no limits to its impact. Ede and Hind and the rest might sneer—*would* sneer, no doubt, if they knew about it—but what they didn't realise was that while they were deriding him and passing him over he was quietly undermining the very foundations of their position. When the report was finished, Jessop would send it to the Human Rights Commission of U.N.O., and action would be taken.

For a long time he sat quietly with the document before him, day-dreaming as he so often did. In his mind's eye he saw a great concourse of world statesmen, each with a copy of his plan. He heard the applause when his name was mentioned; he listened to speeches acclaiming his vision, sharing his indignation. Sweeter still, he saw himself receiving congratulations from the very people who had scorned him. He dwelt on that. He would be modest, he decided, in his moment of triumph. As far as he was concerned, bygones should be bygones. All the same, he reflected, Ede could hardly help feeling pretty foolish when the text of the document came in over the office tape, with the matter-of-fact catch-line, "Jessop Plan. Full. Not for release before 18.30 G.M.T." He'd feel even sillier when he found himself personally arraigned in the Plan before the bar of world opinion.

Jessop would have liked the fantasy to stay bright, but it faded like a rainbow and with a sigh he unscrewed his fountain pen. For more than an hour he wrote with fierce exhausting concentration, filling sheet after sheet of foolscap with his neat careful handwriting. Occasionally as he wrote he smiled to himself at a particularly telling phrase; occasionally he frowned in anger. Sometimes he spoke snatches of sentences aloud and even declaimed them, waving a hand in the air as though addressing an invisible audience. Once or twice he pushed back his chair and walked agitatedly up and down the room in a fever of composition, his eyes ablaze.

He was barely aware that the presses had started running until a boy came in with a copy of the first edition. That brutally snapped the thread of thought. He picked up the paper and glanced through the headlines. Afterwards he sat perfectly still, his gaze focused on the middle distance, his eyes unseeing. His attitude suggested sleep.

He was aroused just before eleven by a distant roll of thunder—forerunner of a storm that had been rumbling around all day. He packed the *opus* into his case, tore off the last of the tape, locked the door of his room and walked downstairs to the office garage, where he kept his Austin. The commissionaire happened to look up as he crossed the lobby and gave him a nod—an offhand nod, it seemed to Jessop.

The semi-basement garage was congested, as usual, and he had difficulty in manouvering his car out. It was a ridiculously inadequate garage. Evans, who was in charge of office management, had said only a week ago and with a rather meaning look that he would have to revise the list of people entitled to use it. Jessop felt pretty sure that if any name were knocked off the list it would be his. Particularly now that he wasn't going to be Foreign Editor. Sycophants like Evans soon got wind of unrealised expectations.

He drove slowly through the southern suburbs, his mind so absorbed with his troubles that when he reached the road in which he lived he could hardly have recalled a single feature of the route by which he had come. The house which he had shared with his mother until her death a month ago was undistinguished. As a young man he had thought it wonderful, but he had grown out of it and now that she was gone he didn't quite know what to do about it. He enjoyed solitude more than most men; he even enjoyed looking after himself, provided someone came in once or twice a week to clean. All the same, a whole house to himself was more than he could manage. If he'd had Cardew's salary, now, no doubt he too could have afforded a luxury flat in Jermyn Street, but he hadn't, and with the housing shortage so bad everywhere he would have difficulty in finding a place suited to his pocket. And he wouldn't dare to press his claim for more money at this stage. They might take the opportunity to dispense with him altogether. That would probably please them better even than sending him to Malaya. Malaya! Nothing on earth would induce him to go there.

He put the car away and stood for a while in the sultry night air, watching the play of lightning against a threatening bank of cloud. The pale roses under the front window looked fresh and beautiful in the flashes. He drew a deep breath, savouring their perfume. He'd miss the garden if he left this place—it had been one of his greatest delights. Not that it meant so much to him now that his mother had died—he'd made it lovely for her as much as for himself, and it seemed an empty frame without her. He felt her loss acutely and unceasingly, for she had been the constant and almost the only companion of his leisure, the one person with whom he had been completely at ease. She at least had appreciated him, she had believed in him. She had nourished his ambitions and fostered his hopes. She had even believed that he might one day become a great editor, and there had been a time when he had half-believed it too. Perhaps it was just as well that she hadn't lived to know his ultimate humiliation.

Drops of rain began to splash around him and he went into the house. It smelt of Mrs. Molloy's furniture polish—not a very cosy smell. He felt hungry, and scanned the pantry for food. There were bottles and tins, left-overs from his mother's housekeeping, but he felt too tired to bother with any of them now. He ate some bread and cheese and drank up the milk—it would only turn sour in the storm. Then he sat down next to the radio and lit a cigarette. He switched it on keeping the volume low in order not to disturb the neighbours. Some foreign station was playing the Grieg piano concerto on records and he heard it through. It was an exciting piece, especially against the background of thunder, and it made his pulse race.

When it ended, he went up to bed. He was physically exhausted, but felt too agitated for sleep. He had not slept soundly at night for years—not since the early days of the war, not since the bombing. Recently his insomnia had been getting worse. Sometimes he took tablets, but he usually found that he lay awake waiting impatiently for them to take effect, and in any case his supply had run out.

For a while he tried to read, but his eyeballs ached and the words were blurred on the page. The bed seemed hard—perhaps he had made it too hurriedly that morning. He must remember to turn the mattress. He put the light out and lay in the darkness, listening to the mounting storm. His thoughts turned to the interview he had had with Ede, and to all the things he had wanted to say and hadn't said. As he built up the scene again, fact and fancy became so intermingled that he could almost believe he *had* said them. He saw Ede embarrassed by his biting sarcasms, wilting under his deadly shafts. When his imagination was drained and he could no longer conjure anything from the darkness, he turned his mind again to the wreck of his career. It was a mental treadmill—hateful yet irresistible. Soon he was writhing and tossing from side to side, talking and counter-talking until his brain reeled and his nerves shrieked with tiredness.

In the end he must have slept a little, for as a clap of thunder rattled the panes he woke from a fearful dream, fighting off tormenting demons that came at him with flames. For a moment, when the lightning flashed, he could see the face of Nicholas Ede at the foot of the bed. He struggled up and lunged at it, sweating and terrified, but it had gone. It had been a different face—a more arrogant Ede, with an evil smile and thick, brutal lips. A gloating Ede.

Jessop lay back on his pillow, and suddenly he felt at peace. Suddenly everything had become clear to him. He knew now why Ede had been so anxious to send him to Malaya. Ede *wanted* him to go the way of Eversley. Ede wanted to kill him. Ede was a murderous megolomaniac, who knew that Jessop was in his way. Ede, the protagonist of the powerful, the greedy, the exploiters—Jessop, the champion of the underdog, the downtrodden and oppressed. And Ede was afraid of him—afraid of what he, Jessop, would say about him. Jessop laughed quietly in the darkness. Well, the plot had been uncovered in time. No doubt Ede had thought that he had a weakling to deal with, an easy victim. No doubt he had taken silence for submission. Again Jessop chuckled. Was there not such a thing as silent strength? He too could make plans. He was not going to allow himself to be killed by Ede—he had a duty to survive, a duty to his fellow-newspapermen, who had no inkling of the danger in their midst. It was now more important than ever that he should finish his *opus*. He *would* finish it. But first he would deal with Ede—yes, and with Ede's fellow-plotters. He would strike at once, and rid the world of these criminals. Not recklessly, no, no! With sly cunning, matching Ede's own.

He lay in creative ecstasy, his mind never more lucid, revolving ingenious schemes. Yes, already he was beginning to see a way. Had not Providence placed in his keeping, for this very purpose, the perfect instrument of execution? Had not Providence even arranged the pattern of events, by calling the miscreants together? Ede, Cardew, Hind, Munro. What did it matter who went first?—let Providence decide that. One by one, they could all be destroyed. And some day, he would receive the thanks of mankind. He would be hailed as a deliverer, a saviour.

To-morrow he must be up early—he had work to do. The prospect of action soothed him. He turned on his side and fell at once into a deep untroubled sleep.

Chapter Five

Shortly before noon next day, editorial executives and heads of departments began to assemble in the Board Room for the morning conference. It was a sombre room, panelled in dark oak from floor to ceiling. Opening out of it was the Directors' Dining Room, where a waitress was now busy laying the table for the Munro luncheon. Beyond was the restaurant.

The first arrivals stood around joking and chatting, very much at ease. The atmosphere at these twice-daily conferences was quite informal. Things were different now from what they had been in the harsh competitive days before World War II, when there had usually been twenty pages or more to fill and advertisers had had to be wooed and readers had had to be clawed away from rivals with stunts and sensations. In those days, as Joe Hind and others could well remember, there had been an air of strain at conferences, with a go-getting Editor rapping out reprimands, a restless Ideas Man injecting a stream of impracticable suggestions into every department, and reporters being dispatched in all directions, often on the most hare-brained missions. In those days the threat of the sack had never been far away and nerves had been stretched taut. The News Editor had been afraid to miss a story and the Foreign Editor to leave a corner of the globe uncovered by his men. Reporters had found it necessary to lie, threaten, blackmail, distort and invent in a cut-throat battle of survival against the other gentlemen of the Press. Sub-editors had gloated over smart-aleck headlines and screamed in ever larger type. In those days there had been almost nothing too degrading for a popular newspaper to do in its wild scramble for circulation.

Now, for good or ill, much of that had changed. There were only six or eight pages to fill each day, because of the shortage of paper. Advertisers no longer had to be wooed; they came, layout in hand, begging for space. Modest profits were assured, provided there were no undue extravagance. Frantic competition for minor scoops was a waste of effort when there was no room to print them anyway. Excessive invention and distortion were no longer safe, for the Press was under other scrutiny than that of Edgar Jessop. A Royal Commission had just reported on its activities, and not wholly in its favour. Evidently it had to watch its step. It must try to be accurate and responsible and serious, the word went round—worthy of a grown-up democracy. By 1949, something of the lassitude and smugness of the Welfare State had settled on Fleet Street. Jobs were safe, and dividends were safe, so why worry? The tension had gone—and with it much of the excitement.

It was, therefore, a calm and contented body of men who gathered round the conference table that morning—except, of course, for Edgar Jessop, and he showed nothing of his feelings. Hind, in jovial humour after a rewarding evening with Miss Brooks, was there for the News Room. There was the Art Editor, with the first batch of news pictures, and the Features Editor, who didn't actually need to be there but was bored and wanted company. There was the Sports Editor, who had dropped in to make sure he got space on Page One for a boxing event that he thought important. There was Cardew, of the sensitive face and elegant clothes, who had just come by cab from the Foreign Office. There was Hutchinson, the Columnist, eager to turn rejected news scraps into cottage pie, and Pringle the Crime Reporter, who wasn't of conference calibre but had been specially summoned because of the new wave of "cosh and run" attacks in town. There was Smith-Randolph, the Leader Writer, sitting back on the Editor's left, faintly aloof.

On Ede's right sat the Assistant Editor, Henry Jackson, an old warrior steeped in printer's ink, and the mainstay of the paper. He was long past sixty, but nobody knew just how long, and he never offered any information on the subject. His face was deeply lined and his hair was quite white, but his mental vigour was certainly unimpaired. He had served the *Morning Call* without sparing himself for more than forty years and his only ambition was to postpone retirement and go on serving it till he dropped. He admired Ede and was trusted by him, and the two men worked well in harness. But whereas Ede applied himself to his editorship with gusto and brilliance, Jackson was content with pedestrian routine and quiet competence. Ede put the paper first but tried, not always with success, to avoid being submerged by it; Jackson put the paper first and last and knew no other life. It was one of the oldest office jokes that even when he was off duty he always seemed reluctant to go home, and grim jests were made about his probable domestic background until it was discovered, to the surprise of all, that he had a sweet and gentle wife of whom he was extremely fond. Nevertheless, the paper was rarely out of his mind except when he was asleep. A newspaperman, in his view, had no absolute claim to a private life. Newspapermen, it was true, frequently married and brought up families; purchased houses and endowment policies; took up hobbies and went on holidays, but all these things were incidental, and in no circumstances should be allowed to impinge upon the job. If a man wasn't prepared to sacrifice his family, his leisure, his health, and if necessary even his life, to get a good story, then in Jackson's view he oughtn't to be in Fleet Street. Service, order and discipline were Jackson's gods. His limitations were recognised, but the staff liked him for his qualities. He was reliable, even-tempered and friendly, and he knew his job backwards. He knew his place, too, and always deferred to Ede when deference was due. He was the prompter, the adviser, the restrainer; never the rival. Ede presided at the table with the good-humoured tolerance of the man who knows that his authority is unquestioned.

When all were seated, Ede nodded to the News Editor and the conference began. Hind started to read from a prepared statement on which, under his direction, the main items of news had been summarised. These, with later additions, would form the backbone of to-morrow's news pages. Since all those present had duplicated copies of the statement in front of them, the recital lacked both surprise and suspense. Nevertheless, it was far from tedious. Hind, lolling back in a nonchalant way with his buttocks overlapping the edge of his chair, his brown suit crumpled as though he had slept in it, a cigarette smouldering between his fingers, put on a first-class act. Not for him the twice-told tale! Paraphrasing freely, he illuminated the bald items of news with touches of colour and humour, glancing repeatedly round at his colleagues to see how they were enjoying the cheerful commentary. Ede, not for the first time, watched him with quiet relish, admiring his expertise. Hind might be a phoney, and he certainly had some regrettable characteristics, but he was always good entertainment.

There were, of course, pitfalls which even so adroit and experienced a News Editor as Hind could not always avoid. From time to time a news item which had already appeared in some paper, or even in the *Morning Call* itself, would creep undetected into the tail of the statement. Then, inevitably, Jackson would pounce. "That's old, Joe," he would say in a tone of finality, and he would then quote the newspaper, the date, and sometimes even the exact position in the column where it had been published. His memory was photographic and prodigious. Hind would grin. There was no arguing with Jackson.

Sometimes an interesting news item would be followed by a barrage of supplementary questions from Ede or Jackson or anyone else who was interested, and a free-for-all would follow. Baiting the News Editor was considered a legitimate sport, in which all but the vulnerable Jessop participated. It occasionally happened that Hind had summarised the news item too quickly before coming into conference, and could not recollect the details required of him. Then he would either declare that the story was thin and valueless, really not worth anyone's attention, or shuffle rapidly through his papers with exclamations of astonishment that he could have overlooked that one piece of copy, or else—by a line of double-talk in which he excelled—attempt to convey the impression that he was actually giving the required answers. Then Ede would shake his head regretfully and the conference would collapse in laughter.

To-day, no such pitfalls yawned, and Hind proceeded for a while without interruption. Food news opened the statement—a dreary sign of the times, this, that an extra pennyworth of meat a week could steal a banner headline. Then came reports of a possible railway strike, on which the Industrial Correspondent was working; a White Paper on the distribution of manpower, and the latest coal production figures.

"That's all the dull stuff," said Hind. He knew what was important but he didn't pretend to like it. "There'll be the usual pre-holiday piece—trains, traffic prospects and so on." He looked inquiringly at the Editor. "I don't know whether we want to follow up Cooper-Wright's attack on the B.B.C. for harbouring fellow-travellers?"

Ede stroked his blue jowl. The Proprietor, who was in America, took a poor view of Cooper-Wright. "I don't think so, Joe—the fellow's probably right, but it's been said before, and we don't want to encourage a heresy hunt. We overdid it this morning—the speech was only worth a couple of sticks." Ede had picked up a good deal of jargon since taking over the editorship, and he was human enough to like airing it. It made him feel that he had been in newspapers all his life. "Carry on."

"Well, we've got the churches, of course." The *Morning Call* was currently campaigning for the repair of the blitzed city churches. "Two interviews."

"And pictures," put in the Art Editor.

"All right," said Ede. "Better run them to-day—it looks as though we're going to be a bit short of stuff anyway." Hind wrote the word "Must" against the item on his statement and proceeded. "The crime wave is still gathering strength," he said. "We've got three more cases to-day—an old woman coshed in Hampstead, a jewel-shop raid during the morning rush-hour, and a hi-jacking in Stepney."

Ede looked across at the Crime Reporter, with no great pleasure. Arthur Pringle was a short, unprepossessing man of forty-five with a narrow head, sandy hair and pale eyes. He had contrived to be taken on by the *Morning Call* at the height of the wartime manpower shortage, largely on the strength of his own hints that he had a pull with some of the "boys" at Scotland Yard. He had since held down the job by the well-worn Fleet Street device of absenting himself as much as possible from the office and surrounding all his movements with an aura of mystery. Although he was hardly ever where he was supposed to be, he was adept at appearing to be on hand if wanted, and important telephone messages always seemed to get relayed to him in time to avoid trouble. During his rare appearances in the office he sought to give the impression that he was engaged on secret business of the most vital nature, and on these occasions might be seen conversing out of the corner of his mouth in dark corridors while casting hunted glances to right and left. Even by Fleet Street standards he was illiterate, but he had a genius for "getting by".

To-day he felt nervous, and blinked back at Ede as though the unaccustomed limelight hurt his eyes. His racket, he suspected, was coming to an end, and perhaps his job as well. On the previous evening the News Editor had detected him in a serious malpractice, and it seemed likely that he had already reported the matter to the Editor. Pringle was the more anxious to create a good impression now.

"The jewel-shop raid is believed to be the work of the same gang that did the Thornton Heath job last week," he confided.

Ede nodded impatiently. "I dare say, but I think it's time we gave the public something more than snippets. You'd better do a feature article, Pringle, summarising the crime wave to date. Clean the whole thing up in one good piece."

"It's the shortage of police," said Pringle.

"Yes, yes, I know. Bring that in, of course, but I want a balanced picture of the whole situation. I'd like to see the article by four o'clock."

"Yes, sir," said Pringle, a trifle stunned and looking like an undersized Atlas bearing the weight of the underworld on his shoulders.

Ede turned again to Hind. "Anything more, Joe?"

"While we're on the crime stuff," said Hind, who had listened to these exchanges with malicious satisfaction, "there's an item here that links up—another judge who wants to re-introduce flogging for robbery with violence. That's the second in a week."

"The third," said Jackson. "If you remember, Latimer set the ball rolling last Monday."

"The third," said Hind with a smile.

The Leader Writer stirred, scenting a topic for editorial comment. "There's no case," he said with Olympian certainty. "The whole thing was thoroughly thrashed out by the Cadogan Committee and they were very emphatic." He proceeded to outline the Committee's main findings and a lively discussion started. Ede was always interested in matters of principle—far more than in the technicalities of newsspaper production. Hind sat back with his head sunk in his shoulders and grinned at the Sports Editor. He was far more interested in technicalities than he was in matters of principle. Jackson had his eye on the clock.

The lines of a leader comment were soon sketched out. Hind was folding up his statement. Ede said, "Is that the lot, Joe?"

"That's about all," said Hind. "Oh, except for a report of buried treasure under an old windmill in Norfolk. I don't know whether there's anything in it but I've sent Golightly up to have a look. It's an exclusive so far."

"Good man," said Ede.

Now it was Jessop's turn. He sat bolt upright with an expressionless face and began to read out the items typed on the foreign news statement in a voice that at times was barely audible. He stuck closely to his brief—he hadn't Hind's flair for dramatic public recital and his one aim was to get through quickly and without incurring criticism. In spite of the revelation that had come to him during the night and the knowledge—reinforced by the rectangular tin in his right-hand pocket—of his superiority to those in authority here, the habits of years were not to be discarded in an instant and he still appeared nervous. As he read he fidgeted with the statement, shifted in his seat, and wondered if people were listening to him. Ede sensed his embarrassment and made a mental note to announce Cardew's appointment that day, if only in fairness to Jessop. The man could hardly be expected to make much of a showing when the colleague who had been preferred to him was sitting beside him. All the same, Ede felt confirmed in his decision. Jessop simply hadn't the personality for a top-ranking job.

One or two people began to stir restlessly. Hardly anyone was interested in the foreign statement, particularly when it was about conferences rather than wars. When Jessop twice stumbled over a Polish name—with good reason, for it was Skrzypczynski!—Hind began to laugh, soundlessly, shaking the table. Jessop shot him a look of hatred and his right hand went to his pocket, finding comfort there. Perhaps Providence would take note of the episode.

"Better get through the rest quickly," said Ede to Jessop, not without sympathy. "What about this Note to Hungary that the F.O. is taking so seriously?" Jessop was about to explain, but Ede was restive and turned to Cardew. "You've got something on that, haven't you, Lionel?"

"Yes," said Cardew, "the position is this . . ." In a few rapid sentences the Diplomatic Correspondent summarised the Foreign Office document. He was a tall, slender young man with fair wavy hair that was brushed as flat as possible to his neat head. He had a pale, rather distinguished face, with high cheekbones and an engaging smile—though to-day he seemed rather solemn. Young though he was—he was still in his late twenties—it was obvious as soon as he began to speak that he had a quick and comprehensive grasp of the matter he was talking about. His analysis was brilliant.

Ede nodded approvingly—that was all plain sailing. Lionel, he knew, would turn in an interesting piece in impeccable prose.

Jessop listened to the recital with averted eyes and a sardonic twist of his mouth. Cardew was slick and fluent—he would take anyone in. As the Diplomatic Correspondent concluded, he said, "There's nothing else of importance," and screwed up his statement, which was covered with doodles. Hind pushed back his chair hopefully and the columnist managed to get a signal of dismissal from Ede and crept out. The Sports Editor spoke up about the Big Fight and got the space he wanted. A tinkle of glass in the adjoining room reminded Ede that Munro would soon be arriving. He caught the Art Editor's eye. "Pictures downstairs, Fred. I can give you five minutes. Right, that's all." The conference was over.

Jessop got up, timing his movements with care. He allowed one or two people to leave ahead of him, but was careful not to be the last out of the room. At the lift, where there were already more of his colleagues than could be accommodated in one load, he muttered something about not being able to spend the whole day there and plunged down the stone stairs to the next floor. Then he turned along a little-used corridor and climbed up by the back stairs to the floor he had just left. He waited a moment or two, to give time for any stragglers to get clear, and again approached the conference room, this time from the opposite direction. The door stood open, the room was empty. He stepped in quickly and walked over to the inner door that led to the Directors' Dining Room. He listened. No sound came from inside. He wrapped a handkerchief round the door knob and opened the door a fraction, peeping in. The room was prepared for luncheon and the far door into the restaurant was closed. He slipped inside, emptied the contents of his tin on to a plate, carried the plate to the sideboard in his handkerchief, and slipped out again. He had done it! He felt a pleasant tingle of excitement, nothing more. Providence, he knew, was watching over him. He had nothing to fear.

Chapter Six

Dawson Munro, Governor and Commander-in-Chief of the scattered group of possessions known as the Outward Islands, was the last of a long line of colonial administrators. His forebears—hard, thrusting Empire-builders for the most part—had believed in the Divine Right of the Munros to administer, and Dawson had inherited the doctrine so completely as to be unconscious of the fact. He was, however, superficially aware of the requirements of a changing world and practised a benevolent paternalism where his ancestors would have relied on a sharp kick in the pants. His liberalism—with a small "l", for it was from the Labour Government that he had received his rapid advancement—took the form of a rather patronising goodwill towards all his fellow-men and an often-expressed belief that even the most murderous of his coloured subjects were "not bad chaps at heart." He was erudite, conscientious, and up to a point able, but he suffered from a monumental complacency and a limitless capacity for self-deception. Scurrilous attacks on him in the vernacular Press of Port Sargasso had not shaken his conviction that he enjoyed the goodwill of the underdog, nor had recent developments in the Outward Islands undermined his certainty that he knew what was best in all circumstances. He was the sort of man who blandly refuses to believe that he has any enemies, and in fact has few friends.

Munro had accepted Ede's invitation to lunch at the *Morning Call* more as a magnanimous return for the useful editorial backing the paper had given him in a critical hour than because he had any nostalgic desire to revisit the scene of his early literary labours. Now that he held a responsible public position his former association with what was, after all, a rather sensational popular daily was slightly embarrassing. Indeed, if the subject of his early career ever arose in the course of conversation—and as he enjoyed talking about himself it quite often did—he usually managed to convey the impression that his scholastic triumphs at Harrow and Trinity had been followed almost at once by membership of the House of Commons and a successful Under-Secretaryship. To-day, as he strode behind a somewhat grubby urchin on his way to the Editor's room, there was nothing in his expression of benevolent interest to indicate that he was familiar with every inch of the place. Nor would his greeting to Miss Timmins, amiable though it was, have revealed to a stranger that they had once been troupers in the same company.

The Editor poured sherry at a small cocktail cabinet in his room and smilingly handed Munro his glass. The Governor was a tall man with a large frame that had not as yet filled out—he was barely forty. To remedy this defect—for he already thought of himself as an elder statesman—he had a habit of thrusting out his stomach, which with his stooping donnish shoulders, gave his figure the shape of an elongated letter S. He boomed in cultured accents, his head patronisingly inclined from long habit, his mild gaze focused to shrewdness by thick lenses. In a surprisingly short time he was embarked on a recital of his recent activities.

Ede sipped his sherry, observed his man closely, and politely waited for an opportunity to get a word in. He was no sycophant, and a Governor *qua* Governor meant nothing to him, but it was almost a physical impossibility for him to be rude to anyone.

"By the way," he managed to say at last, "I thought I'd ask Iredale to join us for lunch, as you assured me you had no objection. You're certain that's all right?"

"Quite all right, my dear fellow," said Munro heartily. "I shall be delighted to see him again. Some people might find him a bit abrupt, perhaps, but I know he's a good chap at heart. He seemed to me to have ability, too." The Governor fingered the heavy gold chain—a family heirloom—that lay across his waistcoat. "At the same time, Ede, I think you were wise not to use those articles of his. He showed them to me, you know—very properly, in the circumstances. They exhibited rather more heat than light, I thought. I didn't object to the personal criticism in the least—in my position you get a good deal of that from the less well-informed section of the Press—but I felt it wasn't quite the moment to rock the boat."

"I dare say not." Ede was slightly annoyed by Munro's tone. It was one thing to make his own decision on a matter of policy—though he wasn't so sure of the soundness of that decision now that he had had an opportunity to reflect on what Iredale had said—but quite another to have it so loftily approved by an interested party. "I gather," he said, "that you and Iredale had one or two rather heated encounters."

"Oh, nothing to speak of," said Munro with the good-humoured tolerance of a headmaster discussing a boy's minor peccadillo with a parent. "Personally I like to see a newspaperman taking his assignment so seriously. So many of them, unfortunately, are far too frivolous. How is Iredale feeling about it all now?"

"Still ruffled, but cooling down. If you happen to feel like talking shop after lunch—and I frankly hope you will—I think I can promise you there'll be no broken heads. By the way, how long are you staying in England?" The Editor's tone was casual. He knew perfectly well that the answer depended on what the Secretary of State had had to say to Munro that morning.

"I expect to fly back on Tuesday," said the Governor complacently.

"Ah! Speculations disproved, in fact?"

"They were always groundless, my dear fellow. I really don't know why the Press always has to take a melodramatic view whenever a Governor is recalled for consultations. As a matter of fact, this whole business has been exaggerated out of all proportion. It's been very unfortunate, of course—very unfortunate indeed—and shocking bad luck for the Clintons." He gave a reminiscent shake of his head. "The family was wiped out, you know. Still, these things do happen in the best-regulated colonies, and between ourselves there was a certain amount of provocation. The Clintons were not the most liberal planters in the colony."

"Would it have made any difference if they had been?" Ede's

feelings towards the absent Iredale were growing friendlier every moment.

Munro appeared to bend his whole judicial capacity to the question. "M'm—yes, I think it might have done. Mind you, I'm not blaming the planters—at least, not altogether. They have their difficulties—one has to admit that. But they don't move with the times, and I must say some of them are extremely headstrong. They give me a great deal of trouble."

"Iredale tells me a few of them actually threatened you."

"Yes, that is so, but I can't feel they meant what they said. Probably their nerves were a little frayed. Two or three of them called at Government House—a sort of unofficial deputation—demanding what they called 'strong measures'. Naturally I wasn't prepared to give them assurances under pressure. Then one of them made the very improper observation that if I wasn't careful my body would be found floating in the lagoon! I know him well—he's a hot-tempered chap with a very trying wife, but he's a good fellow really. He'll probably ask me over for a drink as soon as I get back."

"I can't say I envy you your job," said Ede. "It almost sounds as though you're conducting a war on two fronts."

"I have to hold the balance. Naturally, a job like mine has its dangers, but someone has to carry on the public service. Three of my ancestors were assassinated, you know . . ." Munro mentioned the fact as though it were the first time in his life he had told anyone. "But then, I daresay they deserved it. Getting on with people is an art. My rule is to try to see the good points of the other fellow, and always to shake hands when the row's over."

Ede smiled. "Admirable counsel! If you ever get tired of your islands, Munro, you might come back and do a little peacemaking here. I assure you that planters have nothing on newspapermen when it comes to temperament." He glanced at the clock. "Well, let's go upstairs, shall we, and see if the restaurant has improved at all since your time. Lionel Cardew will be joining us—he's our new Foreign Editor from to-day. You'll find him very well-informed.

I've asked Joe Hind, too—he's always good company. You remember him, I expect?"

"The Falstaff of the *Morning Call*? Yes, I remember Joe. A capital fellow. Is he drinking as hard as ever? I'm afraid that's a thing I can't agree with . . ." As Munro followed the Editor to the lift, the echoes of his voice boomed round the lower corridors.

Chapter Seven

There is no more disturbing influence in a newspaper office than a roving foreign correspondent home on leave between assignments. The office draws him irresistibly, but he has no work to do there unless some emergency arises, no hours to keep, not even his own desk to sit at. He haunts the Foreign Room, in it but not of it. He browses through the morning papers, restlessly scans the tape, flirts with the secretary and wisecracks with anyone who comes in. When he is obviously becoming an unbearable nuisance he drifts out disconsolately and wanders idly from room to room, looking in vain for a colleague with sufficient leisure to join him in a "quick one". He is a mild joke around the place. People meeting him in corridors say, "Good Lord, are you still here?—I thought you'd gone to China," and he grins sheepishly and says he expects to be in China by Thursday. Then they slap him encouragingly on the back, their minds clearly elsewhere, and rush away. Long before lunch-time, he profoundly wishes he were already in China.

It was in something of this frame of mind that Bill Iredale made his way back to the Foreign Room at about the same time that the Editor was pouring out Munro's first glass of sherry. Miss Burton, the secretary-typist, had gone to lunch, and so had the tape-machine boy. Edgar Jessop was there alone, sitting quietly at his desk, waiting for the sudden hubbub that would tell him his plan had worked. He stirred as Iredale entered. He was quite glad to see Bill—in fact he felt as though he would like to take Bill into his confidence. Bill would understand—he had had a raw deal too. He knew what it felt like to be humiliated. But then, Bill hadn't had the revelation. Better, perhaps, to keep his own counsel.

Iredale drew up a chair, stuck his feet on a desk, and felt for his pipe. This was the first opportunity he had had of a quiet *téte-á-téte* since Jessop's interview with the Editor on the previous evening.

"Any news, Ed?" he asked. "About you, I mean?"

"I didn't get the job," said Jessop in a flat tone. It wasn't so important now, of course, but it wouldn't do to let that be seen.

"Oh, bad luck!" Iredale felt genuinely sorry. His friendly relationship with Jessop was so old-established, so deeply-rooted in common professional experience, that he had long taken it for granted. They both belonged to the depleted Old Guard of the paper—and ink, like blood, was thicker than water. As reporters they had collaborated on the same stories, sharing triumphs and failures; jointly, they had faced sudden crises in the early morning hours; they could recall the same great occasions, the same people, the same office jokes; they had passed through the same exacting school. Even after Iredale had gone abroad, the bond had continued, for Jessop in the Foreign Room had often handled his dispatches and had kept in constant touch by cable. That had meant a great deal to Iredale during the war, when the friendly encouraging telegram from London had been like air to a diver. Of the two, Jessop had had the more positive sentiment, for in the early days he had felt something like hero worship for Iredale's independence and self-reliance, the qualities he lacked. He had been eager and hopeful then; Iredale couldn't fail to notice that he had become shut-in and morose and bitter, but he was well aware of Jessop's professional disappointments as well as of his recent personal loss, and continued to think of him as he had been, rather than as he was now. As he looked at Jessop's drawn face, he felt the old twinge of compassion for a man whose hopes had always outrun his achievements and who lacked the blessing of the strong—inner repose. The fact that Iredale could well see Ede's point of view in passing Jessop over for the job of Foreign Editor didn't lessen his sympathy for his old stable companion.

He prodded the bowl of his pipe thoughtfully. "Who *is* getting the job?" he asked. "Do you know?"

"Cardew, of course. To get anywhere on this paper you have to make love to the Editor's wife and then she sees that you get promotion!"

Even Iredale, hardened though he was to newspaper scandal, looked a bit taken aback at that. "Easy, old man! That's going rather far, isn't it?"

"It's true," said Jessop. "You wouldn't know about it, you've been out of the country, but everybody else does. Cardew's always taking her out—and this is his reward. Just imagine it—Cardew!" He drew fiercely on his cigarette. "Why, only a year or two back I was teaching him his Fleet Street ABC. Do you know, when he came here he hardly knew the difference between a galley and a spike. I remember Ede bringing him in . . ." Suddenly the Editor's fruity, confident voice seemed to fill the room as Jessop plunged into bitter mimicry. "'Oh, Jessop, I want you to meet Lionel Cardew. He's just joined the staff and he doesn't know much about newspapers. I want you to teach him all you can about the technical side. Take him under your wing, there's a good fellow."'

Iredale couldn't repress a smile. Jessop's talent for mimicry was always amusing, even though his targets were not always kindly chosen.

"And that's just what I did," Jessop added. "I took the so-and-so under my wing and hatched him out and now I've got to take orders from him and pretend that he knows best."

Iredale sat silent for a moment, frowning. He didn't know Cardew well, but what little he'd seen of him, he'd liked. In any case, there had been special reasons, he knew, for giving Cardew an opportunity on the paper, and he couldn't let Jessop's remarks pass without protest. "He may not have known the difference between a galley and a spike, Ed, but by God he knew the difference between a Spitfire and a Messerschmitt. He didn't get that D.F.C. and bar for nothing. I reckon he more than earned any special consideration he got." He saw that Jessop had turned pale, and wished the subject of Cardew had not come up. "It must have been galling for you, though," he added. "I know just how you feel. What happens now? Didn't Ede offer you a break at all?"

"He wanted to send me to Malaya, if you call that a 'break'."

Iredale's face cleared. "You don't say!" He sounded delighted. "Well, that's fine, Ed. What are you hanging about for? Take my advice, old boy, and go. Shake the dust of the office from your feet—it's a wonderful place to be a long way away from. You'll feel a new man out there."

"Eversley is a dead man," said Jessop darkly. "I don't believe Ede would be sorry if I came to a sticky end too. He's always had it in for me."

"Don't be bloody silly," said Iredale. He flung an empty tobacco tin into the waste paper basket with unnecessary violence. When Jessop got that sort of hump there was really nothing to be done about him.

Suddenly the door opened and Katharine Camden's well-groomed head appeared. "You haven't got Joe Hind, have you?" she asked, glancing round. Iredale pretended to look under the desk and said, "Sorry!" He was about to suggest a drink when he remembered his lunch appointment. Regretfully he watched the door close behind her.

"Nice girl," he observed.

Jessop snorted. "I thought you were sore with her about that article."

"I was, but she talked me out of it last night. I met her in the Crown. Have you ever noticed the way she walks? Beautiful action!"

Jessop had noticed. He always noticed attractive women, but that was as far as it went. He had never been able to overcome his natural diffidence sufficiently to do anything about them, except weave romantic fancies. He couldn't even manage the fluffy ones, let alone the sophisticated beauties. "She's not my type," he said.

"Is she tied up with anyone, do you know?" Iredale tried to make the question sound offhand.

"I don't think so. She's always with the crowd. She used to go around with O'Shea . . ." Jessop broke off with a jerk, as though he'd suddenly touched a live wire.

"O'Shea? Ah, yes, I remember him. Tall fellow with a long chin. Wasn't he killed when that bomb blew up?"

"Yes," said Jessop.

"Tough luck for her. I suppose she's still getting over him." Now that Iredale's interest was aroused he realised that he'd never heard the full story of the office bomb. It took a long time to catch up with things missed during the war—there had been so many of them. "Were you here when it happened, Ed? It must have been quite a night."

"It wasn't at night," said Jessop, fiddling nervously with a piece of copy. "It was just before morning conference. The bomb fell in the well on the Saturday night and blew up on the Monday morning. Delayed action."

"Oh, was that it? It must have made a hell of a row when it fell—wasn't it reported?"

"No. It should have been, of course. There was a rota of wardens—we all took turns. We had to patrol during raids, just in case something like that happened. As a matter of fact, I was on duty myself at that end of the building on the Sunday night—if the bomb had fallen then I'd have heard it and we'd have been all right. But, as I say, it must have dropped on the Saturday night, when a chap named Archer was supposed to be doing his spell. I don't think you ever met him. The blighter was playing pontoon in the shelter."

"Bad show, eh? Was there a row about it?"

"The directors took a very poor view from their safe country retreats," said Jessop sardonically. "They stopped asking for Archer's deferment after that. He was killed in Normandy. With all those deaths on his conscience, I'm not sure it wasn't the best thing that could happen to him." Jessop's hands were still busy with the piece of copy. "Actually," he said after a pause, "it was lucky for me that Archer *was* playing pontoon on the Saturday, or they might have thought I was responsible. But nothing dropped while I was on deck—I'd swear to that any time, in any place." He had become very intense.

Iredale looked at him in mild surprise. "Okay—nobody said it did." He glanced up at the clock and gave a low whistle. "I must be off."

"What's the hurry?" asked Jessop. "You're not running after Katharine Camden, are you?"

"No such luck. I'm lunching with Governor Munro, believe it or not!"

Jessop stared at him, a look of incredulity spreading over his face. "*You*—with Munro?" He choked back his rising panic. This was frightful. Iredale was on the side of the angels. Iredale was a good fellow—his friend—almost his only friend. "I don't get it," he said. "I thought you and he were at each other's throats."

"It's a fool idea of Ede's. As a matter of fact, I believe I'm on his conscience a bit. Anyway, he seems to want us all to shake hands and be friends. I can't say I'm looking forward to the session."

"It's more than *I'd* do with Munro," said Jessop slowly. Delay—that was the only thing that would help now. The conversation must be kept going somehow. "He always used to behave as though he was God Almighty when he worked here, and he hasn't changed. He passed me in the corridor a few minutes ago and he looked straight through me."

Iredale took his feet off the desk. "You go to Malaya, old son," he said lightly. "You'll be appreciated there."

Jessop leaned forward, willing him to stay. "It's all very well, Bill—I can't suddenly go off like that. I'm not footloose the way you are. I've got things to do here. Just look at this for a moment and you'll see what I mean." He opened his dispatch case and took out the *opus*, smoothing out a dog-eared corner of the folder. "It's nearly finished—it's a report I'm doing on Press methods in Britain for the Human Rights Commission of U.N.O. What chance would I have of getting on with it in Malaya?"

Iredale, with one eye on the clock, allowed Jessop to press the bulky manuscript into his hand. He had known that Jessop did some scribbling in his spare time, but it was a rare privilege for anyone to be shown the results. He glanced curiously at the title page.

"My idea," Jessop explained, "is that the Human Rights Commission should lay down common standards of Press behaviour for all countries—and make sure that they're enforced, of course."

Iredale raised his eyebrows. "Isn't that a bit dangerous? *And* impracticable, I would have said. Still . . ." He paged rapidly through the manuscript. "Gosh, you've been busy. All in your own fair hand, too."

"The Press is a sewer," Jessop declared. "It's got to be cleaned up."

Iredale laughed. "You need a drink. I'd like to read this, Ed, but it'll have to be later on." He pushed the *opus* back across the desk. "My God, it's five past one. Ede'll shoot me. So long—don't fall down the sewer!" He jumped up and rushed from the room.

Jessop sat still, waiting. Tiny beads of sweat gathered on his forehead.

Chapter Eight

At ten minutes to one, while Ede and Munro were still getting acquainted and Iredale and Jessop were discussing the bomb, Lionel Cardew had dropped into the News Room to tell Hind about a home news angle to one of his diplomatic stories. His new appointment had not yet been announced, but he knew it was going to be at any moment. In the circumstances, he might have been expected to seem pleased with life, but the look of anxiety that had been noticeable at the conference had now settled more deeply on his usually sunny features. The fact was that he was torn apart with worry. His affairs were in a mess.

Cardew was a man whose whole life and outlook had been changed by his war experiences. In September 1939, he had just left his public school and was about to go up to Oxford to read for his degree before entering the diplomatic service, thereby following a firm tradition of the upper middle class family from which he came. With the outbreak of war he had scrapped all his plans and rushed impulsively into the Royal Air Force. He had had the youth, the intelligence and the dash to make a first-class fighter pilot, and in 1940 he had been one of "the few" in the Battle of Britain. Twice he had been shot down and survived; twice he had been decorated. The final inevitable crash had left him with a considerable "bag" of enemy planes to his credit, a broken body, and an exhausted nervous system. He had been ill for two years and had then been invalided out of the service, an honourable veteran of twenty-two.

His people had wanted him to resume his studies, thinking that a year or two at Oxford would have a tranquilising and stabilising effect on him, but the Foreign Office no longer had any appeal for him. His highly-strung, mercurial temperament had boggled at the thought of the cloistered life, the pre-occupation with precedent, code and protocol. Post-war diplomacy would no doubt demand courage, flair and the lively, nimble brain, and all of these he had, but it would also require orthodoxy and restraint. As a diplomat one could be eccentric but not erratic; brilliant but not independent. Violent feelings must be curbed, their expression confined to the raised eyebrow, the measured reproof. Cardew rightly doubted his patience and prudence. When an opportunity had occurred, after a meeting with Nicholas Ede at a party, he had given a new twist to the family occupation by joining the *Morning Call*. Very soon he had been appointed Diplomatic Correspondent.

He had enjoyed the next few years. The atmosphere of the office had proved informal, human, and alive. Ede had befriended him and watched over him. Rosemary Ede had admired and encouraged him. The work had been fascinating. He had attended all the crucial post-war conferences and written about them with verve and spirit. When at times he had seemed a bit too brilliant, taking a line too much of his own, Ede had restrained him with affection and understanding.

Now all that pleasant chapter had ended, not because of his new appointment—as Foreign Editor he would have a new and wider field for his gifts—but because his personal life had got out of hand. He knew that he faced a crisis, and must make a quick decision.

He had just begun to explain his errand to the News Editor when a slip of paper was brought in announcing his promotion. Hind, all bonhomie, clapped the ex-Diplomatic Correspondent heartily on the back. "Splendid news, Lionel," he said genially. "I've always felt you were the man for that job."

Cardew winced slightly, but his smile was polite. "Thanks," he said. He had little in common with the News Editor.

Hind glanced up at the clock. "Pity we can't celebrate," he said. An idea seemed suddenly to flash into his mind, and Cardew guessed what it was. "You're going to this Munro lunch too, aren't you?"

"Yes."

"Then why don't we pop up there now and have a quick one before the others arrive?"

Cardew could think of no reason for refusing. "All right," he agreed. These office luncheons were informal affairs, and it was recognised that whoever arrived first would start pouring the drinks.

"Of course," said Hind as they went up in the creaky old lift, "it won't be so easy to fill your old post. It isn't every Diplomatic Correspondent who can stand up to the Foreign Office." Now that Cardew was so obviously on the up-and-up there could be no harm in laying it on a bit. "Any idea who's to succeed you?"

"Not the remotest." Cardew was not disposed to become expansive with Hind. He felt in a false position, and it made him uncommunicative.

The Directors' Dining Room looked pleasantly hospitable. The table, laid for five, was gay with flowers. On a sideboard stood a generous assortment of bottles, flanked by a plate of stuffed olives and a dish of salted almonds.

Hind went straight to the bottles. If they were quick they might manage a second drink before the others arrived. "What'll you have, Lionel?"

"Sherry, please," said Cardew. Hind poured the drink, then mixed a generous gin-and-French for himself.

"Well," he said, lifting his glass, "here's luck—and may you always know the answers at Conference!" He gulped his drink and gave a deep "Ah!" of satisfaction. His small greedy eyes swept the sideboard. "Have an olive."

"Not for me, thanks. I don't like the things. You go ahead." Cardew helped himself delicately to a few almonds.

"I can't understand anyone not liking olives," said Hind. "They're one of my weaknesses. I always remember a night in Malaga . . . Did I ever tell you about that, I wonder?" He carefully selected a large olive, popped it into his mouth and chumped it up.

"*What* about the night in Malaga?" asked Cardew in a bored tone as he strolled over to the table to look at the menu card. He had no interest in the News Editor's reminiscences, which were usually lecherous. Suddenly there was an agonised cry behind him and the sound of shattering glass. He swung round in alarm. Hind's face was fearfully distorted and his great frame was swaying. Before Cardew could reach him he had crashed to the floor. His muscles were twitching and there was froth on his lips.

After one shocked glance Cardew dived for the telephone and dialled the News Room. Soames, the Assistant Editor, answered. "This is Cardew. Get a doctor quickly and send him to the Directors' Dining Room. Hind's had a fit or something. Hurry!" He dropped the receiver, knelt down beside the unconscious man and loosened his collar. Hind was obviously in a very bad way. His eyes were fixed and glistening; his skin felt cold and clammy. Cardew, leaning over him, became aware of a faint smell of bitter almonds. A scared look came into his face.

A moment later there was a booming laugh in the corridor and the door opened. "As a matter of fact I think it was all bluster," Munro was saying as he preceded Ede into the room. "I don't think he meant it at all . . ."

Cardew looked up at them. "Hind's ill. I've sent for a doctor. He's pretty bad."

"Oh, dear me," said Ede with quick concern, and dropped to his knees beside Hind.

"We had a drink," said Cardew shakily. "He ate an olive and collapsed at once. It all happened in a few seconds."

Ede was trying to find a pulse. His face was very grave. "Who's getting the doctor?"

"I asked the News Room."

"Better hurry them up. I can't feel anything here."

There were more footsteps in the corridor and Iredale came hurrying into the room, an apology for lateness on his lips. He stopped short suddenly and stared at the tableau. "What's the trouble . . .?" he began.

"It's Hind," said Ede over his shoulder. "He's . . ." He broke off, and for a moment there was complete silence. Then he got slowly to his feet. "I'm very much afraid the poor fellow's dead."

Chapter Nine

News of the tragedy swept quickly through the office and brought the editorial wheels to a sudden halt. People collected in small groups, outwardly grave yet inwardly excited, as after a declaration of war. Members of the staff who were just going out to lunch spread the sensational tidings in the street; others, just coming in, were swiftly apprised and swelled the undercurrent of commotion. There was a dearth of hard facts, but according to Pringle, who had precipitately dropped his feature article on the crime wave and had been nosing about on the fringe of the police cordon upstairs, it was definitely murder—"no doubt about it, old man." Significant arrivals at the front entrance of the building were recorded by a dozen heads thrust from windows above the crawling Fleet Street traffic: a man with a brisk walk and a black bag, a squad car with a full quota of policemen, an ambulance, and another police car bearing three plain-clothes officers. Yes, it looked as though Pringle was right. The brazen infiltration of reporters from rival papers was noted, not without indignation. Up from the seething pavement below came the patient, appealing tones of two uniformed constables—"*Move* along there, please, *move* along."

To Jessop, sitting alone in an ecstatic glow, the information he had been waiting for came from someone shouting in the corridor to someone else who passed—"They say it's Hind!" Jessop smiled quietly. A very satisfactory choice by Providence, in view of Hind's behaviour that morning! He felt no compunction—only the sort of elation that comes from reading a communique recording an enemy disaster. This was his first victory over the powers of evil. Now he must show, by wise discretion, that he was worthy to be the instrument of Nemesis. He went out in search of a group to which he could unobtrusively attach himself.

Up in the Directors' Dining Room investigations had begun. Plain-clothes men were taking photographs, dusting doorhandles and furniture for the chance fingerprint, and packing up china, glass and cutlery for closer scrutiny at leisure. Hind's body still lay on the floor, a napkin over the contorted face. Ede had answered the first obvious questions, and he and his guests had been shepherded downstairs until the police were ready to see them.

Chief Inspector Alfred Haines, of Scotland Yard's Criminal Investigation Department, took a stuffed olive from the plate on the sideboard, drew out the plug of red pimento with a pair of tweezers, and sniffed cautiously at the opening. He passed the olive to his colleague, Inspector Ogilvie, with a significant glance, and repeated the operation with a second and a third. Each gave off the characteristic odour of cyanide.

"You're right, doctor." he said to the elderly man beside him. "They all seem to have been tampered with. Ingenious method, I must say." Haines was a solidly-built man of medium height, fiftyish, with shrewd grey eyes under bushy grey brows and an expression of benevolence that seemed out of place in an officer who had earned the reputation of being one of the Yard's most formidable detectives.

Dr. Mather, who had arrived on the scene too late to do anything but report a homicide, nodded sagely. "Yes, you're up against a clever fellow. I've heard of chocolates being used, but these things must have been much easier to fill, and they're just as effective. You notice how the plug keeps the smell in. I don't suppose that poor chap knew that anything was wrong until he'd crunched the thing up—and then it would be too late. It's deadly stuff." Looking pointedly at the olive in Haines's fingers he added, "It should be handled with gloves."

"Don't worry," said Haines. "I'll wash in a moment."

"The Nazis used to carry it round with them when they were on the run at the end of the war," Mather went on. "I once saw an SS general die of it in under thirty seconds, but that was hydrocyanic acid—these crystals would take a little longer to absorb." He picked up his case. "Well, I hope you get your man, Inspector. It's a good job the brains aren't all on one side, eh? You know where to find me if you want me." He gave Haines a friendly nod and departed.

The Chief Inspector looked round for Sergeant Miles. "You can get these olives packed up now, Sergeant. Don't touch the plate—I'd like to have that gone over for prints before it's moved."

"Right, sir." Using the inspector's tweezers, Sergeant Miles began to put the olives into a small container. He picked them up gingerly, as though they might explode in his fingers. He was an earnest-looking young fellow, with a heavy jaw and a schoolgirl complexion.

Haines joined Ogilvie, and for a time they watched the routine work proceeding. Haines was wearing a faintly rueful expression. "Pretty bare, eh, Inspector?"

Ogilvie nodded. They had made their own careful examination of the room, but superficially it was entirely without clues. No initialled handkerchief had been conveniently dropped under the sideboard; no lipstick had fallen from a handbag, or wallet from a pocket. Experts might succeed in probing some of the room's secrets after hours of labour in dark room and laboratory, but it looked as though there were to be no short cuts.

"Let's go and talk to the manageress," said Haines. He motioned to one of his men. "All right, Johnson, you can take the body away now."

Miss Hewson, who ran the restaurant, was sitting alone at a table, waiting to be interviewed, her hands nervously clasping and unclasping in her lap. She was a thin, worried-looking woman of middle age, with fading auburn hair and prominent teeth.

Haines and Ogilvie drew up chairs and the Chief Inspector came straight to the point. "About these olives, Miss Hewson. Where did they come from in the first place, where were they kept, and who had access to them? I should like to know their whole history."

Miss Hewson's agitation found relief in speech. "Inspector," she said in a high-pitched voice, "I don't know any more about them than you do. The only thing I can tell you positively is that they didn't come from *my* kitchen."

"They didn't?" Haines stared at her in surprise.

"Definitely not. I often do provide olives, because I know Mr. Ede likes them, but one has to make a change now and then, and to-day I gave them salted almonds instead."

"But you do keep olives in your pantry?" put in Ogilvie, his dark eyes alert and his pointed nose twitching with interest. He was a good ten years younger than Haines and looked his complete antithesis, having a thin, fresh-coloured face, lean body, and elastic step. A naturally impatient man, Ogilvie had sometimes thought his Chief almost too deliberate in his methods, almost over-inclined to reflection, but experience had shown him that Haines was usually justified in the end.

Miss Hewson gave the younger man a toothy smile. "I do keep them, of course," she said, "but the only ones I have now are two unopened jars—you can see them if you want to. I buy them in small jars so that once they're opened they get finished straight away, and we haven't had olives here for a fortnight. Oh, no, someone brought those olives in from outside, though how they got on to the sideboard is a mystery to me."

"What about the plate they were on?" asked Haines. "Where did that come from?"

"That's another thing." Miss Hewson seemed more indignant now than upset. "It was a plate from the table—Mr. Ede's bread plate. Someone had been interfering with the table after it was laid. I saw that at once."

"How do you mean, at once?"

"Well, it was about five past one, actually. I couldn't understand why Mr. Ede hadn't rung the bell for lunch—he usually rings it as soon as he comes up—so I popped my head in to make sure the bell was working Poor Mr. Hind was lying on the floor and I heard Mr. Cardew say something to Mr. Ede about olives, and then of course I looked and saw them, and I noticed that Mr. Ede's side plate had been taken."

Haines nodded approvingly. Miss Hewson evidently had an eye

for detail in spite of her present nervousness. "If, as you suggest, some unauthorised person put the olives there, have you any idea when that could have been done?"

"Well, it must have been after half-past twelve," said the manageress. "That I can be certain of. Evelyn finished laying the table at half-past, and I went in as I always do to make sure everything was just as Mr. Ede would like it. There were definitely no olives on the sideboard then."

"You're quite certain of that?" Haines pressed her. "It may be very important."

"I'm positive, and so is Evelyn."

"Did either of you go into the room again?"

"Not until after everything had happened."

"Do you think you'd have noticed if any unauthorised person had gone in from the restaurant?"

"Not necessarily," said Miss Hewson. "I shouldn't think any of the staff would have done because they're all very busy at that time, but one of the customers might have. In any case, there's a door from the Board Room and another from the corridor."

"Yes, so I see." Haines pondered. "I suppose you're quite an expert on food, Miss Hewson. Did you happen to have a look at the olives?"

"Yes, I did. They were very nice ones—the best quality stuffed Spanish olives, and beautifully fresh."

"Are they difficult to get hold of?"

"Oh no, you can buy them anywhere—at a price, of course."

"M'm. Well, thank you, Miss Hewson, you've been very helpful. Now perhaps we could have a word with Evelyn?"

"I'll send her in," said the manageress. She was obviously relieved at having cleared the restaurant of responsibility for such a shocking occurrence.

Haines got up. "Will you talk to the girl, Ogilvie? I expect that story's all right, but you'd better check it thoroughly. Have a squint round the pantry, too. I'll go and see Ede."

Chapter Ten

It was a strained, tense group that the inspector found waiting for him when Miss Timmins, her cheeks pallid around their hectic spots of rouge, showed him into the Editor's room. Discussion of the tragedy had come to a standstill. Ede was sitting at his desk, his face cupped in his hands, brooding on the incredible event and still seeking a way round some of the more alarming implications. Cardew, his own anxieties temporarily submerged, seemed numbed by the swift violence of Hind's death at such close quarters. He was just beginning to realise the narrowness of his own escape. Iredale was leaning over a low table, turning the pages of a mid-day paper with hardly a pretence of interest. Munro, sunk in an easy chair with his long legs stretched out, was rather regretting that he had consented to come in the first place. Jackson, who had been taking an active part in the conversation, was just going off to see that the broken routine of the paper was resumed without delay. An almost untouched plate of sandwiches and a bottle of whisky on Ede's table were an ironical reminder that luncheon had been the object of the gathering.

When Haines entered there was a general stir. Any news would offer a welcome respite from the weary treadmill of their thoughts. Almost before he was in the room Ede said anxiously, "Well, Inspector, what's the position?"

Haines never allowed himself to be hurried, particularly at the beginning of a case. "If you could just give me the names of these gentlemen again, sir . . ."

"Of course, Inspector. Mr. Dawson Munro, Governor of the

Outward Islands: Lionel Cardew, our Foreign Editor from to-day; William Iredale, one of our foreign correspondents."

"Thank you," said Haines, studying each man in turn. His shrewd eyes rested for a moment on Munro. "I seem to remember having read something about you in the papers lately, sir."

"That's quite possible, Inspector." Of the four, Munro was clearly the least shaken by Hind's death.

Haines grunted. The inclusion of a V.I.P. among the lunch guests wasn't going to make the investigation any easier. At the same time, it suggested an obvious line of inquiry.

"Well, gentlemen," he said, taking up a position by the window, "as I suppose you all realise, we're dealing with a case of murder. The olive that Mr. Hind ate contained poison, and the poison must have been put there deliberately."

"How very shocking!" remarked Munro, who never doubted that his observations on any subject would be acceptable.

"Naturally," the Inspector went on, addressing Ede, "we're still very much in the dark about how it happened, but we have established that the olives did *not* come from the restaurant. They were taken into the dining-room by some unauthorised person some time after half-past twelve to-day. We have to concentrate, therefore, on a single half-hour. It's obvious, I think, that whoever planted the olives knew all about your little luncheon party, and that he was very familiar with the inside of the office. That seems to point to a member of the staff, or at least someone closely associated with the paper. The first question I want to ask you, Mr. Ede, is who knew about the luncheon?"

Ede shrugged his shoulders helplessly. "Anyone might have known. These office luncheons are a fairly regular institution and there's nothing at all hush-hush about them. Any or all of the guests may have mentioned it." He looked at Cardew and Iredale, who both nodded. "Then the restaurant staff knew, of course, and I've no doubt Hind mentioned it in the News Room. My secretary, Miss Timmins, knew—it was she who telephoned the invitations. I don't know whether she managed to contact everyone the first time—if not, she may have left messages with other people. In any case, she's had the names of the guests on her pad for a couple of days and she's the Charing Cross of the office. Everyone stops by her desk. I should hardly think it a very promising line of inquiry, Inspector."

Haines agreed. "I'm just trying to get a rough idea of the dimensions of the problem," he explained. "Can you tell me when the invitations were sent out?"

"Let me see—it was about a week ago that I rang you, wasn't it, Munro? Then Miss Timmins asked Cardew and Hind the day before yesterday, and I asked Iredale myself yesterday evening."

Haines jotted down a note. The murderer had evidently had plenty of time to make his arrangements. "Very well. Now we come to the second point—access to the dining-room between half-past twelve and one o'clock. Have you anything to say about that, sir?"

Ede slowly shook his head, "Nothing very helpful, I'm afraid. A newspaper office is a free-and-easy sort of place, you know—people are moving about the whole time and no one pays any particular attention to what anyone else is doing. In any case, a good many of the staff must have been going in and out of the restaurant at that hour. The Directors' Dining Room wasn't locked—it would have been quite a simple matter for any one of them to have slipped in from the corridor. Or from the Board Room, of course," he added, and his eyes were troubled. "Our editorial conference broke up at just about twelve-thirty, and I suppose someone could have hung back after the others had gone. If you wish, I can give you a list of those who attended to-day."

"I'd be glad if you would," said Haines. He considered the matter for a moment. "It may not have any bearing if, as you say, any other member of the staff could have got in easily, but I'd like to see the list, all the same. Well, now, let's pass on. There's the question of the poison. We don't know yet exactly what was used, but it was some form of cyanide crystals. There wouldn't be anything like that around the office, would there, as far as you know?"

Ede was about to disclaim any knowledge when Iredale broke in quickly. "There would indeed. The Process Department uses something of the sort for making blocks—cyanide of potassium, I think. At least, it did in the old days."

Ede gave Iredale a sharp look. "I didn't know that, Bill."

"I'm sure a lot of people do know," said Iredale. He suddenly wondered whether, in all the circumstances, he'd been wise to volunteer the information, but having done so he met the inspector's interested gaze with frankness. "The reporters probably do, anyway. They go out on stories with photographers, and when they get back they're naturally interested to see how the pictures have turned out."

"Quite so," said Haines. "Do I understand that you've actually seen this cyanide yourself during a visit to the Process Department?"

"I did see it once, years ago of course. There was a big drum of it: it looked like grey mothballs."

"Well, you've certainly given me a valuable piece of information, Mr. Iredale. I shall have to look into that right away." The inspector made another note and gently cleared his throat. He looked soberly round at his audience. "There's one point about this tragic affair which I'm sure must have occurred to you all. How could the murderer have been sure that Mr. Hind would be his victim?"

Munro untwined his legs. "That's one of the things we've been discussing, Inspector. A fascinating problem! In my view, a number of possibilities present themselves . . ."

"I don't think we need make the problem more complicated than it is," said Ede. "I confess I hadn't realised it myself, but it seems that when Hind attended these office luncheons—which was quite often, as he was very good company—he was usually the first upstairs. So Mr. Cardew tells me."

"You mean he was a particularly punctual man?"

Cardew, to whom the question had been addressed, looked embarrassed. "It wasn't exactly that. The fact is that Hind was usually ready for a drink about one o'clock, and by arriving first he could help himself."

"I see. Was this—er—little trait of Mr. Hind's generally known?"

"I imagine so," said Cardew, still more uncomfortably. It seemed a bit hard to dwell on the man's foibles at this stage. "You must have known it, Bill."

Iredale nodded. "I guess everyone knew it. The reporters certainly did. Hind used to joke about it himself."

"And while we're on this particular subject," said Ede, "there's something else you should know, Inspector. Hind happened to be extremely fond of olives. I can vouch for that, because I am too."

"Was his liking for olives also generally known?"

"I should think a lot of people must have known. A newspaper office is a bit like a large family—we get to know each other's habits rather intimately."

"It wasn't difficult to know Hind's tastes," said Iredale dryly. "He was taken out to lunch a good deal, and naturally he was pretty forthcoming about them."

"Taken out by whom? By his colleagues?"

"By reporters, mostly." Iredale refrained from adding that the reporters had been encouraged to put the cost of entertaining the News Editor on their expense accounts.

"H'm." The inspector appeared to be weighing the information he'd been given with great care. "The suggestion is, then," he said at last, "that whoever wanted to get rid of Mr. Hind knew enough about his habits to be able to bank on his being the first person to eat an olive to-day?"

"It looks rather like that," said Ede.

"Well, you may be right, of course." Haines sounded very far from convinced. "If so, then all one can say is that it was an extraordinarily reckless gamble. No one could possibly have been certain of a thing like that. The murderer must surely have been prepared at least to risk other deaths."

There was a moment's heavy silence. Then Ede said, "Yes—I suppose we are all, in a sense, survivors." He looked doubtfully at the inspector. "It's difficult to conceive of such callous indifference right here among us."

"I can understand how you feel, sir," said Haines sympathetically, "but such people do exist. You probably remember that case only a few weeks ago, when someone planted a bomb in an aircraft and destroyed twenty people or more just to make certain of killing one individual. We may well be up against that type of mind here. In fact, on the evidence so far, it seems most likely. But that still leaves us with the vital question unanswered. Who was the *intended* victim—who was the person on whose account the whole plan was made? In spite of what you tell me about Mr. Hind's known habits, I don't think we can take it for granted that he was the one. At least, we must allow for other possibilities."

"We must allow, in fact, for four other possibilities?" asked Iredale.

"Just so."

"Oh, come," said Munro, "surely not? Speaking for myself, I really can't imagine . . ."

Haines interrupted him. "It's very natural for you to take that view, sir, but I dare say if Mr. Hind were here with us he'd be equally reluctant to think that anyone would want to kill *him*. For that matter, why *should* anyone have wanted to? Can any of you gentlemen make a suggestion?" He gazed round at the circle of unhelpful faces. Realising that if they had anything to say they'd be much more likely to say it in private, he prepared to close the discussion. "Well, Mr. Ede, it looks as though there may be a long and complicated inquiry ahead of us. I'm afraid you're going to find us a great nuisance around the place before it's finished."

Ede nodded gloomily. "It looks like it, Inspector, but I don't see how it can be helped. Provided you don't get in our way while we're bringing out the paper, we're at your disposal. I'm sure we're all as anxious as you are to get to the bottom of this atrocious business. I still find it almost unbelievable." His pink cheeks had an unaccustomed pallor. "If you need a room to work in, there's an empty office on the second floor that should house most of your sleuths. Miss Timmins will show you where it is. If you need anything or anyone, just dial 425 on the house telephone and she'll look after you. Don't hesitate."

"That's exceedingly kind of you," said Haines.

Dawson Munro produced a large old-fashioned watch from his

waistcoat pocket. "Well, Inspector, with your permission, I'll be off. I'm a very busy man, unfortunately."

"I should like to have a private word with you before you go, sir," said Haines. He had no intention of letting his V.I.P. slip away like that. "Perhaps you wouldn't mind stepping down now for a few minutes?"

"Very well, if it's necessary," said Munro graciously. He turned to the Editor. "Good-bye, Ede. I'm extremely sorry about all this. Most distressing for you."

Ede took the clammy hand extended by the Governor. "I'm afraid it's been anything but a pleasant reunion."

"Don't give it another thought, my dear fellow. Things like this can happen in the best-regulated newspaper offices." Munro gave the Editor an encouraging smile, nodded to Iredale and Cardew, and followed the inspector out. Ede came with them to give Miss Timmins a brief instruction. A few minutes later the two men had been shepherded into the vacant second-floor office.

"Now then, Inspector, what is it?" asked Munro affably as they found seats.

"Well, sir," said Haines, "in spite of what you said upstairs I can't help feeling you may be the reason for all this business. You've been having some political trouble in your part of the world, haven't you?"

Munro smiled tolerantly. "My dear Inspector, you're surely not trying to suggest that one of my Islanders followed me to London to poison me at a luncheon? You said yourself that whoever is responsible must be familiar with this office and is probably a member of the staff, and I agree with you."

"I know, sir, but you get some queer tie-ups in politics, particularly these days. People like your Islanders have friends and supporters all over the place. Of course, this isn't my province . . ."

"Just so, Inspector. You can take my word for it that you're alarming yourself unnecessarily. If I were you I should stick to fingerprints."

"I probably would if I had any," said Haines dryly. "Anyhow, sir, I shall have to make a special report about you. When an important personage narrowly escapes being poisoned at a party, the question of whether or not it was a coincidence that he happened to be there is obviously one of the very first things we have to look into. You haven't, I suppose, received any specific threats against your life?"

"Nothing specific, no. The police did find a homemade banner with the words 'Death to the Governor' on it after they'd dispersed a group of rioters about three weeks ago, but I took that as an indication of political disapproval rather than as a personal threat."

Haines suppressed a smile. "No doubt you get used to living in that sort of atmosphere and think nothing of it."

"One becomes philosophical."

"I suppose so. Apart from these political attacks, there hasn't been any individual who has at any time made threats against you—either out there or here?"

"Oh, no. At least . . ." Munro hesitated. "I had a little trouble with one of the planters, but it was a passing affair. I expect he's forgotten about it by now. In any case, he's in Port Sargasso so he clearly couldn't have had anything to do with this business to-day."

Haines nodded. He was reluctant to consider the more fantastic possibilities at this early stage of the inquiry. "What about people in this country, sir? You don't, I suppose, happen to know anyone who works in this building?"

"Oh, yes, Inspector," said Munro. "It hasn't any relevance to your investigations, I'm sure, but I—er—I used to be on the staff of this newspaper about fifteen years ago. There are still quite a number of familiar faces around."

Haines eyebrows shot up.

"But as far as I am aware," added Munro with a smile "none of them would want to kill me."

"No old scores to pay off, sir?"

"Fifteen years would be a long while to keep an old grudge on ice—and I'm not the sort of person who makes enemies. As far as I can remember, when I left here I enjoyed the goodwill of everyone."

"And you haven't been in contact with any of your old colleagues since you left the paper?"

"Not in recent years. Oh, apart from Mr. Iredale, of course—I saw quite a bit of him in the Outward Islands during the recent riots. The paper sent him out there to report on the situation, you know."

"No, sir, I didn't know. Were your relations with him quite friendly?"

Munro considered the question carefully. "Fundamentally I think I can say yes. We had—er—superficial differences . . ."

"About what, sir?"

"Oh, the local situation, you know—the riots . . ." Munro's tone dismissed the subject.

"I'd be grateful if you could be a little more explicit, sir. What exactly happened? Was there a quarrel?"

"With a newspaper correspondent? Hardly, my dear Inspector. No—Mr. Iredale became rather difficult and I had to disabuse his mind of certain misconceptions. The political situation in the Outward Islands is very complex, and only those with long experience of the people can really form a balanced judgment." The Governor launched himself happily into a favourite subject. "To understand it fully you have to go back to the emancipation of the slaves. In the late eighteenth century . . ."

Haines broke in hurriedly. "May I take it, sir, that Mr. Iredale was not in any way violent? I just want to get his attitude clear."

"His language was a trifle uninhibited," said Munro. "I was obliged to reprimand him, and he has a quick temper. However, it all blew over very quickly. You can see that for yourself—otherwise we should hardly have been lunching together."

"A meal doesn't necessarily imply amicable relations," observed Haines. "The plate held olives, if I remember—not an olive branch."

"You're letting your imagination run away with you, Inspector," said Munro, annoyed. "I see what you're driving at, of course, but the suggestion that Iredale may have tried to poison me because of a political difference, however acute, is utterly ridiculous. We simply don't *do* things like that in this country—and in any case, Iredale's not that kind of chap. I'm sure he bore me no malice at all." Munro again pulled out his watch. "And I'm afraid I've far too much to do, Inspector, to waste time on such improbable theories."

"All right, sir," said Haines, getting up, "I'm sorry to have detained you. By the way, how did you get along with Mr. Hind when you and he were colleagues together?"

Munro looked surprised. "Oh, quite well—he wasn't a bad sort of fellow. A bit uncouth, perhaps. I hadn't seen him for years, of course, until to-day."

"The place must seem strange to you after all this time," said Haines. "Did you manage to find your own way to the Editor's Room before lunch or did someone take you up?"

"I was taken up by a boy," said Munro stiffly. "Good gracious, Inspector, are you now considering *me* as a potential murderer?"

Haines was unperturbed. "Some day, sir, when both of us are less busy than we are now, I hope you'll tell me about the political situation in the Outward Islands, and I'll tell you about my methods of criminal investigation. I don't doubt that we shall both learn a great deal." He accompanied Munro to the door. "Where can I get you in case of need?"

"At my club, the Acropolis. I shall be leaving England on Thursday."

"I'll wish you a safe journey, then," said Haines politely.

"Thank you, Inspector."

"And if our people do offer to keep an eye on you until you leave—well, I think I should accept if I were you sir. To tell the truth, I don't like the look of this case at all."

Chapter Eleven

Nicholas Ede spent most of the afternoon driving into Surrey to break the news of the tragedy to Mrs. Hind. He could have sent a deputy, but he was a naturally considerate man with a strong sense of responsibility for his staff, and he felt it his duty to go. After it was over he was glad that he had done so, but the painful interview left him feeling limp. Back at the office there was no respite. The absent Proprietor had to be informed by cable of what had happened. The rest of the Directors had to be prevented at all costs from rushing up to the office and adding to the confusion. Several appointments had to be cancelled and new ones somehow squeezed in. It was the most rushed and wretched afternoon that Ede could remember.

The inspector had taken Ede very much at his word and was using Miss Timmins constantly. He had mobilised strong forces for the investigation, a fact that was reflected in the increasing dislocation throughout the office. The Process Department had been turned upside down under Ogilvie's supervision, and it seemed doubtful whether any news pictures would catch the first edition. The people who had figured on the conference list that Ede had given to Haines were receiving special attention, and as they were all key men the effect on work was calamitous. Attendance at the afternoon conference was so thin that Jackson—who had taken over editorial control for the time being—was obliged to abandon it altogether and finish planning the paper in private conclave with the Night Editor. There had been so such upheaval in the office since the day the bomb exploded.

Just after five o'clock a message came through from Haines

asking if the Editor could make it convenient to call upon him. Ede went quickly downstairs, trying hard to control his irritation. On the way, he dropped into the News Room to see how Soames was getting along as Hind's replacement. He found a reporter sitting at the News Desk, and Soames in a corner deep in conversation with a stranger who had all the marks of a plain-clothes detective. In the Reporters' Room two similar conversations were going on. Work had virtually ceased. Ede went on his way fuming.

Haines greeted him with an apologetic air. "I'm sorry to have to trouble you again quite so soon," he said.

"It doesn't matter about troubling me, Inspector, but you're certainly playing hell with the office. Your men are as thick as locusts. I told you I was anxious to co-operate, but is this invasion really necessary?"

"I'm afraid it is," said Haines. "You see, sir, the way things are turning out we really have no alternative but to treat every employee of the paper as a suspect. We're having to interview everyone."

Ede looked startled. "The whole staff? But, good gracious, there are more than two hundred of them!"

"So the Secretary of the company has informed me," said Haines ruefully. "What makes it more difficult is that some are on holiday, some are sick—and then, of course, there are others who used to be employed here and aren't any longer. And it's all got to be done in a hurry."

"What exactly are you trying to find out?"

"Primarily, which people have an alibi for that half hour when the olives were taken into the dining-room, and which haven't. It's a complicated job, as you can imagine, checking stories against each other. That's why I've got so many men at work."

Ede still seemed staggered by the magnitude of the effort. "You mean that there's no shorter way than this mass onslaught?"

"Not that I can think of. You see, Mr. Ede, there are no material clues at all. I haven't had the detailed report from the Yard yet, but I have to assume that that room won't tell us anything."

"Still, where's this going to get you? When you've found out where everyone was, you'll still have an enormous number of suspects on your hands."

"I know, sir," said Haines patiently, "but it'll be a beginning. This office is like a cul-de-sac—we're beginning a drive through it towards the dead end, with the whole staff in front of us. As people can prove their innocence, we let them go past us. The alibi is only one test—we shall hope to use others. At last, if we're very lucky, everyone will have passed through except just one man or woman—and he or she will be the murderer. It's tedious for us and exasperating for you, but it's the only possible method. By the way, you'll be interested to know we've checked up on the cyanide. Mr. Iredale was quite right about that."

"Oh?" Ede sensed more trouble.

"Yes. I've just sent a sample of the stuff to be analysed. There's enough of it in the Process Department to poison the whole of Fleet Street."

"Surely it's not just lying about?"

"Well, not quite. It's stored in a separate room, and it's supposed to be kept under lock and key when it's not in use. I've satisfied myself, though, that almost anyone in the office could have found an opportunity to help himself to a handful if he'd wanted to."

"That's bad." Ede frowned. The safe keeping of cyanide could hardly be considered an editorial matter, but he wished he'd known about it. "Well, we must see that the precautions are tightened up from now on, Inspector, though it's rather like shutting the stable door. Was this what you wanted to see me about?"

"Well, no, sir, not exactly. I really wanted your personal assistance. As I mentioned just now, we've got to apply other tests to our mass of suspects in addition to the one of opportunity. Motive is obviously going to be of the greatest importance—whoever put that poison in the olives did it for a pretty substantial reason. I want you to tell me whether you know of anyone in the office who disliked Mr. Hind—or any other member of the luncheon party—sufficiently to wish him out of the way."

Ede was silent for a moment. He had feared all along that this onus would be put on him. "You place me in an extremely difficult position, Inspector," he said presently.

"A man has been killed, sir."

"I know, I know. But I'm not sure how far that justifies me in telling you things that throw suspicion on members of my staff—things that may have no bearing on the case at all. You're really asking me to gossip."

"That's it, sir. I know it goes against the grain, but if you don't, others will—and without your sense of responsibility. I'd sooner have it from the fountain head."

Ede still hesitated. "A motive doesn't necessarily imply guilt. I shouldn't like to think you were going to rush off and arrest the first man who has had trouble with Hind."

"You'll have to trust my discretion, sir. We don't do things like that, you know. An arrest is a very serious matter. Apart from anything else, I have my own reputation to think of."

"All right, Inspector," said Ede reluctantly. "I don't like it, but I'll tell you. There *has* been something on my mind since Hind's death, though I don't suppose for a moment it's of any significance. Hind came to me yesterday evening and reported one of his men for a rather serious offence. Arthur Pringle, our Crime Reporter. I dare say you've met him on cases."

"Pringle? The name's familiar, but I don't think I've ever run across him. We don't see quite as much of crime reporters, you know, as some of them like to pretend. What's he been up to?"

"Faking his expense accounts, according to Hind. Of course, as I expect you know, reporters' expense sheets often have as little foundation in fact as some of their stories. They reckon to make a bit on the side, particularly on out-of-town jobs; it's a well-understood Fleet Street convention. I don't much like the practice myself, but within reasonable limits it has to be accepted. If a reporter spends fifteen shillings in a pub standing drinks while he's on a story, and charges twenty-five shillings for 'hospitality' or whatever the current euphemism happens to be, there's nothing anyone can do about it, after all. But Pringle appears to have overstepped the bounds. Hind discovered that he's been charging large sums—amounting in all to some hundreds a year—for stories that he hasn't covered at all. The fact is, I'm afraid, that he's been given too much latitude, and he's abused it. It seems that Hind had warned Pringle once before, and this time he felt he couldn't let it pass. He came to me and said that in his view Pringle was nothing but a crook and should be dispensed with."

"I see," said Haines gravely. "You were certainly right to tell me of this. Did Pringle know that he was going to be reported?"

"Yes. Hind told him yesterday afternoon."

"Do you suppose that he knew to-day that Hind had already mentioned the matter to you, or might he have supposed that it was still in abeyance?"

"I'm afraid I've no idea."

"Have you seen Pringle about it yourself?"

"Not yet. I was proposing to wait until I had a moment to go over his expense sheets and see just what the offence amounted to. Goodness knows when I shall have an opportunity now." Ede looked very perturbed. "There's a tradition on the *Morning Call* that we don't sack anyone unless we're left with no alternative, but if Pringle has really gone as far as Hind said, I'm afraid I'll have to get rid of him. Professionally speaking, he'll be no great loss. However, that's of no interest to you. You asked me point blank whether I knew of anyone with a possible motive. Reluctantly, I've told you."

"And I'm obliged to you," said Haines. "I shall have to talk to Pringle, of course. I should like to see those expense sheets myself, if I may."

"Very well," said Ede wearily, "I'll send them down to you. Mind you, Inspector, I don't for a moment think that Pringle had anything to do with this business. He's not a very prepossessing individual, but I can't believe he'd kill Hind out of revenge, or even to keep him quiet. It's too melodramatic altogether—even for a crime reporter."

"I dare say, sir. Well, now, is there anything else you can tell me about Hind's relations with his colleagues while we're on the subject?" Haines looked at the Editor with a quizzical expression. "Is there by any chance a lady in the case, for instance?"

"Where Hind was concerned," said Ede with an expression of distaste, "I imagine there was always some lady in the case, but the private affairs of the staff are none of my business."

"I appreciate your feelings, sir. At the same time, if Hind was abnormally mixed up with women, that obviously has a bearing on the investigation. Was he a philanderer? Is that what you're trying to tell me?"

"That's what I'm trying *not* to tell you, Inspector."

"Quite so, sir. Do you happen to know which lady was the latest object of his attentions—or would you prefer me to inquire elsewhere about that?"

"Oh, if you're going to be told I may as well tell you. He's been going around with one of his reporters—a girl named Sheila Brooks. She hasn't been here long and I don't know a great deal about her. A mere child, I believe—I'm sure she can't have had anything to do with this business."

"She may be able to give us some useful information, all the same," said Haines, making a note. "Now is there anything else you can tell me about possible motives?"

"Nothing," said Ede shortly.

"I understand that Mr. Iredale had some trouble with Mr. Munro."

A look of exasperation crossed Ede's face. "Iredale had a row with Munro in the course of his duty, Inspector. He also had a row with me over the same matter. He would no more have murdered Munro because of it than he would have murdered me. That was an incident, not a motive."

"I see, sir. Well, we'll leave it at that for the moment. Oh, there's one other thing. What about Mr. Cardew's relations with Mr. Hind?"

Ede stared. "They were quite normal as far as I know. Why do you ask that?"

"It must have occurred to you, sir, that Mr. Cardew occupies a unique position in this case."

"Because he happened to be present when Hind ate the olive?"

"Did he just *happen* to be present? We don't know that. As

things stand at the moment, he appears to be the one man who could have planned to kill Hind and carried out the murder without any risk that the wrong person would be killed."

"I've never heard such damned nonsense," cried Ede, shaken at last out of his natural politeness. "If Cardew had had anything to do with it, do you suppose he'd have allowed himself to become so conspicuous? I'm quite sure it was pure chance that took him up with Hind. You're on the wrong track altogether. Good God, man, if you go on like this you'll poison the whole atmosphere in the office."

"At least I shan't have poisoned a colleague," said Haines grimly. "I wish, sir, you could see this case from my point of view. Of course you don't like all this prying and suspicion, and neither do I, for that matter, but it's unavoidable."

"There's such a thing as moderation," said Ede.

"If you mean by that that some people can be automatically ruled out because they're nice people, I'm afraid not, sir—not by me. You said just now that I was on the wrong track, but the fact is that I'm not on any track at all. I've no evidence—none. I've a couple of hundred suspects, but they're just faces to me, and they all start equal. What I do know is that one of them is a murderer—as clever and ruthless and dangerous a murderer as I've ever come across. He's on my mind a great deal, Mr. Ede. He's probably sitting somewhere out there now, behaving as innocently as you or I, with all his tracks covered and nothing to worry about. He's probably watching me, laughing up his sleeve and thinking as you do that I'm causing a great disturbance and not getting anywhere. He's got everything in his favour. In all my experience I've never known a tougher problem. That's why I can't afford to be squeamish. If it's humanly possible I'm going to drive him to the end of that cul-de-sac before he does any more harm, and the only way to do it is to go on probing without any regard whatever for people's feelings. You see, sir, if Hind *wasn't* the intended victim, the murderer is more than likely to try again. As far as we know he still has cyanide in his possession. Very soon there may be one survivor less! That's the thought that haunts me."

Chapter Twelve

Half an hour later Inspector Haines was sitting back in his chair and surveying Mr. Pringle with faintly malicious pleasure. "So you're the Crime Reporter?"

"That's right, Inspector," said Pringle jauntily. "Glad to meet you. I don't know how it is I've never run across you before. Anything I can do to help?"

"That remains to be seen, Mr. Pringle. I'm always open to suggestions—provided, of course, you don't try to make them the basis of an interview."

Pringle looked quite shocked. "That's understood. This is a private talk, eh?" He cast a wary glance round the empty room, and drew his chair a little nearer to the inspector's desk. "I think I can tell you a thing or two. I've been working things out. It's going to be a very sticky case."

"So far I'm with you," said Haines.

Of course, you don't know the office the way I do. You haven't got the dope. That's where I can help you. I don't shout the odds around the place, but I don't miss much. I keep my eyes and ears open." He leaned forward confidentially and words oozed from the corner of his mouth. "Has it occurred to you, Inspector, that the poison may not have been intended for Hind at all?"

"The thought had crossed my mind."

"It had, eh?" Pringle wagged his sandy head in admiration. "I've always heard you were pretty smart. Mind you, it *could* have been Hind. Between ourselves, Inspector, he was a nasty bit of work. Women, you know—and he liked talking about it. Of course, we mustn't be narrow-minded. I'm a married man. You're a married man. We don't expect perfection." Pringle winked. "All the same, he went too far. He seduced one of the waitresses."

"Really!"

"Yes, a girl named Rose. She was a nice little thing—he took her on Epsom Downs. She married a G.I. and went to Arkansas."

"That seems to let her out, then."

"Yes, but there are plenty of others. There's old Jackson's secretary—he's the Assistant Editor, you know. Girl named Penelope." He made the word rhyme with "envelope". "Hind gave her the works all right, and she's still around. He had a try with Katharine Camden, but she was out of his class—I don't think he got anywhere. Then there's an old flame of his in the Art Department—girl named Phyllis. He told me about her when he was tight. *That* all started when she showed him something in the dark room."

"Mr. Hind certainly seems to have got around."

"Oh, he tore pieces off right and left. But there's a lot more dirt in the office that doesn't concern Hind. Those little kids wouldn't have had the nerve to poison him—they took everything lying down. What you want to look for, Inspector, is the big stuff. Let me tell you something." He inched forward until he could lean his cuff on the desk. "There's an eternal triangle in this office." He pointed significantly to the ceiling. "Upstairs."

"Is that so?"

"It certainly is. Have you met Ede's wife?"

"No."

"You should. She's a real smasher. And do you know whose girl-friend she is?" Pringle paused impressively. "Cardew's. Lionel Cardew's."

"You have my whole attention," said Haines.

"Good. I'm glad to be able to collaborate. We'll break this case wide open between us, you see if we don't. Anyway, that's the lowdown. Ede doesn't know about it—he's one of those saps that work evenings. He thinks Cardew's a pal of his—thinks he can trust him with his wife. But I've seen Cardew and Mrs. Ede together. Cardew showed her over the office, you know, not long ago. Talk about friendly! She called him 'sweetie' every other word. They go out together too. On the river—that sort of thing. It sticks out a mile. I reckon she's his mistress."

"That's interesting," remarked Haines. "Possibly slanderous."

Pringle was startled. "Oh, come off it, Inspector, this is in confidence. I wouldn't say a word about it to anyone but you. Anyway, there's your triangle."

"I'm still not clear," said Haines, "exactly what it is you're suggesting. Who do you think meant to kill whom, and why?"

"Just work it out for yourself, Inspector. After all, there's no smoke without fire. Maybe Ede found out about his wife at last and tried to bump off Cardew. Maybe Cardew got tired of working someone else's claim and decided to get rid of Ede. Maybe Mrs. Ede hates her old man and planted the stuff herself—she comes to the office now and again. More likely she got Cardew to do it for her, though. Of course, these are just suggestions—sort of raw material for you to work on."

"You're certainly full of ideas."

"I know what's going on, that's why," said Pringle complacently. "I have my spies."

"All the same, Mr. Pringle, I think for the moment I prefer to concentrate on Hind. A man who behaved as you say, he did no doubt made enemies. He seems quite a likely victim to me." Haines's mask of good-natured interest suddenly dropped. "By the way, how did *you* get on with Hind?"

"Eh?" The pale eyes blinked. "Well, as I told you, Inspector, I couldn't really approve of him."

"Did he approve of you?"

Pringle looked hurt. "What are you getting at, Inspector?"

"I have my spies too. I'm told that you and Hind had words yesterday evening."

"Oh, that!" Pringle gave an uneasy laugh. "I thought for a moment it was something serious. He got a bit shirty about some expenses I'd put in—that was all. He must have been feeling liverish."

"Did he not say he intended to report you to Mr. Ede?"

"He did say something of the sort, as a matter of fact, but I don't suppose he meant it. Hell, he was once a reporter himself—he knows about expense sheets."

"What about them?"

"Well, everyone makes a bit on their expenses. After all, what's a copper here and there?"

"It depends who the copper is," said Haines grimly. He lifted his notes and disclosed a bundle of green slips, which he waved menacingly in Pringle's direction. "These, Mr. Pringle, are your expense sheets for the past four months."

Pringle's jaw dropped. He was conscious of an unpleasant sensation in his stomach. He felt in his pocket for a bottle of indigestion tablets he always carried, popped one in his mouth and put the bottle back. "Oh," he said.

"I've been having a look through them," Haines went on. "They're fascinating. There's an item here, for instance, for July 3rd. 'Hospitality—Yard turn. £4 7s. 6d.' I presume you were entertaining the Commissioner that evening!"

Pringle pretended to peer. "You can hardly expect me to remember what it was for after all this time," he muttered. "Probably just drinks with the boys."

"What boys?" asked Haines. "Do you by any chance mean the police?"

"Well," said Pringle resentfully, "you know how it is. We're all in the pub together . . ."

"We? I don't remember ever having been bought a drink by you, Mr. Pringle. I should be very reluctant to recall such an occasion. Could you name a Chief Inspector, an Inspector, a Sergeant, or even a constable of the C.I.D. for whom you've ever bought a drink? Just one." His tone was pleading. "I assure you the information will go no farther."

Pringle wriggled. "Look, Inspector," he said, "stop kidding, will you? You know how it is. All the chaps do it. It's the recognised thing."

"I see. You mean the Press Bureau at the Yard gives you the stories, and you charge them up to the office in drinks that you don't buy. A very cosy racket, I must say."

"It's always done, anyway," said Pringle sullenly. "As for Hind saying he'd report me, that was just bluff. No self-respecting Editor would give it a thought. Anyway, he was a fine one to talk—what about all the free lunches we used to buy him? He was just being difficult. He never liked me."

"That I can understand," said Haines. "Well, now, let's take another item. 'June 12th—Missing Child at Farnborough—£14.' I admire the rotundity of your figures. You—er—you seem to have spent nearly a week on this story. Who was this missing child? Farnborough—let me see—no, I must say I don't recall the case."

"It was a private tip I had," said Pringle, beginning to edge his chair back from the inspector's desk. "It turned out that there wasn't anything in it, but I had to look into it all the same. It actually costs more when the story's a stumer—you must know that."

"Who gave you this tip?"

"We never disclose the sources of our information," said Pringle with dignity.

"What was the alleged child's name? What hotel did you stay at? Of whom did you make inquiries? Well, Mr. Pringle, I'm waiting."

Pringle's front collapsed. "All right," he muttered. "You win, Inspector. I didn't go. I needed the dough, and the paper's got plenty. It made up for the times when I didn't charge enough."

Haines tossed the green packet back on to his desk. "In fact, Mr. Pringle, you're a cheat and a thief. Well, now we know where we stand. Do you still think the Editor would have considered this of no importance?"

Pringle licked his dry lips. "What are you going to do? I've got a boy in boarding school—he's doing well—it'll be hard for him if I get into trouble. It was really for him that I did it."

Haines gave an exclamation of disgust. "I'm not going to charge you, if that's what you mean—not with fraud, anyway! Mr. Ede can take care of that." He selected another paper from the pile on his desk. "I've got a report here of the order in which people who attended the editorial conference this morning left the Board Room. It seems that you were the last to leave."

Pringle, whose thoughts were still concentrated on how to get out of the expenses jam, looked puzzled. "I *was* a bit behind the others—what of it?" Suddenly he caught up with the situation. "I say," he said with a squeak of alarm, "you surely don't think *I* killed Hind?"

"Since you ask me," said Haines, "I think you're as likely a person as anyone I've met so far. You're a pretty unpleasant piece of work, Mr. Pringle. You had a grudge against Hind, and a good reason for silencing him. You've been doing your utmost to throw suspicion on others, which you naturally would do if you were guilty. Yes, you seem to me a very promising candidate. Did you by any chance know there was cyanide in the Process Department?"

Pringle swallowed. "No," he said.

"That's a lie if ever I heard one," said Haines cheerfully. "I suppose you didn't know Mr. Hind liked olives, either?"

Pringle hesitated, his pale eyes darting a glance across to the inspector and away again. "I did happen to know that," he said.

Haines smiled. "You're a very simple man, Mr. Pringle, aren't you?"

"I didn't do it, anyway," said Pringle. Consciousness of truth gave his voice an honest vehemence at last. "I swear I didn't, Inspector. I may have been a bit careless about those expenses, but I wouldn't kill a man. I wouldn't know how to begin."

"Not after all those drinks with Chief Inspectors, Mr. Pringle?" Haines looked disdainfully at the Crime Reporter and his tone suddenly changed. "Get out," he said.

Chapter Thirteen

The inspector waited until the door had closed behind Pringle and then called up Miss Timmins on the house phone. "Will you see if you can find Miss Sheila Brooks for me and ask her to come and see me?" Then he had a wash. After Pringle, he felt he needed it. He couldn't get it out of his mind that there *might* be something in that story about Cardew and Mrs. Ede. That's what happened when people threw dirt—some of it stuck.

He greeted the girl who knocked at his door some ten minutes later with a solicitude that was only in part tactical. Here, presumably, was a damsel in distress, and he was by nature chivalrous. She was also extremely pretty, if one liked that blonde chocolate-boxy type. He didn't, as a matter of fact, except on chocolate boxes. As he looked at her, he thought how little he would have wished to see his own daughter, who was about the same age as Sheila Brooks, with such vivid fingernails, such drastically plucked eyebrows, and such an expression of calculated hardness. However, his gaze was so benevolent that she could have guessed nothing of what was passing in his mind.

"I'm sorry to have to bother you with questions at a time like this, Miss Brooks," he began, as soon as she was comfortably seated. "I'm afraid Mr. Hind's sudden death must have been a great blow to you."

He saw the girl's lips tremble. Blinking, she felt in her bag for a cigarette and fumblingly lit up, and presently her face was again set in a sophisticated mask.

"It's bloody, isn't it?" she said, puffing out a cloud of smoke that almost hid her from view. "Have you any idea who did it?"

Haines shook his head. "Even if we had, Miss Brooks, we'd hardly be announcing the fact to up-and-coming young newspaper reporters. Now, if you don't mind, *I'll* ask the questions."

"Why pick on me?" she asked resentfully.

"Because," Haines told her, "I hope that as a friend of Mr. Hind's you may be able to help us."

She looked at him coldly for a moment and then her shoulders lifted in a shrug. "All right—go ahead."

"I'd like to know a little about yourself, first. How long have you been working on the *Morning Call?*"

"About a month."

"Quite a newcomer, eh?" He smiled disarmingly. "I suppose you started your career on a local newspaper—that's the usual way, isn't it?"

"As a matter of fact, I didn't," said Sheila. "I skipped that part. I came straight here."

"Oh? How did you manage that?"

"I knew Joe—Mr. Hind," she said in a flat voice.

Haines's expression seemed to invite further confidences.

"At least," she amended, "my father knew him. He's Joe's bank manager—he was, I mean. I'd always wanted to work on a newspaper, and when I heard that one of the bank's clients was News Editor of the *Morning Call* I got Dad to talk to him, and Joe took me on for a month's trial."

"That was quite a stroke of luck."

"Yes, I suppose it was." With startling naïveté she added, "Joe told Dad that it was difficult to find vacancies, but after we'd had a talk he said he thought he could make use of me."

Haines grunted. "Was your father keen on the idea, too?"

"Not really. Dad's a bit old-fashioned, but I talked him into it."

Haines grunted again. He was a bit old-fashioned himself, and he couldn't help feeling that this young woman's craving for excitement and romance might have been directed into safer channels. "And Mr. Hind looked after you, I suppose?"

Sheila nodded. "He was frightfully decent. He taught me practically everything I know."

"And you became very friendly?"

She gave him a defiant stare. "Yes."

"He took you out sometimes, I suppose—to lunch and so on?"

"Yes, but I don't see what that's got to do with anything."

Haines saw no need to tell her that it had to do with olives. "Did you ever quarrel with him?"

"Certainly not. Why should I? He was always very nice to me."

Haines gazed thoughtfully at this pretty chit who had been let loose among the wolves of Fleet Street. There wasn't much point, he felt, in probing her relationship with Hind, and he'd had enough of that sort of thing for one day. Quite possibly she had been the man's mistress, thinking it part of the adventure. She *might* have quarrelled with him, in spite of her emphatic denial. He might have given her cause for jealousy—even in so short a time as a month. But nothing that had been said in this interview so far gave the inspector reason to think that the late Joe Hind's girl-friend had either the intensity of feeling or the calibre to plan and carry out a skilful, coldblooded murder, even if she had had a motive. A fit of the sulks or a slap in the face would have been more in her line. No, he was wasting his time. She would, he believed, fade quickly from the case, and—now that her patron had gone—probably from Fleet Street too.

Perfunctorily he put a routine question. "Have you any idea yourself who might have wanted to kill Mr. Hind?"

The forget-me-not blue eyes opened wide. "Of course not. How could I have?"

"You knew him very well. You must have heard him speak of other men—if not of other women. Do you know of anyone who was on bad terms with him?"

Sheila slowly shook her head. "That was the thing about Joe—he always got on so well with everybody." Then she suddenly remembered. "Oh, there was Bill Iredale, though. Joe and he nearly had a fight in the Crown last night."

Haines sat forward with a jerk. "What about?"

"Well, it sounds absurd," said Sheila, "but I think it was about me." She appeared to find the recollection not wholly unpleasant.

"About you? Why, did you know Mr. Iredale?" New possibilities suddenly teemed in Haines's fertile imagination.

"That's the absurd part," said Sheila. "I don't know what it had to do with the Iredale man, because I'd hardly set eyes on him before, but he suddenly said some awful things to me about Joe as we were going out. He had the hell of a nerve. Joe was furious and so was I. I really thought they were going to hit each other."

"Do you remember what it was that Mr. Iredale said?"

"Not exactly—but he was definitely the aggressor. He seemed to be trying to warn me against Joe. I think he must have been a bit tight." A note of excitement was creeping into Sheila's voice and Haines began to wonder if after all he had under-rated her suitability for Fleet Street reporting. "His eyes were full of hate and he was leaning forward, glowering, and looking just as though he'd like to throttle Joe. It was quite frightening, really—I can't think what would have happened if Katharine Camden hadn't separated them."

"How long did this quarrel last?"

"Oh, it was all over in a moment or two. It had flared up, you see. But it was terribly fierce while it lasted."

Haines gave a brief nod. It didn't look as though he were going to get any more hard facts out of the girl, who obviously fancied herself as the central figure in an exciting drama. He would get his information from Iredale.

"Well, I won't keep you any longer, Miss Brooks," he said. "You must forgive me if I've seemed inquisitive about your personal affairs. We're doing our very best, you know, to find out who killed Mr. Hind."

She sensed dismissal, but she didn't want to go. It was all right as long as she kept talking, but she feared the outer loneliness. "It won't bring him back, will it?" she said. She looked very forlorn now—a confused, miserable child who'd got into deep water and didn't know how to struggle out. As she turned to leave, Haines saw that tears were running down her cheeks. She sniffed a "Good-bye" and he stood and watched her till she turned the corner of the corridor.

Chapter Fourteen

Haines had rather taken to Iredale during their short encounter in the Editor's Room. He had liked the man's quiet solidity, the rough cut of his features, the astringent frankness of his manner that yet kept something in reserve. As he regarded his visitor now across the desk, his first impressions were confirmed. The deep blue eyes met his with a leisurely, speculative glance; the powerful body was at ease. Here was a man, Haines would have said, with good nerves and no inner tensions—a man who'd come to terms with life. Restful, reliable and definitely likeable. At the same time, he'd shown a capacity for sudden anger. He was a formidable man. He couldn't be lightly written off as a suspect, as Sheila Brooks had been written off. Coolness and rugged charm meant nothing—the post-homicide behaviour of murderers followed no pattern. The only thing that was absolutely safe to go on was evidence, and that was precisely what was lacking.

Having studied his visitor for a moment or two, Haines got down to business. "I understand, Mr. Iredale, that you had a quarrel with Mr. Hind last night."

Iredale gave him a slow glance, applied a match to his curved briar, and dropped the stump into the waste-paper basket at his side. "I thought it wouldn't be long before you got around to that, Inspector," he said ruefully. "Yes, we did have a bit of a scene."

"What about?"

"Do I have to tell you? It's not a thing I like talking about."

"You'd be well advised to."

Iredale pondered. "Well, it starts a long way back—about twelve years ago, I suppose. I was a reporter then, and Hind was my chief.

He already had a reputation for being a womaniser, and I think he was rather proud of it. He was born in the wrong century—he ought to have been a feudal baron, with the right of first night. Anything young and pretty was grist to him, and he didn't bother to step outside the office for his material. He took what came to hand . . ."

Haines nodded. The consensus of evidence on this aspect of Hind was conclusive. At that moment there was a knock at the door and Sergeant Miles came in with an official-looking envelope. Haines murmured "Excuse me" and glanced through the document, his brows drawing together in a deep frown as he absorbed the contents. Then he said, "All right, Sergeant, thank you," and thoughtfully put the paper aside. "I'm sorry, Mr. Iredale—where were we?"

"Talking about Hind's weaknesses. Well, of course, I didn't worry about his behaviour—young reporters aren't exactly censorious, and it seemed no business of mine. Then, not long before the war, it did suddenly become my business. A girl came over from Dublin on a sort of exchange basis. She was a journalist on one of the Irish papers, and she wanted to see how reporting was done on a big London paper. She was a charming girl—lively and gay and very Irish. She was about twenty-two, and I was a little older. Well, she just hit me for six. Hind saw that I'd fallen for her, and the blighter sent me up north to do an industrial series. While I was away, he started his monkey tricks. I expect she was flattered—I don't know the details. All I do know is that he put her in the family way and got some quack to fix her up. Things went wrong, she became ill, and she went back home in a shocking state. Next thing I heard, she'd taken two hundred aspirins and pegged out."

"And you've borne him a grudge ever since, eh?"

"Not actively. Life's too short—and I haven't seen him for years, except for the briefest periods. At the time, of course, it was different. I hated his guts after Molly died, and I switched to the foreign side because I couldn't bear the sight of him. I had plenty to do, and gradually the whole episode practically went out of my mind. Then, yesterday evening, I was having a drink in the Crown and there was Hind with his latest girl-friend, Sheila Brooks. I knew the form directly I clapped eyes on them. She was pretty, and the right shape, and as unsophisticated as they come. Just Hind's meat, in fact. Seeing him working on her brought everything back. As they walked by I said something about him being up to his old tricks, and advised her to watch her step. Naturally he didn't like it, and—well, we practically had to be separated. And that, Inspector, is the whole story."

"Except that to-day he was murdered," said Haines.

"That's a part of somebody else's story. I won't pretend I'm sorry. I think he got what was coming to him—but I didn't do it."

"I wish I were certain of that," said Haines.

"I wish I could make you certain. With a motive like mine, I don't know how I can. But I'll tell you this—I wouldn't have used poison. It's not in my line." He sat still, quietly smoking. "And if I *had* used it," he added as an afterthought, "I certainly wouldn't have drawn attention to myself by telling you there was some of the stuff in the office."

"That all depends, Mr. Iredale," said Haines grimly. He picked up the document which Sergeant Miles had brought in. "I've just had word from the Yard that the cyanide in the Process Department is *not* the stuff that was used for the murder. Our research people have analysed it, and also the poison in the olives, and the two are slightly different. About things like that they never make mistakes."

Iredale shrugged. "So what? I'm not sure that I follow what's in your mind. I didn't say the Process Department stuff was used, I only said it was there. I was trying to be helpful." In spite of his casual tone, he seemed worried.

"That's certainly what I supposed at the time," said Haines. "Now I have to consider the other possibility—that having your own private store of cyanide, you deliberately drew attention to another source, to which anyone might have had access, in order to spread suspicion more widely."

Iredale looked disgusted. "I wish to God I'd never mentioned the stuff."

"I'm not making any accusations, of course," said Haines, putting the document away. "However, these little things do raise questions in one's mind. How was it you arrived late at the luncheon, Mr. Iredale?"

"I was only a few minutes late. Now what are you getting at?"

"It occurred to me," said Haines mildly, "that if by any chance you *had* put cyanide in the olives, it might have been understandable that you should hang back a little."

"I don't see why. I wouldn't have been obliged to eat a poisoned olive myself, simply because I was there punctually."

"Do you like olives?"

"Yes."

"Then you might have felt it would be suspicious to refuse, and have hung back to avoid the necessity."

"Good Lord, what a tortuous mind you have!"

"Not tortuous enough for this case, I'm beginning to fear. There's another point. If *I'd* arranged to murder a colleague, I think I'd have tried to arrive after the deed was done—as you did. Less unpleasant, don't you think?"

"I doubt if I'd have been squeamish at that stage. Anyway, Inspector, it was by pure chance that I was delayed. I got caught up with Edgar Jessop in the Foreign Room—he was keen on my seeing a manuscript he'd been working on, and I couldn't rush away without offending him. I wasn't hanging back, as you put it, at all—as a matter of fact I was doing my best to get away."

"I see," said Haines reflectively. "In that case, it seems that you owe Mr. Jessop a debt of gratitude. Without knowing it, he may have saved your life." Haines consulted his file. "Jessop—ah, yes, he's the Assistant Foreign Editor." The inspector sat back and began to fill his own pipe. "Well, that seems to be all for the moment." He looked keenly at Iredale. "What do *you* think about this murder? You seem to have quite a lot of sense, and you know most of the people in the office. I'd like to hear your opinion."

Iredale smiled. "Ought you to collaborate with a suspect? Or are you just giving me rope?"

"There are nearly two hundred suspects," said Haines. "I must talk to someone. Well, have you any views?"

Iredale considered. "Only that it was a pretty crazy thing to do. In a newspaper office, of course, that doesn't point to anyone in particular."

"The sort of craziness that would risk killing four people to make sure of one must be uncommon even in a newspaper office."

"Yes, of course, but there's plenty of the sort of abnormality that might lead to that kind of thing."

"You're not serious?"

"Why not? You don't have to look far along this street for mild attacks of megalomania, do you now?—and that's merely the way it takes a few of the people at the top. You've got to remember that a lot of the men who gravitate to a newspaper office are artists, in a rather seedy sort of way. Chaps with an unsatisfied creative urge. A good many of them become disappointed artists. They get angry and frustrated and envious. Most newspapermen over the age of thirty are bitter about something. The majority of us just subside into drink or idleness and call it a day, but the odd chap might go really crackers."

"Have you ever known it happen?"

"I've known plenty of close shaves—nervous breakdowns, and that sort of thing. It isn't a healthy life, you know—there's too much artificial excitement, too much tension, too much exaggeration of unimportant things. I've known a man get drunk every night for a week because he didn't get a by-line on a story that he thought deserved it. There's no sense of proportion, and the atmosphere's always highly charged. I'm not suggesting that a newspaper office is just a rather specialised sort of lunatic asylum, but I do think it's as likely a place for a really crazy murder as any I know."

"Well, it's an interesting point of view," said Haines thoughtfully. "A possible line of approach, I suppose, though I'm afraid we have to concentrate on humdrum routine in our business." He smiled. "If you feel that way about the office, you must have been quite glad to get away to something a bit quieter."

Iredale laughed. "Oh, we carry our temperaments with us." He thought of his quarrel with Munro and shot the inspector a suspicious glance, but the grey eyes seemed innocent of guile. "Still, when you're on your own you *can* take a breath now and again. I know I shall be relieved when I've put a couple of thousand miles between myself and Fleet Street."

"I dare say," said Haines, getting up. "I don't want to appear discouraging, Mr. Iredale, but it may be some little time before that happens."

Chapter Fifteen

Edgar Jessop had passed a peaceful supper-hour loitering alone beside the river and was now returning at an equally leisurely pace to the office. The quiet beauty of the evening was in keeping with his mood, for he was still soothed by the afterglow of achievement and the knowledge that he would never again be tormented by Hind. For the time being, his mind was as placid as the Thames itself.

In the efforts of the police, so far as they were known to him, he found cause for supercilious amusement—exactly as Haines had foreseen. Scotland Yard were obviously quite at a loss, or they wouldn't have spent all day systematically combing through the staff. Jessop himself had been briefly questioned by one of Ogilvie's assistants, but the detective had lost interest in him as soon as it became clear that he didn't even claim to have an alibi. A few harmless questions about his position in the office—but clearly a formality. His smile was serene as he turned towards Fleet Street. Where did they expect to get by such means? They must know by now that hardly anyone had an alibi. He was one of a great crowd, and in numbers there was safety.

Providence, he felt, had shown good judgment in picking on Hind—and even better in selecting himself as its instrument. Not many people would have thought of such an ingenious plan, with all the details so perfectly worked out. The only pity was that he couldn't tell everyone how clever he'd been—they'd have realised then how greatly they'd underrated him.

The fact that it was Hind who'd died must have misled the police completely—put them right off the scent. He himself, after all, had never had a public quarrel with Hind; nobody had any inkling of how he'd detested the man. There was nothing to connect him with Hind's death, nothing at all. There was no reason to suppose he would be questioned any more. As far as he was concerned, the elimination of Hind was a closed chapter. Success had given him a wonderful feeling of confidence. He was a different man altogether.

He sauntered in past the front box, a faint smile still illuminating his face. The commissionaire on duty looked up. "Oh, the inspector's been asking for you, Mr. Jessop."

The smile faded. Jessop felt no apprehension, but he was slightly startled all the same. "Thanks, Sarge," he said. He couldn't imagine what Haines would want him for. Some trifling routine matter, no doubt. He climbed to the second floor and knocked boldly at the door on which hung a big card with Haines's name on it.

The inspector called "Come in" and turned from the window as he entered. "Yes?" he said. "Who are you?"

"I'm Edgar Jessop. I understand you've been asking for me." Jessop looked at the inspector with interest. So this was his main adversary—the mercenary hired by his enemies to fight their battle. Well, he looked harmless enough—he might well be somebody's kindly old uncle rather than a policeman. Jessop felt fully equal to dealing with him.

"Ah, yes, Mr. Jessop, I'm glad you've called in." Haines pulled up a chair for him. "There was just one small point I wanted you to clear up for me."

"Of course, if I can," said Jessop.

"I believe Mr. Iredale was with you just before lunch to-day?"

"That is so," said Jessop. There was something about the inspector's level gaze that he found disconcerting after all, and to his annoyance he felt his pulse beginning to hammer.

"He had a luncheon appointment—you knew that, of course?"

"Yes—he told me." Jessop sat very still, waiting. Could this be a trap of some sort?"

"But he was about five minutes late. I gather you detained him." Haines accompanied the question with a friendly smile and began putting his papers together. This was the merest routine, and he was tired. He'd had a long day. "Is that so?"

Jessop hesitated. An appalling possibility had suddenly leapt into view—the possibility that he might be lifted out of the anonymous crowd and have one particular action of his subjected to suspicious scrutiny. If the inspector thought that Iredale had been kept away from the lunch deliberately, he'd want an explanation.

"I don't know that I detained him," said Jessop with a forced smile. "We were just talking, you know."

Haines stopped fiddling with his papers, and his face lost its benevolent expression. He looked at Jessop quickly and began to light his pipe. "It's not of any importance, of course," he said between puffs. "Mr. Iredale said something about a manuscript you insisted he should look at."

Jessop felt a stirring of his old resentment. The suggestion that he had pressed his *opus* upon Iredale was true enough, but there had been no call for Bill to be so slighting about it. In fact Bill oughtn't to have mentioned it at all; it had been shown to him in confidence.

"I asked him if he'd care to see it," said Jessop, "that's all. He seemed interested and we discussed it for a bit."

Haines frowned. "I'd like to get this quite clear, Mr. Jessop. Mr. Iredale distinctly gave me the impression that he was late for lunch because you pressed your manuscript upon him and he felt he couldn't leave without discourtesy."

Jessop flushed. "That's absurd," he said. "We're old friends—I shouldn't have minded at all."

"Evidently he thought you would. He *was* in a hurry to get away, I take it?"

"Not particularly. As a matter of fact, it didn't seem to me that he was very keen on going to the lunch."

"I see." Haines concentrated on his pipe for a few seconds. "All right, Mr. Jessop, that's really all I wanted you for. I should be grateful if you'd keep the subject of this interview to yourself. Thank you for coming."

Jessop went out moodily. The afterglow had faded. He felt angry with Iredale. He'd made a great effort to save Iredale's life—yes, at some risk to himself, that was clear. And what was the result? Disparaging remarks about his *opus*. The sort of thing one might expect from Cardew or Ede. They were all alike—he couldn't get a square deal from anyone. His eyes narrowed, and his hand sought comfort in the flat tin he carried in his pocket. His thoughts, that had been so tranquil, began to turn again to violence.

Chapter Sixteen

On his way into the building next morning Haines stopped to have a word with the commissionaire at the box, a grey-haired veteran of some ancient war whom everyone called "Sarge," though his name was Vickers.

"Just come on duty?" asked Haines pleasantly.

"A couple of hours ago, sir. Eight till four's my shift." The man spoke with a brisk cheerfulness that was obviously natural to him; then suddenly his face dropped and his tones became hushed and confidential. "This is a bad business, eh, sir? Never 'ad anything like it 'appen in all the time I've been 'ere."

"I don't suppose you have, Sarge."

"Couldn't sleep last night for thinkin' about it." Vickers moved a little closer to the inspector. "One thing I can tell you," he said earnestly. "It wasn't no stranger what did for Mr. 'Ind. We'd 'ave knowed if there was anyone in the building what 'adn't no business there."

"I was going to ask you about that." Haines had had no reason to change his view that the killing of Hind had been an "inside" job, but the possibility that the murderer might have been someone only indirectly or formerly connected with the paper could not be excluded. "How do you manage to keep a check on everyone?" he asked.

"It's 'abit, sir. Like the coppers at the 'Ouses of Parliament, we gets to know all the faces pretty quick. Mind you, we can't say at any pertickler time which of the staff's in the building and which ain't. They come and go so fast it ain't possible to keep track. But strangers, now—that's different. Anyone coming in 'ere that we don't know gets stopped, and believe me, there ain't no sneaking in. We 'ave to be careful, you know—lot o' mad people come to newspaper offices. You'd 'ardly credit it without you saw it yourself. Only last week we 'ad a girl said she was in telepathetic communication with the planet Venus. According to 'er, she'd learned the songs what they sing up there, and so 'elp me, she wanted to sing 'em to the Editor." Vickers scratched the side of his chin reminiscently. "Nice bit of 'omework she was, too—aside of being quite balmy, o' course. When it comes to customers like that we've got eyes in the back of our 'eads. 'Ave to 'ave."

Haines smiled. "So there weren't any strangers in the office yesterday morning?"

"Well, sir, there was one or two called in, but they didn't amount to much. We 'ave a waiting-room over there, see. What 'appens is they send a slip up to the News Room stating their business, and one of the reporters comes down and talks to 'em, and then if they've got anything to say what's worth anything, they're taken upstairs. But nobody went upstairs yesterday morning at all. Reg'lar poor lot, they were."

"I see. Tell me, Sarge, suppose someone had called who had worked here once but didn't any longer, would you have noticed him, or would he have got by like one of the staff?"

"I reckon we'd notice him even more than we would a stranger," said Vickers, adding wisely, "There's nothing like a familiar face what didn't ought to be there to make you look twice. Anyway, no one like that called yesterday morning."

"What about friends and relatives of the staff—wives and so on?"

Vickers shook his head. "No, sir, not yesterday."

"Well, it's something to know that. Thank you, Sarge." Haines nodded and went on his way satisfied.

He found the second-floor office looking more like the statistical section of a big business house than the headquarters of a murder investigation. Extra desks and chairs had been brought in, and more than a dozen plain-clothes men were hard at work among piles of papers, notebooks and coloured filing cards, completing and collating the results of the inquiries they had made on the previous day. There was a steady hum of activity in the air. Sergeant Miles was dictating in a gruff undertone to a man at a typewriter. Nothing in this quiet methodical scene indicated that the aim of all these people was to hang a man by the neck until he was dead.

Inspector Ogilvie, conductor-in-chief of the statistical orchestra, came forward as Haines entered. He was in his shirt-sleeves, he was beginning to need a shave, and his eyes showed signs of fatigue.

"Had a tough night, Inspector?" asked Haines sympathetically.

"As a matter of fact, sir," Ogilvie confided, "I'd hardly noticed it was over. We didn't finish the interviews till eleven, and we've been piecing the bits together ever since. We're getting near the end now, though—I think I'll be able to give you the complete picture in a few minutes. By the way, the fingerprint report has just come in. It's disappointing, as usual."

Haines took the document over to the window and skimmed through it. The findings were very much what he'd expected. The plate on which the olives had been found had only a few smudged prints. The mass of prints on furniture and door-handles were equally useless. One or two good prints on some of the plates and cutlery probably belonged to the restaurant staff, and were being checked.

"I don't know why we still bother with these things," said Haines. "Criminals know too much—I don't think I've had a helpful fingerprint since the year the war ended, not on this sort of case, anyway. We'd do better to cast a horoscope!" He handed the document back to Ogilvie. "It's fairly clear what happened. The chap must have taken the olives along in some container, tipped them out on to the plate, and carried the plate to the sideboard in a handkerchief or something. After all, why *should* he leave prints? He wouldn't hang about—I dare say the whole job only took about twenty seconds. He wouldn't need to touch anything but the plate. Well, there we are, Inspector. I must say I'm much more concerned over the cyanide report. I really did think we'd traced the stuff."

"That shook me, too," said Ogilvie. "After all the work I'd done in the Process Department, it was like a stab in the back. If that supply's ruled out, I'm blessed if I know where we start looking."

They sat down by the window, and Haines told Ogilvie about his own interviews on the previous day. Presently the hum in the room began to die down and men began putting on their jackets. There was an air of expectant achievement, such as that which precedes the declaration of a poll. Sergeant Miles came over with a bunch of typed sheets. "That seems to be it, sir." He passed it to Ogilvie, who paged through it.

"Well, Chief," said the inspector, "here is the position. There are one hundred and ninety-two people who normally work in this building. That's the figure the Secretary gave us, and I've checked all the names with the pay-roll. There are five more who've left within the past two years, and they've all got alibis. By the way, one of them is Lambert, the Foreign Editor who changed his job. He's on holiday in the Scilly Islands."

"Fine—it's a pity a few more weren't," said Haines.

"Oh, we haven't done badly out of holidays—there were fourteen away altogether. They didn't give us much trouble, and they're all okay. We checked by telephone with the hotels. Three people were away ill yesterday, and they're all accounted for. Seventeen people didn't come on duty till the afternoon, but one or two lunched in town, and they haven't all got alibis. To cut a long story short—you'll see all the details for yourself—we're satisfied that one hundred and twenty-four people have complete alibis for the period twelve-thirty to one o'clock—in fact, from twelve-twenty—I thought I'd better allow a little margin to be on the safe side. That leaves sixty-eight members of the staff without alibis—fifty-two men and sixteen women."

Haines gave a low whistle. "Sixty-eight! I'd hoped it would be fewer than that."

"I was pretty tough about it, sir, as you said. In some cases there are only a few minutes of the half-hour not vouched for by others, and of course quite good stories to explain how the time was spent, but not stories that could be checked." He passed the bundle of papers across.

Haines began to go through the list. "At least," he said, "I don't seem to have been wasting all my time. No alibi for Iredale, Cardew, Pringle, Jessop . . ." He ran his finger slowly down the long column. "By jove, though, it's pretty formidable, isn't it? The women don't seem to come out too well."

"No," said Ogilvie, "I think that's because they're mostly secretaries and so on, and they go off to powder their noses before one o'clock. A lot of them eat in the restaurant at about that time, anyway, and one of them could easily have slipped into the Directors' Dining Room on her way up."

Haines's eyes were still on the papers. "Now I would have thought that Miss Timmins would have had her nose to the grindstone for that half-hour, with Ede still around."

Ogilvie shook his head. "She was one of the powderers. She went out for a couple of minutes after Ede had taken Munro into his room. In any case, she sits alone in her office—we couldn't get any corroboration."

"Of course not. Ah!—no alibi for Sheila Brooks."

"She just missed it, sir. She was positive she was in the Reporters' Room all the time, but on investigation we found she went up to the library to get a reference book. She's an eyeful, isn't she?"

Haines grunted. "None for Katharine Camden, either."

"No—she was wandering around the office looking for Hind."

"H'm. Let's see, there were a couple of girls . . ." Haines found the note he had made during his conversation with Pringle. "Rose—oh, no, she's the one that went to Arkansas. Penelope—that'll be Penelope Walker, number 38. Oh, she's out, I see. And Phyllis somebody—Phyllis Stokes, that'll be, I suppose. She's out, too. Well, so much for Mr. Pringle!"

"Suspects, sir?" Ogilvie never liked to feel that he was not being kept fully informed.

"Not really. Victims, I'm told, of Hind's baser instincts. Hallo, no alibi for Ede? Wasn't he entertaining Munro?"

"Not until a quarter to one," said Ogilvie. "He went back to his room at twelve-thirty as soon as the conference was over, had a word or two with the Art Editor, and then rushed off to see the

Features Editor. I've never known such a place for rushing about—it's a ruddy anthill. Munro's all right, of course. I checked very carefully on him, as you said, but it appears that he was under observation from the moment he stepped over the threshold."

Haines nodded. "Well, I congratulate you, Ogilvie. You've done a good job on this—very thorough."

Oglivie didn't seem so satisfied with his work. "I think it's sound enough, sir, but where do we go from here?"

"I think *you'd* better get a bit of shut-eye, Inspector—and those chaps of yours. After lunch, I suppose we'll have to start combing through these sixty-eight again. We may not be able to rule any of them out, but some of them must be a good deal less likely than others. These office boys, for instance—what possible motive could they have had? Anyway, I'd say this was a man-sized murder."

Ogilvie shrugged. "*I'd* say, sir, that after nearly twenty-four hours we haven't a clue."

Haines looked a bit grim. "I'm afraid that's about the literal truth," he said.

Chapter Seventeen

The atmosphere in the Reporters' Room late in the afternoon did not suggest any deep feeling of deprivation as a result of Hind's death. Though the late News Editor had been held in professional respect by most of his staff, it was now evident that there had been little affection for him. Yesterday there had been a certain solemnity in the air, for even to reporters, who thrive on sensation, murder on the premises is disquieting. But discussion had soon become detached and even a shade callous, and the incident was now no more than an uneasy background to conversation. Sheila Brooks, to everyone's relief, had absented herself for a few days.

Work was proceeding in a very desultory fashion, for with the approach of the August holiday, news had dried up. In any case, the fussy, conscientious Soames had not yet got into his stride as Hind's successor, and the reporters were taking advantage of the lull. Haycock, a veteran with a bald and shiny scalp, was somnolently turning the pages of a copy of *Life*. Golightly, a lanky, restless man of thirty, was back from his treasure-hunt, which had proved a flop, and was inscribing what appeared to be a motto or legend in coloured inks on a piece of cardboard. Grant was winnowing an enormous stack of competition postcards on which readers of the *Morning Call* had been invited, for a prize of ten guineas, to state "How I proposed" or "How he proposed" in a hundred well-chosen words. Rogers, a smart, good-looking youth and one of Nature's irrepressibles, had been out all morning, and was now preparing to transcribe an interview. Katharine Camden, who had been covering an archery contest, was bored at having to write it up and was ready to be diverted by anyone or anything.

Pringle, seated a little apart from the others, was consuming weak tea and charcoal biscuits and trying by the nonchalance of his manner to convey the impression that there was nothing remarkable about his presence in the office at an hour when he would normally have been coining expenses *in absentia*. He hadn't quite decided yet whether to close down his racket and hope that Ede would forget about it in his preoccupation with Hind's murder, or whether to go ahead and cash in as quickly as he could before he was sacked.

Besides Pringle, there were a couple of intruders. Bill Iredale, who was finding the Reporters' Room increasingly congenial, had dropped in after lunch and was sitting next to Katharine at the desk of the absent Sheila. Jessop was there too, driven out of the Foreign Room by Cardew's presence. All that day, hatred had been rising in him like a head of steam. The trouble was that this time he couldn't leave the choice to Providence, and he had so many enemies that it was difficult to decide where to strike next. His anger was easily diverted to some new person by a chance remark or action—like Cardew occupying the desk that he should have had. He sat quietly, trying to focus his resentment, while the conversation flowed round him.

Rogers wound a sheet of paper into his typewriter with an air of disgust. "I'm told the Big White Chief is getting peeved about all the prying in the office," he remarked to no one in particular. "Funny, isn't it?"

"What's funny about it?" asked Katharine.

"Well, he's a fine one to object to prying. D'you know what I've been doing all morning? I've been trying to persuade the broken-hearted family of a Miss Henrietta Peacock to tell me the full story of why she threw herself over a railway viaduct. Now whose idea was that, I'd like to know?"

The tone of grievance struck an answering chord in Jessop. "That was Jackson, as a matter of fact," he said. He was the only one present who had been at morning conference. "Jackson can never forget that he was a contemporary of Northcliffe. I think he's a hypocrite." Jessop began to mimic the Assistant Editor's rather precise manner of speaking. "'It might be a good idea, Soames, to send one of your young men out on this story. A little human interest is what we need. No intrusion into private grief, of course—just tell him to get the facts!'"

"I agree it's shocking," said Haycock, who had once worked on the old *Morning Post* and remembered more dignified days. "Still, Jackson's nothing like as bad as Hind was. *He*'d have sent you to interview a man on the gallows."

Pringle, his voice crumby with charcoal biscuit, said, "There's such a thing as respect for the dead, old man."

Rogers, whose thoughts had been on Miss Peacock, suddenly seemed to become aware of Pringle's presence. "There's such a thing as the Crime Reporter doing crime stories," he said. "I thought suicides were your pigeon, Arthur. Are you on holiday or something?"

"I'm collaborating on the case," said Pringle with dignity. "I've been asked to stand by."

Katharine glanced across at Iredale and they exchanged smiles. Rogers sat back. "What view have you and the inspector formed of the case, Sherlock?"

"I'm pledged to silence," said Pringle.

Haycock looked up from his paper. "It's an ill wind . . ." he said. He had never liked Pringle.

"It's all very well to sneer, old man," said Pringle. "If I wanted to, I could tell you things that would make your hair stand on end."

Haycock stroked his shiny scalp. "Then you're wasting your time in the newspaper business."

Rogers cackled. "You're an old twister, Pringle. You don't know a thing."

"I don't pretend to have solved the case," said Pringle modestly, "but I have my own convictions about it."

"That's nothing to the convictions you'll have when the inspector finds out about *you*," said Golightly from the sidelines.

Pringle looked startled. "What's that?" he squeaked, spattering bits of charcoal biscuit over his teacup.

"You know, I believe Eric's got something there," said Rogers thoughtfully. "Murder for a scoop! Arthur Pringle, first with the news at last. Read all abaht it!"

Pringle looked round at the circle of amused faces. "I don't think that's very funny, old man."

"You wouldn't, if you did it," said Golightly. "And after all, crime *is* your profession, Arthur. I dare say your place is bulging with cast-off cyanide if we only knew."

"If he did do it," said Rogers, still as though Pringle weren't there, "we've got to hand it to him—it begins to look like the perfect crime. But with all his training he'd know the snags, of course, like leaving fingerprints on plates and doorhandles and all that stuff."

"It's no joking matter," said Pringle solemnly. He cast a backward glance at the door and lowered his voice. "We think it's possible there may be more foul play practically at any moment. One of us in this room may be the next on the list. The poison's not been found yet, remember." With gratification he saw that for the moment at any rate he had gained the attention of his audience. "I'm jolly careful what *I* eat and drink, I can tell you that."

Katharine said, "I once knew a man who died from a surfeit of charcoal biscuits. It wasn't a pretty death."

Loud guffaws echoed round the room, and Pringle lapsed into a huffy silence. Golightly, who had not allowed the conversation to distract him from his creative efforts with the coloured inks, got up and hung his finished handiwork on a nail. "How's that?" he asked. The illuminated text read: "The hireling scribes of the newspaper press, who daily pawn the dirty linen of their souls for the price of a bottle of sour wine and a cigar."

"Who wrote that tripe?" asked Grant from behind his embankment of postcards.

"Ruskin. Classy, isn't it? What a prig!" Golightly surveyed the text with pleasure. "I wish someone would give *me* a cigar," he said wistfully, walking back to his seat. "Anybody remember Havanas?" As he passed Grant, he picked up a block of about five hundred unexamined postcards and dropped them unemotionally into the waste-paper basket.

Suddenly the News Room door opened and Soames came in with a newspaper clipping in his hand. He was a great man for clippings—an ardent follower-up of other papers' stories. He gazed round to see who of his staff was the least engaged and the cover of *Life* caught his eye. "Oh, Mortimer, the *Standard* says old Harcourt is resigning at last. You might give him a tinkle." He grinned at Jessop and Iredale as he passed. "What's all this—Foreign Room sending observers? It's nice to be some people, I must say." The News Room door closed behind him.

"When the wind's in the north," remarked Golightly, "they say you can hear old Soames's scissors as far away as the Elephant and Castle."

"He used to hate clippings when he and I were reporters together," said Iredale.

"Ah, change and decay!" observed Rogers sententiously. "Now he's drunk with power." The description of the mild, painstaking Soames was so inapt that even Pringle smiled.

For a few moments there was comparative quiet. Then the restless Golightly walked over to the notice board and stood there studying the Duty List: "Why have they put you on late turn to-morrow, Mortimer? Something special happening?"

"I've got to cover a dinner for Ede," said Haycock. "He's the guest of honour at the International League of Editors."

"Bad luck, you hireling scribe!"

"It *is* rather trying—I hate wearing a dinner jacket in hot weather. It's a pity some of you young fellows don't polish up your shorthand—I always get these jobs." Haycock had been a fine descriptive writer in his day, but nowadays he rarely got a "break". He went over to a telephone box, grumbling to himself.

Jessop sat frowning. He was thinking how pleasant it must be to be a guest of honour. Ede was always gadding about, always enjoying himself, always at the centre of things. Some people were born lucky.

Iredale leaned back, rocking gently on two legs of his chair and watching Katharine. She was sitting still with her fingers on the keyboard of her typewriter, and didn't seem to be concentrating. "How's the archery?" he asked her.

"I wish you'd go away," said Katharine. "I shall never get this thing finished. I can't even think of an 'intro'."

"Why not draw a bow at a venture?" said Iredale airily.

"Smarty! Why not give me a useful suggestion?"

"Nothing easier," he said. "How about this? 'Robin Hood and his Merry Men lived again to-day (Wednesday) when youths and maidens in Lincoln green filled the glades of Sherwood Forest . . .'"

"The contest was at Elmer's End," said Katharine coldly. "Now I see why they thought it better to send you abroad."

"My mind wasn't entirely on it," he admitted. "How about a drink when the pubs open?"

"What, again?"

"It's a nice habit to get into." He prodded tobacco into his big pipe and flung the empty tin on to the desk.

"Somebody ought to buy you a tobacco pouch," said Katharine. "Don't you ever have a birthday?"

"I've lost three pouches in a year," Iredale said. "Now I stick to tins."

"You smoke rather a lot, don't you?"

"Only an ounce a day. Wonderful stuff, tobacco." He grinned. "It takes care of all the appetites."

Katharine smiled, her eyes on the typewriter. From across the room Rogers called, "*I* can hear you two whispering. Watch that man, Katharine, he's a beast with women. He'll have you in a sarong before you know where you are."

"*I'd* advise you to watch your drink if you're going out with him," said Pringle. "One small piece of cyanide . . ."

"Oh, for Pete's sake!" cried Katharine. "Let's forget cyanide for an hour or two."

The News Room door opened again with a bang and Soames bustled in. "There's a good story at Baldock, Pringle. George Teviot, the artist, has been found murdered. Better get up there right away."

Pringle stuffed the charcoal biscuits into his pocket. Baldock, eh?—he ought to be able to make a bit out of a trip up there.

"That's torn it," said Rogers gloomily. "Now poor old Haines will be on his own." Pringle left the room to the sound of more unseemly mirth.

Chapter Eighteen

By the evening, Edgar Jessop had made his choice and knew whom he was going to kill next. A method had come to him as a revelation during that half-hour in the Reporters' Room, and the method had suggested the victim. It was, he felt, an appropriate stroke of justice that cyanide which had originally been intended for the liquidation of defenceless creatures should now be used in the same manner to destroy a man who had been put in a position of authority. He was happy about the choice. All that remained was to work out the details.

The difficulties were formidable, but Jessop took them as a challenge. As he sat in the Foreign Room after supper, his *opus* temporarily laid aside for this more pressing business, he had no doubt that he would be guided to overcome them. Probably he was the only man who *could* overcome them. His exhaustive knowledge of office routine and his familiarity with the old building would serve him well.

He dissected the problem with the patient cunning of the paranoiac. He must get the stuff into position without being seen. He couldn't do that to-morrow, because there'd be too many vigilant eyes watching. But he couldn't do it right away either, because if he did the cleaners would find it when they came in the morning. No, the poison must be laid after the cleaners had been, and before the staff began to arrive. It would be necessary, he saw, for him to spend the night in the office. There shouldn't be any difficulty about that—he had done it plenty of times before. Fortunately he had an old razor in his drawer, so he would be able to make himself presentable after the job was done. Then he would only have to wait and mingle with the incoming staff and once again his identity would be lost in the crowd. That was the plan in broad outline. By the time the boy arrived with the first edition of the paper, Jessop had not only gone over the main plan in his mind but he was satisfied with the details as well. He felt sure he had overlooked nothing.

The artistic perfection of the scheme gave him real creative pleasure. He would enjoy carrying it out. The confidence of obsession surged through him. The faint misgivings which he had experienced during his talk with Haines were forgotten. It had been unfortunate that Iredale should have interposed himself, unwittingly, between plan and performance on the first occasion, but nothing like that could happen this time. Haines would never get on the right track—he would have nothing at all to go on. Jessop picked up the paper that had just been brought in, and contemptuously scanned the few lines about the progress of the Hind case. The report had dwindled to a couple of sticks. Routine phrases, through which failure stared. The story was as dead as Hind himself. The police wouldn't admit it, of course, but they had reached the inevitable impasse. How could they hope for anything else, when in the nature of things there were no clues? This time, again, there would be no clues. Only stupid people left clues.

He folded the paper and stuffed it into his jacket pocket, next to the tin of cyanide. He would read it during the long wait. He found his razor and a battered tube of shaving cream and put them into his dispatch-case, wrapped in a hand-towel. He switched off the tape-machine and stood there for a moment, thinking. Obviously it was impossible for him to have an unbreakable alibi, but it might be helpful if he could contrive to give the impression that he had gone home at the usual time. He strolled along to the Reporters' Room and found the two night men playing chess with a recklessness which foreshadowed the imminent collapse of both sides. Jessop, who had been an accomplished player himself, watched for a while in silent amusement. When two bare kings faced each other he gave both players a slap on the back and got up. "After that exhibition," he said, "I think I'm ready for home." He returned to the Foreign Room. Just as he was putting his key in the door to lock up, the Night News Editor walked by. "Good-night, Charlie," Jessop said. "If I hear a fire engine I'll give you a ring!"

He went downstairs and walked briskly across the lobby to the garage entrance, ignoring the commissionaire who glanced up automatically as he passed near the box. The commissionaires were his only danger, and deliberate confusion seemed to be his best policy. He went through into the garage. His car was sandwiched between Cardew's Riley and a vintage Morris that had come in during the day. He squeezed past the Riley. At least Cardew wouldn't be taking up this space much longer! He collected some cigarettes and a pocket torch which he always kept in the car against emergency, and went up through the lobby again and out into Fleet Street, still ignoring the commissionaire. A hundred yards up the street there was an all-night milk bar, and he had a milkshake and bought a packet of sandwiches to take away with him. For a quarter of an hour he strolled up and down in the warm night air. Then he returned to the office. This time the commissionaire, buried in the first edition, barely raised his eyes. By to-morrow or the day after, it was most unlikely that he'd remember whether he'd last seen Jessop going or coming—not that anybody would think it worthwhile to enquire.

The staircase was round a corner, just out of sight of the box. Instead of going up, Jessop went down. The floor below ground level was a storage basement; the one below that was the old air raid shelter. It was years since Jessop had been down here, but the place seemed to have changed surprisingly little since the blitz. Perhaps they were keeping it intact for the next blitz, he thought sardonically. Even the big black S for shelter and the downward-pointing arrow on the wall had been left untouched. In the shelter itself there was a great deal of junk, the overflow from the floor above, but Jessop found he could remember his way about there as though the bombing had been yesterday. The big, high room was divided into compartments by thick blast walls, and some of the old iron cots with their canvas hammocks were still in position. He would certainly be undisturbed here, unless by rats. He folded his jacket into a rough-and-ready pillow, placed his dispatch-case beneath it, and slipped into the bunk. He would need no covering, for the air was stifling. In any case, he didn't expect to sleep much. He was about to light a cigarette when it occurred to him that the ash might give him away if the improbable happened and the police ever thought of looking here. He mustn't take any risks.

He lay quietly on his back, his hands under his head, as he had done in that very place on hundreds of nights before. How persistent, he reflected, was the faint odour of mustiness, the unique shelter smell. The place must have been thoroughly cleaned at the end of the war, yet after all this time the smell still clung to the canvas, taking him straight back to the nights of bombing. He could remember so vividly the details of that strange, troglodyte existence. It hadn't all been hideous, of course. There had been laughter and good-fellowship, as well as fear. Everyone had been friendly then, even the people who now despised him. That had been a time when *they* had needed companionship as well. There was no horror like loneliness.

He could still remember the joy of washing upstairs in cold water after the fetid, nerve-racking night; the acrid, dust-laden air outside, that yet tasted so sweet; the fierce exhilaration at being still alive; the heavenly aroma of coffee and bacon at the A. B. C. across the way. Astonishing how much a stale odour could bring to the mind! With each nostalgic sniff of the musty air he could feel around him again the crowded presence of his colleagues; he could hear the thin whiffle of cards being dealt and re-dealt hour after hour, and the jingle of coins as stakes changed hands, and the infinite variety of snores.

All the same, terror had predominated. He remembered the sudden tug at the heart as the spotter on the roof gave the "imminent danger" signal on the buzzer for the doubtful benefit of those whose duty had kept them upstairs. He could feel the sudden suspension of talk, the tense waiting, the horrible earth-shock when a heavy bomb hit the ground not far away; the inexpressible relief when the buzzer sounded a reprieve. Worst of all had been the threatening crescendo of approaching explosions as a whole "stick" of bombs straddled the area—first, the barely perceptible distant crump, then the louder menacing boom, then the crash that shook the building and started the lights flickering and caused plaster and mortar to fall from the walls and the roof. The next one was going to be a direct hit . . . "Wait for it," someone would say, or, with desperate humour, "I'll go three spades if I live." And then the distant boom again, the passing of danger, the chatter of voices and the too-bright laughter.

Jessop had died a thousand deaths on those nights. He had been torn to bloody charred fragments a thousand times in the agony of his imagination. He had died from water and from gas and from choking sewage effluent; he had lain crushed under beams; he had been buried under tons of debris; he had seen his living body consumed by flames. Up there on warden duty in the lonely corridors, with bombs splashing all around into the sea of fire that was London, he had known the uttermost abyss of fear. But he hadn't succumbed, he told himself now—he hadn't failed his colleagues, as Archer had done. He had retained his self-respect—he had shown that he could "take it" with the next man. He had earned, and had a right to expect, the good opinion of the world. So he told himself—so he had long told himself—driving down the hideous unbearable truth into the dark recesses of his subconscious mind, repressing his guilt at the cost of sanity itself.

He had been cool and confident when he had entered the shelter a bare half hour ago, but now his nerves were on edge and there was an ache behind his eyes. He wished he had not begun to think about these things. The printing machines throbbed overhead like a squadron of heavy bombers. When, after tossing and turning for hours, he eventually dozed, nightmares racked him. He was walking through a blacked-out upper floor, a steel helmet on his head, a warden's lamp at his belt. The air was hot with smoke and fire, and thick with the dust of disintegrating buildings. Outside in the street, voices were shrieking in pain. The guns were thundering. Every time a bomb whistled he cowered back against a wall, yawning with fear. He was supposed to patrol to the end of the building, to listen for the clatter of incendiaries and the heavier thud of missiles that failed to explode. Instead, he was suddenly running downstairs, stripping off his warden's uniform, throwing away his torch. A figure rose in his path—a gross, simian figure with blood on its face. "Get back," it cried, with the voice of Hind, pointing upwards into the smoke. Then the face became Ede's face. "If a bomb falls in the well I shall send you to Malaya," it said menacingly. There was an ear-splitting noise and the earth rocked. Out of the flames appeared Archer, with a rope round his neck. "It wasn't me, it was Jessop," he shrieked. Then two men who looked like Haycock and Golightly pushed Archer off the top of the building and his head came off and went spinning down the street among the tangle of fire-hoses. In a moment the scene changed and there were demons all around, demons with huge distorted features in the likeness of Cardew and Hind and Ede, and they were all prodding at him with red-hot spikes and crying in chorus, "You're the man, you're the man!" One of them struck at him with the metal base of the spike and he woke in pain, thrashing violently on the canvas, his forehead bruised by sudden contact with the iron framework of the cot. He lay panting in sweat and anguish. If only these nightmares would stop! It wasn't true what he'd dreamed. His enemies were seeking to destroy him with false accusations. He had done his duty that night. Archer had been the culprit, and Archer had paid. There was nothing on his conscience. Nothing. NOTHING! He turned on to his face with a groan.

Presently, when he was calmer, he remembered what he had to do. He switched on his torch to see the time and found that it was nearly seven o'clock. He had slept far longer than he'd thought. The machines had stopped, the building was silent. The last of the night men had gone—in the whole office now, there was no one but the commissionaire. The tin of cyanide was firm against his thigh. It took resolution to leave his hiding place, to go out on this mission which for a few minutes would be so dangerous, but now that the time had come he didn't falter. With the help of Providence, he would scatter his enemies. He put on his jacket and crept cautiously upstairs . . .

When he returned to the shelter half an hour later he felt like a commando back from a hazardous exploit successfully accomplished. His plan had gone like clockwork, and the job was done. Now there was nothing for him to do but relax and wait patiently for news. Elatedly he picked up his dispatch-case and made his way to a first-floor cloakroom, locking himself in. The cleaners had not yet reached this floor—he had plenty of time. He washed and shaved—just as he had done after so many blitz nights. His eyes had a pouchy look, but they were often like that after a bout of sleeplessness, and it was unlikely that anyone would notice. When he had finished his toilet he went back to the shelter. This was the really trying part—waiting for the working day to start. It would be fatal for him to be seen around before the office filled up. The hours passed slowly. He had no longer anything to read. He ate the last of his sandwiches, but still felt hungry. He would go somewhere pleasant for lunch, he decided, and have a slap-up meal with wine. A private celebration of the coming event. He had earned it.

At about ten o'clock he suddenly heard footsteps on the landing above the shelter, and the sound of workmen's voices. He gathered up his belongings in momentary panic and crouched motionless in the bunk as the voices came nearer. If the men descended to the shelter they might well see him. Perhaps he ought to leave now, by another exit.

Gradually his alarm faded—some stores were being taken from the floor above, that was all. After a few heavy bangs on the ceiling the footsteps receded and the voices died away. He felt relieved, but shaken. It would be good to get away.

As the hands of his watch moved to eleven he emerged from the shelter for the last time. He walked up the back stairs to an upper storey, crossed to the main staircase, and was soon on the editorial floor, moving briskly, telling himself that he must now behave as though he had just arrived by car from Beckenham, as though nothing unusual had happened. The dispatch-case in his hand provided some corroborative detail. He put his head inside the Foreign Room door and said "Good-morning" to Miss Burton and the tape-machine boy. Cardew hadn't arrived yet.

"You're early, Mr. Jessop," the girl said, with a friendly smile.

Jessop looked at the clock. She was just making conversation. With nothing particular to do in the mornings, especially since his mother's death, he had often looked in at this hour whether he was on duty or not. "I thought I'd do some shopping," he said. He hung his dispatch-case on a peg and strolled out. He felt established now. He had just arrived, like all the other people there—that was accepted. The sight of a couple of plain-clothes policemen jarred him a little. They seemed very active again. Surely they'd finished with their interrogations by now—what more could they possibly expect to learn? Anyway, *he* had nothing to say to them—and he didn't at all want to get into conversation with them, not just now. By to-morrow his movements would have merged into everyone else's, but at present he felt conspicuous. He'd do well to make himself scarce. He still had to run the gauntlet of the commissionaire's box. He walked downstairs to the front lobby, stopping by the door which led from the garage, with one eye on Vickers. He must be nonchalant as he passed Vickers—just as he would have been if he *had* called in to leave his things and was going out again for a morning's shopping. Vickers didn't seem to be looking his way—he was busy admonishing a boy for some misdemeanour. Jessop braced himself and walked casually past the box without looking at it, out through the door, and into the busy street. He didn't even know whether Vickers had seen him or not. In any case, he felt quite safe now, and in the highest spirits. He crossed the road and joined a bus queue.

Chapter Nineteen

That day passed quietly at the office—more quietly than any since Hind's murder. Though sporadic police inquiries were continuing, the tide of detection appeared to be ebbing. There were rumours, not altogether discouraged by Haines in his talks with the Press, that the Yard didn't expect to solve the case on present evidence. The fact that Haines and Ogilvie spent almost the whole day in discussions with various high officials, including the Assistant Commissioner, rather bore out this view. Long discussions, the Fleet Street crime reporters agreed, were almost always a bad sign.

Nicholas Ede spent a busy day, for the Board of Directors had insisted on meeting to discuss the lamentable happenings in the office. Jackson had his hands full too, attending to numerous delegated duties, including the arrangement of office representation at Hind's funeral. Otherwise, the tempo of activity was slow. A party of schoolgirls, touring the building in the charge of "Sarge" Vickers, marked the beginning of the summer holiday doldrums. A lunch-time meeting of the trade union chapel could muster only seven people, four of them Communists. Soames was finding it increasingly difficult to keep his reporters occupied. Jessop, being off duty until four o'clock, lazed in the Embankment Gardens after his excellent lunch. Cardew was finding his new job even less bearable than he had expected, and was rapidly coming to the conclusion that he could no longer postpone action to resolve his personal problem.

Even the conscientious Miss Timmins was affected by the imminence of the holiday week-end. As soon as six o'clock struck, she put the cover on her typewriter and prepared to leave. It was early for her, but she was seizing the opportunity provided by the Editor's dinner engagement to visit her sister. She felt in need of a nice quiet talk with someone who had nothing whatever to do with the office, and Ethel was just the person. The past few days had been gruelling for Miss Timmins. She had had to share the burden of the Editor's anxieties. She had had to make an extra effort to smooth his path, and to put up with his unaccustomed irritability. Inspector Haines had been exacting. The hot weather was very trying, too. She would go to Wembley, she decided, on the top of a bus. There would be a cool breeze—just what she needed.

She dabbed powder on her moist face and listened for the sounds that would tell her the Editor had returned to his room. He was somewhere around the office, and she couldn't leave without making sure that there was nothing else he wanted. Presently she heard his outer door open. She waited a moment or two—she didn't want to give the impression that she was in a hurry to rush away—and then she went in.

To her surprise, it wasn't the Editor after all—the outer door was just closing on Lionel Cardew. Miss Timmins looked slightly annoyed. People weren't supposed to use that door, but the privileged Cardew had got into the habit of popping in and out that way and there was nothing she could do about it since Mr. Ede didn't mind.

At that moment Ede returned. He saw that his secretary was made up for the road. "Good-night, Miss Timmins," he said, with a cheerful smile of dismissal.

"Good-night, Mr. Ede. I hope the speech goes well." She returned to her own room and put on her hat. She was just feeling for her keys when Soames came in, a great sheaf of papers in his hand and the usual harassed look in his eye.

"It's no good, Mr. Soames," she said firmly. "He's just going to have a shower and after that he's going straight out to dinner. You'll have to see Mr. Jackson or else wait until to-morrow."

"I wouldn't keep him more than a couple of minutes," Soames

pleaded. From Ede he could expect quick decisions; Jackson, with only delegated authority, might be inclined to leave things over.

"Sorry," said Miss Timmins in a tone of finality. "The station's closed down."

Soames muttered something about the "monstrous regiment of women" and went off grumbling to look for Jackson.

Almost at once, Iredale stuck his head in. This time Miss Timmins was less abrupt. "Well, and what do *you* want?"

Iredale gave her a leisurely smile. "Hallo, sweetheart. Is this your half day off?"

"Sauce!" said Miss Timmins. "If you want to see Mr. Ede, I'll put you down for six o'clock tomorrow. He's just going out."

"Okay," said Iredale. "It was only about my future—nothing at all of importance!" He grinned and vanished.

A flicker of a smile crossed Miss Timmins' tired face. She'd better go now, before anyone else tried to gatecrash. She gave a last methodical glance round the office. Suddenly there was the sound of a heavy bump from the Editor's room. What on earth could the man be doing? She went quickly to the communicating door and opened it a fraction. "Are you all right, Mr. Ede?" she called. She listened, and heard ugly, choking noises. She went in and stopped with a gasp, her hand flying to her mouth. On the floor, across the threshold of the shower-room, lay the convulsed and naked body of Nicholas Ede. In the air there was a peculiar odour, unmistakable after all the talk there had been about it. She turned and rushed frantically into the corridor. "Mr. Jackson!" she shrieked. "Oh, Mr. Jackson!"

The Assistant Editor was out in the corridor in a twinkling. "What on earth's the matter, Miss Timmins?"

"Oh, Mr. Jackson—it's Mr. Ede. I think—I think . . ." Miss Timmins crumpled up.

Chapter Twenty

Half an hour later a trio of grey-faced men sat in the Assistant Editor's room, each silently occupied with his own thoughts. Jackson seemed dazed by the blow. All he could think of at the moment was the tragic waste, the personal and professional loss, if the worst happened.

Oglivie was tactfully avoiding his Chief's eye. He sensed what Haines was going through, and felt great sympathy. It could have happened to anybody, but Haines was unlikely to be reminding himself of that fact.

The Chief Inspector's features were set in deep lines. He had liked Ede. He had felt a responsibility for him, as indeed for everyone else in this place. It was useless to tell himself that he had done everything in his power to make an occurrence such as this impossible, and that he had given the Editor the plainest of warnings; it was no consolation to know that at every stage of the inquiry he had been in the closest consultation with his superiors and with able, experienced colleagues. The fact was that *he* had been the man officially entrusted with the case, the man on the spot, and that under his very nose the murderer had struck again, unhindered, while the laborious process of elimination creaked on its way. It was distressing and humiliating beyond words. He would have liked to plunge into work, to stop the treadmill of his thoughts, but he was temporarily condemned to inaction. A decontamination squad had arrived from the Yard, but had not yet completed its preparations for entering Ede's room.

The tense silence was broken at last by Jackson. "I suppose there *is* just a chance?" he muttered, hardly daring to look at the inspector.

"We can only wait," Haines said. "I'm afraid the poor fellow looked pretty bad." At least, he reflected, no time had been wasted after the alarm had been given. Emergency treatment had been prompt, and the ambulance had arrived within five minutes. Ede had appeared to be a man with a strong constitution, and he couldn't have taken in so very much of the stuff or he would never have reached the door of the shower-room before collapsing.

Ogilvie tried to be reassuring. "They always say that if there's any sign of life at all when the doctor gets to work on a cyanide case, there's a chance."

Haines grunted. He felt it somehow safer not to speculate on the possibility of Ede's recovery—it was too much like tempting Fate.

The phone rang, and all three men leaned forward with a jerk. Jackson was nearest, and fumbled unsteadily for the receiver. It was an inside call—a query from the Subs' room about some technical matter. For the first time in his life, Jackson behaved as if he didn't care whether the paper came out or not. "For God's sake, man, don't worry me with that now," he cried in exasperation. "Use your own judgment." He flung the receiver down.

Haines sat back. "Surely those chaps outside must be ready by now," he said rather fretfully to Ogilvie.

"I'll go and see, Chief." Ogilvie was half-way to the door when the phone rang again.

This time Jackson handed the receiver over after a moment. "It's for you, Inspector." Specks of moisture glistened on his forehead and his white hair looked damp.

Haines took the phone. "Chief Inspector Haines here. Yes, Sergeant . . . Say that again, I can't hear very well . . . They do!" He looked across at Jackson with shining eyes. "Right. Yes, you'd better stay in case there's a chance later . . . All right. 'Bye."

He hung up and took a long, grateful breath. "They think he'll live."

"Thank God!" said Jackson with deep fervour. He blinked several times, took off his spectacles, wiped them and put them back. "Oh, that *is* good news. Has Mrs. Ede been told?"

"Yes—she's there with him now." Haines was smiling, and looked ten years younger. "You know, Mr. Jackson, if he does pull through, there's not much doubt that he'll owe his life to you. If you hadn't gone straight in and pulled him clear when you did, he'd have had no chance at all. Are you quite sure you're not feeling any ill effects yourself?"

"Positive, Inspector—you needn't worry about me. I recognised that smell at once and held my breath—I'm sure I didn't take any of the stuff in." Jackson sat back and heaved a sigh. "Oh, what a relief!"

Haines nodded. With Ede off his mind, he had suddenly become preoccupied with the implications of the murderer's new stroke. Now that it was clear that Hind had not been the sole target, various possibilities suggested themselves.

(I) Hind's death had been a mistake, the accidental result of a method aimed at Ede. But this seemed unlikely, because Ede had been host at the luncheon and no one could reasonably have supposed that he would be the first to eat anything.

(2) Hind's death had been a mistake, the olives having been intended for either Cardew, Iredale or Munro.

(3) Hind's death had been intended, but only as the first incident in a campaign which was later to include Ede.

Haines frowned. He had no grounds for choice between the second and third possibilities, but in either case the murderer must have had a motive for killing at least two people. What possible motive could link Ede and one of the other four as victims? And would the murderer's whole purpose have been accomplished if Ede had died? Was the campaign over—or was a new offensive brewing? Speed of investigation was obviously imperative.

The door opened suddenly and a plain-clothes man came in. "We're ready to fix you up now, sir."

"Okay, Phillips." Haines got quickly to his feet. "You'd better come along too, Ogilvie—it's not very easy to see in those masks." He turned to the Assistant Editor. "Perhaps you'd tell Miss Timmins the good news? I want to have a talk with her as soon as possible, and it'll do her more good than all the smelling salts in the world."

Jackson beamed. "It will be a pleasure."

The two policemen followed Phillips across the corridor to the men's cloakroom, where a decontamination point had been improvised. Another man was there with a lot of apparatus. In a short time the four of them were dressed in special suits and gas masks, and Phillips led the party into Ede's room. The windows were wide open and the atmosphere had no doubt cleared considerably during the past half hour, but Phillips and his assistant were taking no chances and began to use their ammonia sprays lavishly.

Haines and Ogilvie went through into Ede's dressing-room suite at the far end of the room. It was, they saw, a well-equipped annexe, consisting of a changing room, a wash-room, and a tiled shower cubicle. Thrown across a settee in the changing-room were the clothes that Ede had taken off, and beside them the evening clothes he had intended to put on. The door of the cubicle was open. The shower had been used, but at first glance everything seemed in order. Heavily encumbered, Haines got down on his knees to examine the floor, sweat pouring down his back. Ogilvie peered round his shoulder. Beside the shower there was a piece of duckboard consisting of half a dozen wooden slats screwed on to two battens. Haines lifted one corner, disclosing a sodden newspaper. It was a copy of the *Morning Call*, of that day's issue. Both men inspected it closely. Haines ran a finger over the wet surface and found it crystalline. The cubicle, he realised, must still be deadly.

It was plain enough now what had happened. Someone who had known Ede's habits must have slipped into the shower-room and put the stuff under the duckboard. Ede had stepped out on to it after his shower, with warm water running off him, and at once the cyanide had given off its deadly gas and knocked him out before he could get beyond the door. Haines was just wondering how Ede could have failed to notice the smell of cyanide on first entering the shower-room when Ogilvie drew his attention to a patent disinfector on the wall. Those things, he knew, gave off a strong perfume of their own, sufficient to conceal the presence of the cyanide as long as it was still dry.

By now the decontamination officers were waiting to spray the shower-room. With a last glance round, Haines place the wet newspaper carefully on the duck-board and carried the whole thing out into the main room. Phillips had brought a gas-proof container into which the inspector dropped the exhibits. The main thing now was to get the suite properly aired, so that the Yard experts could come in and make their detailed examination.

It took Haines and Ogilvie a little time to divest themselves of their special clothing and wash away all traces of cyanide. When they got back to the Assistant Editor's room, Jackson was waiting for them. He had sent a message in to Miss Timmins, who was making a good recovery in the Women's Rest Room under Katharine Camden's ministrations. "Well, did you manage to find out anything?" he asked eagerly.

"There's no doubt how it was done, Mr. Jackson," said Haines, mopping his forehead, "but that's about as far as we've got at the moment." Briefly, he described what they had seen in the shower-room.

"Good Heavens!" exclaimed Jackson, as Haines finished, "how unbelievably horrible!"

"Proper execution chamber," observed Ogilvie. "Just like the ruddy Nazis."

"Well, we'd better get on," said Haines. "I'd like to know more about that newspaper, Mr. Jackson. What time would it have been available in the office?"

Jackson, who had been frowning down at his desk as though trying to capture an elusive memory, looked up slowly. "I'm sorry, Inspector—what did you say?"

Haines repeated the question.

"That depends on what edition it was," Jackson told him.

"It had three stars," said Haines, "if that's any help."

"Ah, then it must have been a West of England paper. Let me see, we were running a bit late last night. The first copy must have been off the presses just after half-past ten."

"That gives us a time limit one way, then," said Haines. "The stuff couldn't have been laid before ten-thirty last night." He was wondering if the cyanide had been actually carried into the room in the newspaper. "Come on, Ogilvie, let's go and see what Miss Timmins has to say. Perhaps she'll be able to tell us something more definite."

Chapter Twenty-One

Though her cheeks were still pale and her eyes red, Miss Timmins managed to face the two policemen with her usual air of efficiency. Self-drilled to cope with recurrent crises, she wasn't going to let even an attempted murder get her down—particularly now that she knew the attempt had failed.

"We need your help badly, Miss Timmins," Haines told her. "The position is this. Between half-past ten last night and six o'clock this evening, someone went into Mr. Ede's room in his absence and put the poison in the shower-cubicle which nearly killed him." He let that sink in. "Tell me, was it Mr. Ede's regular practice to take an evening shower at the office?"

"Only when he was going out and had to change," said Miss Timmins.

"Did many people know that he was going out to-night, do you suppose? Members of the staff, I mean?"

"I should think quite a number. I told Mr. Soames because of getting a reporter to cover the dinner, a if one reporter knows a thing like that there's no reason why everyone shouldn't know."

"Quite so. Well, now, Miss Timmins, assuming that someone did go into Mr. Ede's room between those two times, when in your view would that have been most likely to happen? What were the opportunities?"

Miss Timmins plucked at the now rather crumpled frill around her throat and her forehead creased in anxious thought. "I can't imagine, Inspector. I wouldn't have thought it was possible at all."

"It may have happened when you weren't in the building, you

know. Let's consider that possibility first. What were the arrangements about locking your room and Mr. Ede's?"

"I have a key to my room," said Miss Timmins, "and Mr. Ede has a key to his. When we leave at night we both lock our own doors, and when we come in in the morning we both unlock our own doors."

"What about the communicating door?"

"That doesn't lock."

"And do you take the keys home with you, or leave them with the commissionaire?"

"We take them with us. Sarge has another set down at the front box, and of course he's got a master key as well."

Haines made a mental note to have the keys checked. "Well, one thing at a time. Do you remember locking your door last evening?"

"Yes—it was about seven o'clock."

"Was Mr. Ede still in his room then?"

"No, he'd gone a few minutes earlier. I heard him lock his door."

"But he may have come back later in the evening, eh?"

"No," said Miss Timmins, "not last night—Mr. Jackson was on duty. Mr. Ede would always come back if there was any special reason, of course, but last night there wasn't, so he talked to Mr. Jackson on the telephone instead."

"Then to the best of your knowledge, Miss Timmins, both doors were securely locked from the time you left last night until you arrived this morning?"

She pondered for a moment. "Well, there would be the cleaners," she suggested.

"Ah, yes, of course. We shall have to go into that. But as far as you and Mr. Ede were concerned, the rooms remained locked?"

"Yes."

"When did you arrive this morning?"

"At ten o'clock. Mr. Ede came in just before eleven."

"The doors were locked when you arrived, and everything in the rooms seemed just as usual?"

"Yes."

"Very well. Now what about to-day? What opportunities would

anyone have had to slip into Mr. Ede's room unobserved between ten o'clock and six? Plenty, I suppose?"

"Oh, not at all," said Miss Timmins, quickly. "In fact, I don't see how anyone could possibly have . . ."

"Think carefully," Haines pressed her. "It was only a question of a moment or two, you know."

"I realise that," said Miss Timmins, "but the only time we were both out at once was during lunch, and then we locked up—we always do. We're most careful about it, because newspaper editors have all sorts of important papers lying about."

"But Mr. Ede must have been out of his own room several times during the day—at conferences, for instance?"

"Oh, yes," she agreed, "he does pop out quite a bit, but *I'm* here all the time and it's part of my job to be a watchdog."

"You can hardly watch his outer door from your room."

"I can hear, though. It's become a sort of second nature to me to know what's going on in there. In any case, it's a rule that that door isn't used by the staff—Mr. Ede sometimes lets people out that way, but they never go straight in to him. Anyone who wants to see the Editor must come into my room first."

"The intending murderer would have wanted *not* to see the Editor," Haines pointed out. "This was an exceptional circumstance . . . What is it, Miss Timmins?" The secretary's hand had fluttered to her lips in a gesture of dismayed recollection.

"I've just remembered—Mr. Cardew was in there. But of course, that couldn't possibly have anything to do with . . ." Her voice trailed off.

"Wait a moment," cried Haines sharply, "Let's get this straight. You mean that Mr. Cardew was there while Mr. Ede was out?"

"Yes. It was just after six o'clock. You see, Mr. Cardew's a particular friend of Mr. Ede's and so he's in a special position. He uses that door more or less as he likes—he's the only one who does. I'd quite forgotten about him. When I heard someone in there I thought at first it was Mr. Ede—he'd been out, you see—but when I looked in I saw that it was Mr. Cardew. He was just leaving."

"Did he say anything to you?"

"No, he'd gone before I had a chance to speak to him, and Mr. Ede came back almost immediately afterwards."

"How long would you say Mr. Cardew was in the room?"

"Hardly any time at all. Only a minute or two." Haines glanced across at Ogilvie. "I think we'd better have Mr. Cardew in," he said.

"Right, Chief," Ogilvie agreed briskly, and went out.

Miss Timmins looked very perturbed as the door closed behind him. "But, Inspector, I'm sure Mr. Cardew couldn't possibly . . ."

"You'll have to leave that to us, Miss Timmins. Now I want you to search your memory once again. Are you *quite* certain that nothing else of that sort happened during the day? You can see for yourself it's most important that there should be no mistake."

"I'm absolutely positive," said Miss Timmins, adding rather coldly, "and I simply can't believe that anyone would have dared to bring poison into Mr. Ede's room knowing perfectly well that there was somebody sitting next door."

Haines stroked his chin thoughtfully. That did take a bit of believing—except that this murderer had shown himself to be an unusually cool customer. He filed the doubt away. "Well, Miss Timmins," he said, "we've arrived at this position, it seems—that from the time you went home yesterday evening until you found Mr. Ede lying on the floor to-night, the only persons who entered or could have entered Mr. Ede's room in his absence were Mr. Cardew, or someone who gained unauthorised possession of a duplicate key? Is that right?"

"Yes."

"And, of course, yourself," added Haines, looking straight at her.

Miss Timmins stared at him blankly for a moment. "Well, really . . ." she began in an outraged tone.

"We have to think of everything, you know," said Haines gently. He was beginning to wonder whether he had paid sufficient attention to Miss Timmins. What was she *really* like beneath that facade of efficiency? Could she, perhaps, be one of those frustrated spinsters with sexual obsessions? Had she been in love with her boss, and for some reason turned against him? There was no blinking the fact that she had had a unique opportunity to put the poison in Ede's room—and poisoning was more often than not a woman's crime. He remembered that she had had no alibi for Hind's murder, either—and, of course, she had known all about the luncheon party. But what could she have had against Hind? Though she was a pleasant enough person, she was hardly a pin-up girl, and it was inconceivable that there could have been any secret relationship between her and Hind. And she certainly couldn't have intended the olives for Ede—she of all people would have known his qualities as a host. Haines decided that he was venturing into unnecessarily deep waters. There would be time enough to return to Miss Timmins when he had disposed of the more likely suspects.

"Anyhow," he said, his scrutiny over, "I'm very grateful to you, Miss Timmins. You've been most clear and helpful. Now if I were you I should go home and try to get a good night's rest. You'll probably feel a reaction in the morning, you know, after all this turmoil. Good-night."

The hint of suspicion had been too much for Miss Timmins. "Good-night," she sniffed, her composure broken at last.

Chapter Twenty-Two

Haines sat tense as a coiled spring, listening to the rapid approach of footsteps along the corridor. The door opened and Cardew came in, looking flushed, with Ogilvie at his heels.

"Sorry I had to send the runners out after you, Mr. Cardew," said Haines. "Not too inconvenient, I hope?"

"Not at all," said Cardew. "I was only at my flat."

Haines nodded. "Take a seat, won't you? I expect you've heard the good news about Mr. Ede?"

"Yes—I'd just phoned the hospital when Inspector Ogilvie rang me." The young man seemed to be making an effort to speak calmly. "It's been an appalling shock."

"It's been a great shock to all of us," said Haines. "However, all's well that ends well, Mr. Cardew. Have a cigarette."

"Thank you." Cardew helped himself from the inspector's case and flicked on his lighter. He inhaled deeply and relaxed.

The spring uncoiled. Leaning forward in his chair, Haines said harshly, "Why did you go into Mr. Ede's room at six o'clock this evening?"

Cardew's mouth opened and shut soundlessly. He was knocked completely off balance.

"Well, Mr. Cardew, why was it?"

Cardew's face had gone white. "I—I'm sorry, Inspector," he stammered, as if groping desperately for an answer that would bear investigation. "I—I just don't remember . . ."

"You don't *remember*! Less than three hours ago, and your mind's a blank! Let me try to refresh your memory about the incident. You went to Mr. Ede's room by his private door just before six o'clock. You stayed there for a few minutes only, and you left the room just before he returned. You must have gone there with some purpose in mind. What was it?"

Cardew was breathing hard. The strain of the past few days, ending in this frightful attack on Ede, had been almost more than he could bear, and his brain was anything but clear. "Let me think, Inspector—just let me think. This awful business has driven everything out of my head. It must have been something to do with work, I suppose . . ."

In a voice full of menace, Haines said, "I suggest that you went there to spread cyanide on the floor of his shower room—to *kill* him, Mr. Cardew."

Cardew sprang to his feet, his eyes blazing. "How dare you say that, you swine?" White and shaking, he stood glaring at the inspector. Ogilvie had risen too, ready for trouble.

Haines sat quite still. "Unless you can give me a proper explanation of what you *were* doing there," he said sternly, "I've no alternative but to consider that possibility. Sit down, Mr. Cardew, and control yourself. You must realise that you're in a very serious position, and blustering won't help you. As far as we've been able to discover, you were the only person to spend any time alone in Mr. Ede's room during the day. You appear unable to produce on the spur of the moment an explanation of what you were doing there. If ever I've seen guilty hesitation on anyone's face, I saw it just now."

"I didn't do it, I tell you—it's a monstrous accusation. Why *should* I?

"What are your relations with Mrs. Ede?" asked Haines quietly.

Cardew looked as though he were about to leap across the desk. "Leave her out of it, damn you, do you hear?"

Haines sighed. "Mr. Cardew, you are evidently under great emotional stress. Now if you'll just try to calm down, I'll give you a little advice. If you think it wiser, you can refuse to answer any more of my questions until you've got in touch with your lawyer. In that case, I shall assume that the information I have about you and Mrs. Ede is correct, and I shall direct my investigations accordingly. You may be sure that we shall soon be in possession of all the facts. Alternatively, you can tell me the truth yourself, in which case I may at some stage have to warn you that anything you say may be used in evidence."

"There's nothing to tell," cried Cardew. "If you've heard anything, it's just filthy gossip . . . Oh, *God*!" He buried his head in his hands.

Haines waited. Ogilvie was sitting back impassively, watching with secret admiration his chief's ponderous but devastatingly effective technique.

Presently Cardew looked up, his sensitive face distorted with the effort to reach a decision. "Very well," he said in a steadier manner, "I suppose I'll have to tell you everything." He hesitated a moment longer, and then plunged. "When I went to Ede's room tonight, it was to tell him that I wanted to resign from the paper."

"So soon after your new appointment?"

"I had to. The—the fact is, I'm in love with Mrs. Ede."

"And she with you?"

"No, no. Everything's been on my side. God, this is humiliating!"

No one helped him out, and presently he took a deep breath and went on. "I've been friendly with Nicholas Ede and—and Rosemary Ede, for some time. He's been frightfully decent to me, and so has she. She—she's very attractive. He asked me along to his home soon after I joined the paper, and I got used to dropping in quite often. I became a sort of friend of the family, and I took her about a good deal. Ede's job takes up most of his time, you see, and he seemed pleased that his wife was being looked after. Everything was all right until about a week or two ago. Then I suddenly realised that I'd fallen in love with her. I knew I was being a crass idiot, but I couldn't help it. God knows what came over me—I lost my head completely. A few days ago I—I told her I was in love with her . . ." He groaned. "I even asked her to come away with me. I must have been mad."

"What did she say to that?" asked Haines, his face expressionless.

Cardew gave a mirthless laugh. "She was *kind*. She treated me like a small boy who'd been asking for too many sweets. It was the most mortifying experience I'd ever known. After I left her I felt like hell. I knew I'd behaved like a swine towards Ede, and I knew I'd made myself ridiculous in her eyes. I felt I never wanted to see her again. I wondered what explanation I could give Ede for not going there any more. I was still thinking about it when he told me he wanted me to be Foreign Editor. I said I would, but only because I hadn't made up my mind what to do. Then to-day I decided that the only thing I could possibly do was to leave the *Morning Call* altogether. I determined to clear right out and make a fresh start. As you said. it was about six o'clock when I looked into his room to see if he was there. I was going to tell him that I was tired of newspaper work and wanted a change. I'd forgotten he was going out to dinner until I saw his dress clothes laid out. There wasn't any point in my trying to talk to him when he was in a hurry, so I went out. I was going to tell him to-morrow. Then about ten minutes later there was a frightful flap in the office and I heard that he'd been poisoned." Cardew looked unutterably miserable. "That's the whole story. Now you know everything."

"I hope so," said Haines. "Am I to understand, then, that Mrs. Ede gave you no encouragement?"

"None at all," said Cardew. "I tell you, I was just a complete bloody fool."

"H'm." In Haines's somewhat limited experience, a woman could usually prevent such a situation arising if she wanted to. He sat quietly for a while, digesting the story. "Well, Mr. Cardew," he said at last, "all this seems to add up to a pretty powerful motive for murder."

"Do you suppose I haven't realised that? God only knows what Rosemary may be thinking. It's bad enough that she should despise me for an idiot, but if she should imagine . . . Oh, God, I couldn't bear it. I didn't do this ghastly thing, Inspector—I swear I didn't. I like and admire Ede. That's what's so damnable about it all. I know things look black for me, but he's one of the last people in the world I'd have dreamed of harming . . ." Despair seemed to engulf the young man.

"Take it easy, Mr. Cardew. You might just as well save your breath, you know. Pleas of innocence on their own won't get us anywhere."

"I'm sorry," said Cardew. "I suppose I'm making things worse." He raised miserable eyes to Haines.

"What *is* going to get us anywhere? I can't prove I didn't do it—I only know the idea is fantastic. I hadn't the means, if that's any use to you. I wouldn't know how to get hold of cyanide if I wanted it."

"The situation would certainly be much blacker," said Haines, "if that weren't the case."

"Well, it is. And anyway, surely the person who tried to kill Ede was the same one who killed Hind? It stands to reason. You can't pin a motive for *that* on to me."

"There is, I admit, an absence of known motive at the moment," agreed Haines cautiously, "but all sorts of things seem to be coming to light, don't they? What are you keeping back about Hind?"

"Nothing."

Haines looked searchingly at him. "Even if that's true, there's such a thing as taking advantage of someone else's murder—*and* method. It's often been done. A murders B; C, who has long wanted to murder D, realises that he has been shown the way and that, with luck, A will be blamed for D's murder too. There seems to be a great deal of cyanide about, and more than one person may have had access to it."

"It's much more likely that there's a lunatic around the office who did both jobs."

"That's also a possibility. The problem is to recognise a lunatic when you see one. Emotional instability, now, is much easier to detect!" Haines gave Cardew a rather grim smile. "Well, we'll let the matter rest there for a while, and I'll make some more inquiries. In the meantime, you'll oblige me by not going anywhere without letting me know. Is that understood?"

"I seem to have no option," said Cardew. He got up and went painfully out, as though he had been scourged. Ogilvie made a tut-tutting noise as the door closed behind him. "When I was seventeen," he remarked, "I remember feeling like that about a girl. At his age, he ought to know better. What do you make of it, Chief?"

Haines hesitated. "I'll know better when I've seen the lady in the case. I think I ought to have a talk with her right away."

"Do you suppose they might be in it together?"

"If they had been, I can't imagine that Cardew would have given so much away. They'd have worked things out beforehand—he'd never have been in that hysterical condition." Haines slowly shook his head. "No, I'm inclined to think that his story about Mrs. Ede is true. He could easily have come away from her feeling frustrated and desperate, and have killed Ede out of jealousy. Then he probably *would* have behaved as he did to-day. Still, we're a long way from proving it. Cardew was the obvious man to go for first, but he may not be the only one in the picture, and for the time being we'd better assume that he isn't." Haines mentally reviewed the most urgent tasks. "Look, Ogilvie, will you find out where Sarge Vickers lives and go and see him now. Get to know all you can about the keys and what's been happening to them lately. See if anyone else had a chance to get into Ede's room at any time. Oh, and find out if the cleaners went into the shower-room this morning. If you get any lead at all, follow it up. And I'll see Mrs. Ede. Okay?"

Ogilvie nodded, pleased at the prospect of getting off on his own for a bit.

"Right," said Haines. "I'll see you here in the morning."

Chapter Twenty-Three

Ogilvie lost no time in getting hold of Sarge Vickers' address, and half an hour later he was climbing the stairs of the block of council fiats in Paddington where the commissionaire lived. Over a cup of cocoa, he told of the attempt on Ede. Vickers was deeply shocked and obviously anxious to help, but the replies he gave to Ogilvie's questions were uniformly negative. There was absolutely no possibility, he declared, of any of the duplicate keys or the master key itself having been given to an unauthorised person, or taken by anyone without permission. Instructions on the first point were strict; and the front box was never left unattended. Vickers had not parted with them himself, and he doubted strongly that either of his henchmen, Sergeants Peach and Granger, who shared the night-shift between them, would have done so. He mentioned that the Proprietor and one or two of the directors had master keys of their own, and Ogilvie made a mental note to look into that, though he couldn't see any hopeful prospects there. In the end, the inspector had to accept Vickers' assurances. The senior commissionaire was evidently a man who took his responsibilities seriously, and he stuck to his ground. Subject to what the two other commissionaires might say, it appeared most unlikely that the murderer could actually have gained possession of a key.

Ogilvie sat considering the position. *Someone* had got into the room. Leaving aside Cardew, and on the assumption that Miss Timmins's evidence was to be believed, there now seemed only one possibility to be investigated—and a slim one.

"Tell me, Sarge, when is Mr. Ede's room cleaned and how do the cleaners manage about keys? Is there any particular drill?"

"Well," said Vickers, "Mrs. Little and 'er ladies, they come every morning sharp at seven—that's in Granger's shift—and 'e gives 'er the master key so she don't 'ave to bother with a great bunch of 'em. She keeps it till the cleaning's finished, around nine o'clock, and then she gives it to me."

"I see. And did she give you the key this morning, as usual?"

"Yes, Inspector, just after nine. She's a very reliable woman—she wouldn't leave it lying about, if that's what you're thinking. She's been cleaning them offices near ten year, I reckon, an' never a complaint from anyone."

Ogilvie took a thoughtful sip of his cocoa. "Would any of the night staff have been still working, do you suppose, when the cleaners arrived this morning?"

Vickers shook his head. "The last of 'em leaves long before that. Hours before."

"Well, would any of the staff have arrived as early as that to start the new day's work?"

"Not they!" said the commissionaire. "Late finishers and late starters, newspaper people are. The boys are the first to get there, an' they don't arrive till close on nine-thirty. Then a typist or so comes tripping along, an' after that they all start rolling in. But while the cleaning's being done, the building's empty."

Ogilvie pressed him. "You told the Chief the other day that you kept track of all strangers calling at the office, but that you didn't always notice the movements of the staff. Supposing that someone you knew quite well *had* decided to pop in at about eight o'clock this morning, just for once—would you have noticed?"

"That we should, and I'll tell you why—'cause it ain't never 'appened. There'd 'ave been something said, you may be sure. Oh, yes, we'd 'ave noticed that all right."

Ogilvie rather thought so too. "Ah, well," he said, getting up, "thanks for the nightcap, Sarge."

Picking up a cab outside the flats, he managed to arrive back at the *Morning Call* just in time to catch Sergeants Peach and Granger at their midnight switchover. For ten minutes he questioned them closely, but they both bore out what Vickers had already said.

Neither of them had given out keys for the Ede-Timmins rooms; neither had parted with the master key in the past few days, except to Mrs. Little. The front box had at no time been left unattended. Granger was as positive as Vickers had been that no member of the staff could have got into the office before nine o'clock without being noticed. Ogilvie satisfied himself that there was no shaking the men, and went off to get a few hours' sleep. One way and another, he reflected, things were beginning to look pretty bad for Cardew.

When he returned to the *Morning Call* just before seven, Mrs. Little was already there, standing before the box in animated conversation with her three assistants. She was a large, cheerful woman, with immense forearms and pudgy red hands. It was evident from her manner that Sergeant Granger had already told them the news.

Ogilvie introduced himself and got briskly down to business. "You won't be able to clean the rooms belonging to Mr. Ede and Miss Timmins this morning," he told Mrs. Little, "but apart from that I'd like you to carry on, all of you, just as you usually do, and I'll follow and watch."

"Now ain't that just like a man!" said Mrs. Little "Sure you wouldn't like to take a pail, Inspector?"

Her flock gave a subdued titter and followed Mrs. Little and the policeman into the lift. When it disgorged them at the main editorial floor Mrs. Little said: "We always start on this floor, see, 'cos it's left in such a state. Goodness knows what some of their 'omes must be like, 'specially the reporters." She led the way to a large cupboard room, where the women donned overalls and began to fill their buckets from a tap. There was an air of festival about them as they chattered and laughed. It was a beautiful morning, they had a handsome inspector with them, and there had almost been another murder. What more could anybody ask?

"Now," said Mrs. Little in a business-like tone, "what 'appens is this. It's the same every day, so you can't make no mistake. First of all I goes round with the key what Sarge just give me, and I unlocks all the doors on this floor." She led her entourage to the

Assistant Editor's room. "I starts with Mr. Jackson and then I goes on to Miss Timmins and Mr. Ede . . ." She stopped, her way blocked by a young and very large uniformed policeman.

Ogilvie said: "Morning, constable," and Mrs. Little looked wistfully at the closed door. "Sure you wouldn't like to go in, sir?"

"Not just now, thank you, Mrs. Little. You can just pretend to unlock them."

She giggled. "Who do you think I am—Shirley Temple?" Reluctantly she passed Ede's room, "Well, then, there's the Leaders and the Sports and the Foreign and the Arty and the Subs and the Reporters and the News. Quite a walk, ain't it?" Ogilvie followed a pace behind her.

"And that's the lot," she said, flinging open the door of Features. She slipped the key back into her overall pocket. "Now we can all get started. My girls know just what they got to do—we 'ave the rooms divided up amongst us, see?"

"Very efficient, Mrs. Little. And who cleans Mr. Ede's room, as a rule?"

"I do it meself. Always. Then I knows it's been done proper."

"Good," said Ogilvie. "Well, now, when you did Mr. Ede's room yesterday morning, did you clean the shower-room as well?"

"O' course I did."

"What exactly did you do to it?"

"I give the tiles and the floor a wash over and 'ung a clean towel on the 'ook and tidied up a bit like. Mr. Ede 'adn't used the shower the night before, so there weren't much to do. Didn't take more'n a few minutes all told."

"There was a wooden thing on the floor by the shower, wasn't there?—you know, one of those things to step out on?"

"Oh, yes, that's always there."

"Did you move it to wash under it, or did you just wash round it?"

"Now look 'ere, young man . . ." began Mrs. Little indignantly.

"I'm sorry," said Ogilvie, with a disarming smile. "You moved it, eh? And when you'd finished, you put a clean! newspaper underneath it, did you?"

Mrs. Little looked horrified. "Whatever would I do that for? Shockin' wet mess it'd make when Mr. Ede come to take 'is shower! No, *I* didn't put no newspaper there." Clearly she pitied the inspector's ignorance.

"I see," said Ogilvie, a gleam of excitement in his eyes. Vital facts had suddenly begun to emerge. The period in which the murderer could have operated was narrowing fast. The newspaper had suddenly taken on an entirely new significance. Whatever the commissionaires might say, it was now pretty clear that somebody *had* been around during the cleaning operations, or soon after. Ogilvie set to work eagerly to discover just what had happened.

"About how long do you spend in each room, Mrs. Little?"

"Ten minutes, near enough," she said. "There's no time for more, with so many of 'em to do. We 'ave to keep a strick timetable, or we'd never get through."

"Quite so. I'm rather interested in that timetable."

"Well, I'll tell you. I starts in Mr. Ede's room about ten past seven, and about twenty past I finishes in there an' goes through into Miss Timmins."

Ogilvie nodded. "And at about the same time, I suppose, the other cleaners are moving into their second rooms, too?"

"If they're not, they ought to be."

"So that at, say, twenty-five past seven, the position would be this. Mr. Ede's outer door would be unlocked . . ."

"Wide open," said Mrs. Little. "Airin' the room."

"That's better still—wide open. And you would be in Miss Timmins's room—with the communicating door closed, I dare say? It's on a spring, isn't it?"

"Yes it is, and it just won't prop open nohow. Shockin' awkward to get through with an armful O' brooms and pails, I can tell you."

"And the other cleaners would all be inside their second rooms at that time?"

"Yes."

"And a little later, you'd all have moved into other rooms, and the outer doors would still be open?"

"That's about the size of it," said Mrs. Little, slightly mystified.

Ogilvie looked thoughtfully at the charwoman. "Do you suppose," he asked, "that anyone on the staff here would have any idea about how you go to work? You know, the routine?"

Mrs Little folded her enormous forearms and stood frowning. "Well, I dunno about *now* Inspector. It was different during the war, O' course. A lot of the chaps that work 'ere used to sleep in the building then—down in the shelter."

"Is that so?" said Ogilvie, with quickening interest. Here was an approach that he hadn't thought of at all.

"Yes—and we used to see 'em when they come up in the mornings sometimes. Talk about scruffy! Lor, you should've seen 'em. We nearly always 'ad a few words with 'em. That's one thing the war did—made people matey, what it didn't make corpses." She sighed reminiscently. "Oh, yes, proper 'ome from 'ome it was 'ere for some of 'em."

"Suppose, Mrs. Little," said Ogilvie, "that the man who tried to kill Mr. Ede had been around the office while you were cleaning—you know, keeping out of your way and watching his opportunity. Do you think he could have got into Mr. Ede's room for a couple of minutes after you'd finished there, without being seen or heard by any of you?"

Mrs. Little stared. "It don't seem all that likely, I must say, but I s'pose it could 'ave 'appened if 'e made sure the coast was clear first, like. There's a fair racket when we're cleaning, an' we certainly don't 'ave no time to stop and look around."

"That's exactly what I was thinking. Now there's just one more thing—what time did you lock up the rooms on this floor?"

The charwoman made a swift calculation. "About a quarter to eight, I'd say."

"Thank you," said Ogilvie, well satisfied. "I'm very grateful for the help you've given me, Mrs. Little. It's been most valuable."

"You're very welcome, I'm sure. I only 'opes you catch the chap what done it." Mrs. Little watched the inspector out of sight and then hurried away to acquaint the other cleaners with the sensational news that the murderer had possibly been in their midst the previous morning.

Ogilvie went down to the second floor office and spent half an hour setting his notes in order in readiness for Haines's arrival. Just after eight o'clock he went off to the front box to have another word with Vickers.

"Look, Sarge," he said, with barely concealed excitement, "there's one thing I forgot to ask you last night and it's important. Suppose someone had decided to stay in the building all night instead of going home—would you have known?"

Vickers looked thoughtful. "Now that's different," he said slowly. "I dare say we wouldn't 'ave done, at that. We don't really know when people go 'ome, 'cept by chance—there's too many of 'em, an' often when we think they're off 'ome they're just slipping into the Crown for a quick one. They're always bobbing in and out—I tell you, we get proper dizzy."

"Is there any patrol of the building during the night?"

"Well, there is an' there isn't, as you might say. Sergeant Peach, 'e usually does a round just before midnight, putting out lights what people 'ave left burning unnecessary, and then Sergeant Granger 'e sometimes takes a turn round the place early in the morning—though only if there's someone else at the box, mind you! Still, there ain't no search o' the place, o' course. Since you ask me, I'd say if anyone wanted to 'ide 'imself in the office all night 'e could do it easy. There's plenty o' places."

"And leave next day without anyone being the wiser?"

"I reckon so, if 'e was a bit careful."

Ogilvie beamed. "Thanks, Sarge. You know, I think we may be on to something." He went back upstairs and completed his notes."

It was just after half-past eight when Haines arrived. "Morning, Inspector," he called to Ogilvie. "Any developments?"

"There *are* one or two things I'd like to put up to you, Chief," said Ogilvie modestly. He had a pleasant sense of achievement, but he was a tactful officer. "Did you manage to get anything out of Mrs. Ede?"

Haines sat down and began to fill his pipe. "I had a useful half hour with her," he said. "She's a very charming woman. Not very big but a lovely figure—what you'd call petite, I suppose. Large dark eyes and a nice complexion."

"She sounds a knockout," said Ogilvie dutifully. Privately he thought that his Chief's description of feminine charms was lamentably uninformative.

"I won't deny she made a strong impression on me," Haines went on, "and I can well imagine an emotional young fellow like Cardew losing his head over her. She's one of those women with a lot of appeal—what they call 'it'—and yet dignity too. Ede certainly picked a winner."

"Did she corroborate Cardew's story?"

"Yes and no. She wasn't willing to let him take all the responsibility for what had happened—that was the main difference. I suspected all the time that he was being chivalrous. According to her, she found his company pleasant and they did have what she called a very mild flirtation—nothing that she would have minded her husband knowing about, she said. That's as may be. Anyhow, she now thinks that she behaved very foolishly, and blames herself for not realising that he might become serious. She says he was so light-hearted that the possibility never entered her head." Haines paused for a moment. "I'm inclined to believe her—it's a common enough situation, and as a matter of fact she struck me as being genuinely fond of Ede. She was certainly brought up sharp by this business yesterday. If you ask me, Ede has been a bit too much married to his newspaper and she'd been amusing herself in what she thought was a harmless way."

"So she's out, Chief?"

"I think so. She didn't behave in the least like a woman who's just conspired with a lover to murder a husband. Her attitude over Cardew was all wrong for that. She was too frank—just as he was, for that matter. She didn't try to cover up for him sufficiently. It seemed not to have occurred to her that he might be under suspicion, until I began to question her about his state of mind when he left her. She was worried enough on his account then—in fact, her behaviour was just what I'd have expected it to be if her story and his were both true. Of course, that doesn't mean we can rule out

Cardew—he might well have done it off his own bat. He's still the only person that we know had access to Ede's room—unless you've got anything more on that?"

"Yes, I think this is where I come in, Chief," said Ogilvie. "I've covered quite a bit of ground since last night." He proceeded to give Haines a detailed account of his unproductive inquiries about keys and of his highly fruitful half-hour with the charladies.

"The way I see it, sir, is this," he said finally. "We know now for a fact that the cyanide wasn't laid before a quarter past seven yesterday morning, when Mrs. Little finished cleaning the room. If we can believe the commissionaires and Miss Timmins, the murderer had no other opportunity once the cleaners had left. In that case, he must have put the stuff down before a quarter to eight, when Mrs. Little re-locked Ede's door. There's additional evidence to support that theory—for one thing, the newspaper that the murderer put down. The only reason *I* can think of why he should do that is that he had to keep the cyanide from touching the wet floor. If I'm right, then it follows that the job was done almost immediately after Mrs. Little left the shower-room, because otherwise the floor would have dried and the precaution wouldn't have been necessary. And there's another point—a man who'd stayed all night in the office, with the intention of going in after the cleaners, is precisely the man you'd expect to have a first edition in his pocket—whereas later on, that would have been most unlikely. I won't say I think it's an absolutely cast-iron theory, but it does seem to me that everything points to the job having been done in that half-hour."

Haines was impressed. "It's a smart bit of reconstruction, anyway," he said. "Good for you, Ogilvie." He puffed away for a few moments, considering the situation in the light of these new discoveries. "Of course," he said at last, "if you're right, Cardew's visit at six in the evening doesn't mean a thing. The floor would certainly have been dry by then."

"How do we know *he* wasn't the night prowler?" asked Ogilvie.

"If he'd laid the cyanide in the early morning," said Haines, "he'd hardly have gone to Ede's room at the very moment when his victim was about to take the fatal shower. That would have been idiotic, and our man's clever."

Ogilvie agreed. "Well, perhaps Cardew *was* telling the truth. He's not the only pebble on the beach, Chief, as you said yesterday. That idea that he took advantage of someone else's murder to do one of his own is feasible enough, I know, but it's a darned sight more likely that one chap did both jobs, don't you think?"

"Oh, certainly," said Haines. "We've got Cardew in our minds as suspect number one because his motive was so strong, but the case against him is full of holes." He sat quietly for a while, considering competing claims. Iredale's actions would obviously need looking into. Pringle's, too. Pringle had had almost as good a motive as Iredale for wanting to kill Hind, and a better one for wanting to get rid of Ede. If Ede had died, Pringle might have kept his job and his racket—as it was, he would almost certainly be out on his neck before long.

"All right," said Haines finally, "for the time being we'll forget Cardew. We'll work on the assumption that the same chap did the two jobs and that the cyanide was laid during that half hour by someone who'd stayed in the office—and we'll see where it gets us. That means checking up on the whereabouts of the sixty-eight people who hadn't an alibi for Hind's murder. Okay?"

"Fine," said Ogilvie, rubbing his hands. "It'll be a lot simpler than it was last time—most of the sixty-eight must have been at home at that hour in the morning, and corroboration should be easy. We ought to finish up with a nice short list." He was eager to get started. "You know, Chief, I have a feeling that we shall be moving in for the kill before very long."

"I wish you wouldn't say things like that," Haines reproved him. "It may not be us who'll be moving in! I can't get it out of my mind that the murderer's still around with the cyanide. Think of it—a couple of whiffs, a spot on the tongue, and there's another body on our hands. There are so many ways he can do it." The inspector's gaze wandered to the ceiling, where four nozzles protruded from the plaster. "Aren't those things up there fire sprinklers?"

Ogilvie looked up. "Yes, they are."

"You see what I mean?" said Haines grimly. "We'd better have them disconnected."

"All right, Chief," said Ogilvie, soberly. "But if you're feeling as worried as that, why not circulate some sort of warning round the office? Keep people on their toes."

"A very good idea," said Haines. "I think I will."

Chapter Twenty-Four

While Ogilvie proceeded to organise a lightning round-up of the sixty-eight, Haines went along to the Editor's room, now completely free from cyanide gas, and supervised the police work there. It had already been established at the Yard that the cyanide crystals adhering to the newspaper had been similar to the poison used in the olives. Various minute specks of dirt which had stuck to the paper were being microscopically examined, but the results, if any, would be useful only at a later stage. Otherwise, it seemed as though Ede's room was going to be as barren of clues as the Directors' Dining Room had been.

As soon as the photographers and the fingerprint men had finished their work, Haines arranged for a careful search of the less frequented parts of the building in case the murderer should have left any traces of his night's lodging. He also rang up the hospital, and was informed that though Ede was now out of danger he could not yet be interviewed. For the moment there was nothing more to do but draft a cyanide warning and wait for Ogilvie's results. Haines returned to the second floor office.

He had hardly sat down when there was a sharp rap at the door and Jackson came in. Judging by the portentous look on his face, he brought news of significance. A sheaf of press clippings fluttered from his right hand like streamers from an electric fan.

"Are you busy, Inspector?" he asked. "I've got something here that will interest you."

"Come right in, Mr. Jackson. What is it?"

"I think it's possible I may be able to help you about the cyanide."

A gleam of excitement lit the inspector's face. "Go ahead, Mr. Jackson—I'm all attention."

"Well, it was that remark of Inspector Ogilvie's about the Nazis and their execution chambers that put me on to it. I felt at the time that it rang a bell, but I had so much on my mind last night I couldn't recall just why. This morning I knew at once what it was I'd been trying to remember. It was towards the end of the war—the first of the concentration camps had been liberated, and one of our correspondents went with a Press party to have a look at it. He brought back to the office a tin of the poison that the Nazis used in the gas chambers." Jackson solemnly handed over the clippings. "I got these from the library," he said. "You'll see a picture there of the actual tin. The stuff was called ZYKLON—I suppose that was a sort of trade name—but in fact it appears to have been cyanide."

Haines took the clippings and perused them in silence. There were several stories on the same theme, some sent from a place called Lublin and some apparently written in the office. The name of the camp was Maidanek, in Poland. Each story carried the byline, "By Our Special Correspondent, WILLIAM IREDALE." As he read, Haines's face grew more and more serious.

"Of course," said Jackson uncomfortably, "it may be just a coincidence."

"It may," said Haines, still staring at the clippings, "but I should hardly think so. After all, the way the stuff was used in Mr. Ede's room was almost an exact imitation of this gas chamber technique. Who'd have thought of that method in the ordinary course of things? No, it rather looks as though you may have hit the nail on the head, Mr. Jackson. What happened to the ZYKLON, do you remember?"

"I don't think I ever knew," said Jackson with a worried look. "All I can tell you is that Mr. Ede had charge of it for a time—that was when I saw it myself."

"Well, we can't ask him—not yet. I'd better see Iredale." Haines dialled Miss Timmins's number, inquired politely how she was feeling, and once more enlisted her help. Then he sat staring at the photograph of the ZYKLON. According to the story, there had been seven pounds of it. The quantity was terrifying.

Jackson got up. "I'd better leave you to it," he said.

"Just a moment, Mr. Jackson." Haines unscrewed his fountain pen and made some alterations in the draft warning he'd been working on. When he'd finished, he passed it across to the Assistant Editor. "I suggest putting that up on every notice board in the office. Is that all right with you?"

Jackson read it through twice. "I suppose so," he said slowly. "It may make the staff rather jumpy."

"That's what I want. The way things are at the moment, there's not a man or woman in this building who's an insurable risk, and that'll be true until we get our hands on the murderer. People can't be too careful." He looked uneasily at the Assistant Editor. "As a matter of fact, I'm not sure that I oughtn't to advise the temporary closing of the office."

"That's impossible, of course," said Jackson sharply. "Good heavens, Inspector, we managed to keep going all through the blitz."

"This could be more lethal than the blitz," said Haines.

Jackson chewed his wispy white moustache. "Surely the man you're after can't be completely indiscriminating. There must be some method in his madness."

"Possibly, but that's no help to us if we don't know what the method is. He may have very sweeping plans. We're certainly not justified in neglecting any reasonable precautions."

"Very well," said Jackson. "I'll have this notice duplicated, and in the meantime I'll read it over to one or two of the directors. If they agree, as they no doubt will, I'll see that it's circulated this afternoon. Shall I leave the clippings with you?"

"If you don't mind," said Haines.

When Jackson had gone, he sat for a while in gloomy reflection. No policeman, he felt, had ever had a heavier responsibility. It was true that so far there had been a certain pattern about the murderer's activities, but it wasn't a rational pattern. He might strike again at any moment on a mere homicidal whim. The fact that he was probably regarded as a good and trustworthy colleague by dozens of people was frightening. Haines was so disturbed that presently he put in a call to the Yard and had a talk with the Assistant Commissioner. After that, he felt better, and turned again to the clippings. He was just thinking it was rather unlikely that anyone would have stored away a tin of cyanide five years ago with the intention of committing a murder at some later date when there was another knock at the door and Iredale came in.

Haines gave him a curt nod and motioned him to a chair. Shock tactics seemed called for. "Mr. Iredale," he said, "I understand that you once brought a tin of cyanide into this office."

Iredale stared. "*I* did?" He looked quite blank; then shook his head with increasing emphasis. "I'm sorry, Inspector, but I haven't the remotest idea what you're talking about."

"It was called ZYKLON."

The blank look slowly faded; recollection came flooding in. A flush darkened Iredale's face as he met the inspector's flinty eyes. "Yes," he said quietly. "I remember now, of course."

"It's a great pity you didn't remember earlier," Haines snapped. "A spontaneous recollection a couple of days ago would have impressed me. As it is . . ." His shrug completed the sentence.

"For Heaven's sake, Inspector, you surely don't imagine that I kept it from you deliberately? I'm sorry I didn't think of it, but that all happened years ago, and we were talking all the time about cyanide, not ZYKLON. I just didn't connect the two things."

"You knew that ZYKLON was cyanide. You say so here, in these articles of yours." Haines tapped the bundle of clippings with the stem of his pipe.

"Yes, but the damned word isn't written on my heart. I tell you I'd forgotten about it—just as everybody else had. I simply didn't associate the two things, and I think it's unreasonable to expect me to have done so after all this time."

Haines grunted. "Perhaps you wouldn't mind telling me just how you came to bring the stuff here in the first place? What was the point?"

"I certainly wasn't planning to decimate the office with it, if that's what you're thinking. I brought it back because it was my job to report facts, and a tin of ZYKLON seemed a pretty impressive fact to me. Before the Russians took us to Maidanek, a lot of quite intelligent people here seemed to think that the rumours about gas chambers were just propaganda. Well, I saw the gas chambers—I went over them, I saw how they worked. I saw the ZYKLON stacked up in a storehouse like so much insecticide. I also saw the pulverised bones of about a million people it had killed, if that interests you. It seemed quite a story to me, but the office played it down at first—they found it too gruesome and almost incredible. So I flew home with the stuff, and a few other unpleasant relics from the camp, and as you can see we went to town on the story." He met the inspector's bleak gaze squarely. "Anything sinister about that?"

"Not necessarily," said Haines. He was wondering if the unnerving experience—an experience which had evidently made a powerful impression on Iredale's mind—could possibly have affected the man's mental balance. "What was the stuff like to look at?"

"Small whitish-grey crystals."

"Was the tin full when you brought it here?"

"Yes—and it was still full the last time I saw it!"

"When was that? What happened to it?"

Iredale made an effort to cast his mind back. "Well, I showed it to Ede first of all, and he got the Art Department to photograph it. Practically everyone in the office had a look at it. Someone called from the F.O., and someone else from the War Office, and a few of the Embassies sent people. It was quite a sensation."

"Where was it kept while it was here?"

"It was in the Editor's room for quite a time," said Iredale slowly, "because of V.I.P.s calling. I think after that it went to the Foreign Room. I don't know what happened to it then—I flew back to Russia. I suppose someone was told to dispose of it in the end. Perhaps it was sent to Scotland Yard!"

Haines glowered. "I'm not in the mood for jokes, Mr. Iredale. Can I take it you've no idea where the stuff is now?"

"None whatsoever."

"H'm. Where were you between seven and eight o'clock yesterday morning?"

Iredale looked surprised. "In bed, I imagine. Why?"

"In bed where?"

"In my flat in Chancery Lane."

"Can you prove that? Any porters or neighbours who heard you come and go?"

"I'm afraid not—it's not that kind of place. As a matter of fact, the whole building's empty at night. It's a block of offices, and I have a pent-house above the sixth floor. It's not a place that most people would want to live in."

"I see. Well, that's all rather unfortunate. Tell me, Mr. Iredale, have you ever spent a night in *this* building?"

Iredale looked surprised. "Once or twice during the war, yes, when I was home on leave and there was a bad blitz. I don't make a practice of it—it's hardly my idea of comfort."

"Did you spend the night before last in this building?"

"Good God, no! I told you—I was at my flat."

"Someone appears to have spent the night here," said Haines, "and laid the cyanide which almost killed Mr. Ede."

"Well, it wasn't me. You can think what you like, but I don't know anything at all either about Hind's murder or about the attempt on Ede—not a thing."

Haines regarded him thoughtfully. "I was inclined to believe your protestations the last time we talked, Mr. Iredale, but you must see for yourself that the evidence is beginning to pile up. Of the four people who attended that office lunch in addition to yourself, you had quarrelled—to my knowledge—with three. Hind died—that was one out of the way. You knew he liked olives and you expected him to be first in the room. You had no alibi. Then Ede nearly died—that would have been another. Again you have no alibi. You now admit—but only after I've discovered the fact for myself and taxed you with it—that at one time, at any rate, you handled the poison which was probably used in both cases. You also admit you're very familiar with the technique of the gas chamber. Munro, of course, is out of your reach, but don't you think that perhaps I ought to offer Mr. Cardew police protection?"

"I happen to be on the best of terms with Mr. Cardew," said Iredale shortly.

"That's something I shall certainly have to look into. Well, that's all for the moment, Mr. Iredale. Don't go far away—I may be wanting you again."

Iredale went out gloomily. It was damned unpleasant being suspected of murder, however preposterous the idea. Facts could be misinterpreted in such a devilish way. Before long, the whole office would be talking about ZYKLON. Still, he wasn't obliged to listen. He left the building and strolled down to the Embankment, wishing he were in China.

After he had gone, Haines sat for a while considering the new situation. It looked as though Iredale had moved up into the position of suspect number one. However, the main thing at the moment was to trace the ZYKLON and link the result with whatever emerged from Ogilvie's inquiries. Lambert, the ex-Foreign Editor, seemed the obvious person to talk to first. Haines had just found out that he was back from his holiday and could be seen any time that day when Ogilvie came in, a look of quiet satisfaction on his face.

"It was just as I thought, Chief," he said, drawing up a chair. "Almost everyone has a water-tight alibi for the night before last. There are only ten people who aren't fully accounted for, and we should be able to get that number down to six or seven before long."

"Splendid!" said Haines. "I've got some news for you, too." He told his assistant about the ZYKLON.

Ogilvie could hardly contain his excitement. "But that's terrific, Chief. Damn it, we ought to be able to get some line on the stuff, even after all this time."

"I wouldn't be surprised," said Haines. "Well, now, what about these names?"

Ogilvie spread out his papers. "There's Iredale, of course—you know about him already. Then there's Cardew. He *is* still in the picture. He says he spent the night at his flat in Jermyn Street, but there's no night porter and I can't get any confirmation. The woman who cleans remembers that the bed was rumpled, but he could have set the scene the evening before if he'd wanted to. That's two. Then there's Pringle . . ."

"Ah, yes—what about Mr. Pringle?"

"He was sent out of town on a job in the afternoon, and he says he spent the night at a pub in Baldock. He may have done, but there's been some difficulty about checking, so I've kept him on the short list for the time being. He's sort of in suspense."

"I bet he is! If he really was at Baldock, that let's him out, of course, but otherwise he's very much in the running. He'd have been sure to know about the ZYKLON—he has a finger in every pie. The chief doubt I have about him is whether he has the intelligence to have worked things out so well. Low cunning, yes, but is that enough? However, we'll see. Who else?"

"There's Edgar Jessop. He lives by himself at Wimbledon. He says he spent the night at home, but again there's no confirmation."

"I'd better see him again," said Haines. "He's one of those quiet fellows—he didn't make much of an impression on me last time, one way or the other."

"The only thing about him," Ogilvie remarked, "is that he was working in the Foreign Room during the war. If the ZYKLON really finished up there, as Iredale seems to think, he'd have had easy access to it."

Haines nodded. "I'm going to see Lambert—perhaps he'll remember something. That's four."

"The fifth is Miss Timmins. She lives by herself, but as she could have got into Ede's room at any time that's hardly of importance in her case."

"We'll keep her in mind," said Haines, "although frankly I don't see her as a Borgia."

"Then there's a young Sub-editor named Bird," Ogilvie went on, "but he doesn't appear to have any possible grievance against anyone and he's new to the office. Two reporters were out of town in addition to Pringle, and we're still checking their movements—I imagine they'll be ruled out in the end. That's eight. There's a fellow in the Art Department who refuses to say where he was. He's in quite a state about it, but I suspect he was only spending the night with a woman. We shall break him down with a little patience, if it's necessary. That's nine. Oh, and there's a fellow named Rowbotham who works in Features. He's enormously fat—he must weigh about seventeen stone. I can't see him playing 'Peep-bo' with the charladies in the early hours."

"And that's the lot?"

"That's it, Chief. Unless we're on the wrong lines altogether, one of these is our man. If I were guessing, I should say it lay between Iredale and Cardew, with Jessop an interesting newcomer because of his ZYKLON contact, Pringle a runner-up until he establishes his alibi, and Bird and this Art Department fellow as outside chances."

Haines grunted. "It's satisfactory as far as it goes, but we're still a long way from making an arrest."

"I'm not so sure," said Ogilvie. "The case is beginning to move—and when ice breaks up, anything can happen."

Chapter Twenty-Five

The Reporters' Room that afternoon was heavy with pre-holiday lethargy and a charged thundery heat. Haycock was in a telephone box, trying to take down a long-range weather forecast on a pad that stuck to his fingers. Katharine was passing the time by helping Grant with his last thousand postcards. Rogers was studying a road map of the West Country and wishing that he could have had the coming Saturday off as well as the Sunday and Monday. An occasional flicker of facetiousness from his corner stabbed the conversational gloom, but the response was poor. Everyone had been sobered by the attempt on the Editor's life. Murder in the office no longer seemed a good story; it was becoming too much of a habit. A threat hung over all, none the less disquieting because it was vague.

Presently Golightly came in, his jacket over his arm, his tie wrenched askew to give him air. "Phew, it's like a Turkish bath in here," he muttered.

Rogers looked up from his map. "How's the drought in Hampshire, old boy?" Golightly had been out of town on a story since early morning.

"It's nothing to the drought in Golightly, I can tell you!" The reporter flung his jacket over a peg with an irritable gesture. His day in the country hadn't improved his temper. "What a bloody place our garage is! That old Morris wouldn't be yours, Kate, would it?"

"It would, as a matter of fact," said Katharine anxiously. "Don't say it's in the way—I parked it most carefully."

"It's taking up a damn lot of room," he grumbled. "It's been there for three days to my knowledge."

"It needs a new battery," said Katharine. "I'm getting one to-morrow."

Golightly grunted. "I should hang on to the old battery and just let the car go!"

"Katharine isn't the worst offender," said Grant, feeling under a moral obligation to come to her support. "Cardew keeps his car there the whole time."

"Oh, him!" said Golightly. "He's one of the over-privileged." He cast a jaundiced eye over the diminished heap of postcards. "I hear they're thinking of running another competition!"

"Don't take any notice of him," said Katharine to Grant. "He's just a troublemaker."

"Quiet, children!" said Rogers.

The News Room door swung open and a boy came in with the peculiar slouch of adolescence, bearing a sheet of paper which he pinned to the notice board. Golightly strolled over with a bored air, gave it a casual glance, and then suddenly bent to read it. "I say," he cried, "take a look at this, all of you!"

Rogers quickly joined him and the others crowded round. The notice, signed by Jackson, read: "A seven-pound tin of cyanide crystals, with a German label and the name ZYKLON in red capitals, was brought to this office in 1944. Its subsequent history cannot be traced. Anyone who has any knowledge of what happened to it is asked to report to me at once. Meanwhile, all members of the staff are warned to be on their guard when eating or drinking with their colleagues or when in proximity to basins, sinks, etc." The notice ended hopefully, "It is requested that no mention shall be made of this matter outside the office."

There was a moment of thunderstruck silence while the notice was digested. Then Rogers exclaimed, "Well, what do you know!"

"I like the 'etc.'," said Golightly. "Very prim." Haycock turned from the board in disgust and went back to his seat. "I don't know what this place is coming to," he muttered. "Now we have to watch our colleagues! It's getting as bad as a police state."

The others were still grouped round the notice when Pringle came in, closely followed by a waitress bearing a large strawberry ice and a packet of charcoal biscuits. "What's going on, eh?" he asked. Katharine silently made way for him and he read the notice, moving his lips like a child learning its letters. "You see!" he said, triumphantly, looking at Golightly. "What did I tell you?"

Rogers was sniffing the ice-cream. "I shouldn't touch this, old man, if I were you. It has a distinct smell of bitter almonds."

No one laughed. Rogers shrugged and went back to his map. "No sale? All right, *be* stuffy. Let's talk of worms and graves and epitaphs."

"Hell, it's getting beyond a joke," said Golightly. "They must be in a flat spin to put a notice like that up. Who brought the stuff into the office, anyway? I wasn't here in 1944. You ought to know, Katharine—you were around."

Katharine was pale. "I've no idea," she said, lighting a cigarette.

"Bill Iredale *brought* it" Haycock volunteered, "from a camp in Poland. I remember the story very well."

"Where *is* Iredale?" asked Pringle. "I haven't seen him about to-day. You don't suppose . . .?"

"You are a rat, Pringle," said Rogers. "Why don't you shut up?"

"I was only thinking . . ."

"Oh, for Christ's sake!" Golightly exclaimed, and slammed his typewriter open. For a few moments there was an oppressive silence, and then, to everyone's relief, Soames came in from the News Room. "Katharine," he called, beckoning her, "there's a story here that's just up your street." She gathered up her belongings with alacrity and followed him out.

"I wish someone would send *me* out on a story," sighed Grant, mechanically turning over his postcards. "It's a good thing we've got the weekend ahead—perhaps that stuff will have turned up by Tuesday and then we'll be able to breathe again."

"It may turn up to-night," said Pringle darkly, "and then we'll never breathe again." He looked round, inviting appreciation of his humour. A copy of Whitaker's Almanack landed with a crash on his desk, spattering him with strawberry ice-cream. "Now will you shut up?" said Golightly.

The door opened and Jessop looked in. He had just come on duty, and was anxious for news. Ever since last night, things had been going wrong—it was almost as though Providence had deserted him. In the first place, it seemed that Nicholas Ede was going to recover, so all that effort had been wasted. Then Ogilvie had rung him up at home that morning and asked him a lot of questions about the night before last. It was just as though the police knew all about the laying of the cyanide—as though someone had spied on him, and told them. And that wasn't all—not by any means. He had had a stroke of very bad luck. He had overlooked something important, and got caught up in a dangerous lie. He had discovered his mistake last night when he had gone off duty, and there had been no way of putting it right. It wasn't very likely that the police would find out about it, and in a day or two it would be forgotten. In the meantime, though, it was worrying.

He put his dispatch case on one of the desks and said, "Anything doing?"

"Hallo, Edgar," said Rogers. "Seen the notice?"

"No." Jessop went over to the board. He stiffened as his eye caught the word ZYKLON, and suddenly he felt that everyone must be staring at his back. He read the notice through twice.

"*You* ought to remember what happened to that stuff, Jessop," said Haycock. "Wasn't it taken to the Foreign Room in the end?"

Jessop fought to control his agitation. This wasn't at all what he'd expected. It had never occurred to him that anyone would remember the ZYKLON after all this time. Why, he'd even forgotten it himself, until a few days ago. Now people would begin to search their memories, as the notice invited them to do—as Haycock was already doing. Someone might recall that *he* had been the last person to handle it. Cardew would almost certainly remember that. In a flash, he saw that there was only one thing to do if suspicion weren't to fall on him. He must get his blow in first. He looked across at Haycock. "As a matter of fact," he said, "I think I do remember what happened to it!"

"You *do*!" exclaimed Golightly.

"What?" asked Pringle.

"Don't tell him," said Golightly quickly. "But for Heaven's sake go and find Jackson before we're all bumped off."

"I suppose I'd better," said Jessop slowly. He was moving towards the door when Soames looked in again. "Oh, there you are, Ed! Inspector Haines is asking for you. He's down in his office."

"Telepathy!" said Rogers. He held out his cigarette case. "Anyone like a pinch of cyanide?"

Chapter Twenty-Six

Jessop went slowly downstairs, his face as expressionless as a sleepwalker's, his mind on fire. The summons was ominous. Perhaps the police had already discovered his mistake. Perhaps Cardew had already seen them about the ZYKLON. Whatever it was, his defences had begun to crumble. His enemies were closing in on him. With almost no warning, he was called upon to face a crisis.

Well, if they thought he was done for, they were mistaken. They couldn't prove anything. To-night he would hide the ZYKLON. In the meantime, he would do anything he could to confuse the police. He was more ingenious than they were, and with luck he still had the initiative. He would conduct this interview skilfully, and pluck safety from danger. He would fight back with all he had. His fingers tightened on the tin in his pocket and once again it gave him assurance. He knocked boldly at the inspector's door and went in. Haines and Ogilvie were both there.

Haines scrutinised his visitor with much more interest than on the previous occasion. Jessop had been one of a crowd then—now he was one of a handful, one of three or four. An innocent-seeming little man, and almost a blank page as far as Haines was concerned. There was no evidence against him whatsoever—and yet he was under suspicion. The machine had ground slowly, but it had ground small.

Jessop didn't wait for the inspector to question him. "I was on my way to have a word with Mr. Jackson about that notice he's put up," he said. "I've only just seen it."

"Oh, yes," said Haines inscrutably. "You know something about the ZYKLON, do you?"

"I certainly do," said Jessop. He turned a worried face to the inspector. "I wish I didn't—it puts me in a difficult position. I hate the thought of making trouble, but when people's lives are at stake . . ." He broke off.

"Quite so," said Haines. "You can trust us not to make improper use of any information you can give us. Go ahead, Mr. Jessop. What exactly can you tell us about the ZYKLON?"

Jessop lit a cigarette. He felt much better already. Haines seemed friendly—evidently Cardew had *not* been in yet. "Well," he began, "Bill Iredale brought the stuff here, of course, and everyone had a look at it. I remember all about it because I was Assistant Foreign Editor and I had a good deal to do with the stories. It was in Mr. Ede's room for a few days, and then it was moved to the Foreign Room, and Mr. Ede suggested to Mr. Lambert—he was our Foreign Editor then—that it would be a good thing if he got rid of it. That was because Mr. Ede happened to see it lying about in the Foreign Room a few days later, and he didn't think it was a good idea."

Haines nodded. He had seen Lambert, and Lambert had told him the same thing. "And then what happened?" he asked, watching Jessop closely.

"Mr. Lambert didn't quite know what to do with it. Somebody said it was just the thing for garden pests and Mr. Lambert asked me if I'd like to take it away, as I was a keen gardener."

"Go on," said Haines quietly. This at least was the truth. This also he had had from Lambert. The fact that Jessop should admit it so readily was impressive.

"I didn't want it," Jessop went on. "It had too many unpleasant associations. Then Mr. Cardew had an idea—he was the Diplomatic Correspondent then. He thought the stuff had historical interest, and that it would be a pity to destroy it. He suggested handing it over just as it was to the National War Museum."

"Really?" Haines looked puzzled. "I had a talk to Mr. Lambert to-day, and he didn't tell me anything about that."

"I don't suppose he'd have known," said Jessop thoughtfully. "No, of course he wouldn't. I remember he hurt himself on a Home Guard exercise just about that time, and he was away for nearly six weeks. I was deputising for him. I don't suppose he gave the stuff another thought after he asked me to take it away, and when he came back, of course, it was gone. I *may* have told him what had happened to it, but honestly I don't remember whether I did or not."

"And what did happen to it?"

"Well," said Jessop hesitantly, "I thought Mr. Cardew's idea was a good one, so he rang up the Museum and asked them if they'd like it. I remember the conversation, because they had trouble with the spelling of the name ZYKLON. Anyway, from what I heard at his end I gathered that they'd like to have it, and later on he said he'd drop it in himself on his way to the F.O. So the last I saw of it was when Mr. Cardew left the Foreign Room with the tin done up in a brown paper parcel under his arm."

"Was anyone else present when this happened?"

Jessop frowned. "I'm not absolutely sure—there might have been a boy in the room but I don't think so, because I remember Mr. Cardew wrapping the tin up himself, and he wouldn't have done that if there'd been anyone around to do it for him."

The inspector grunted. "Well, we'd better get on to the Museum right away."

Ogilvie had already looked up the number, and in a few seconds Haines was talking to the Director. Jessop sat impassively. He was quite enjoying the interview now. He knew he had done very well, and he met Ogilvie's scrutiny evenly. He listened with the right amount of interest while Haines probed for information on the phone. His face assumed an appropriately concerned look as it became clear from the tenor of the conversation at Haines's end that he wasn't making much progress.

Presently Haines said, "All right, sir, we'll have to leave it at that," and replaced the receiver with a significant glance at Ogilvie. "As far as they know, they never had it."

"That's very odd," muttered Jessop. "Of course, Mr. Cardew might have left it somewhere—or even taken it home and forgotten about it. It was very easy to forget things in those days."

"He might have taken it home and *not* forgotten about it," suggested Haines, deliberately inviting an accusation.

"Oh, no . . ." said Jessop, looking shocked. "You're surely not suggesting that Mr. Cardew . . ." He stopped short. "I never thought of that," he said slowly. "But I'm sure he wouldn't . . ."

"Why are you so sure? Have you a high regard for Mr. Cardew?"

"I don't think he'd do a thing like that," said Jessop.

Haines looked at Ogilvie. "I think we'd better have Mr. Cardew in again, all the same." Ogilvie nodded and went off to find him.

"Well, now, Mr. Jessop," said Haines amiably, "I gather that Inspector Ogilvie has already talked to you about your movements the night before last."

"Yes," said Jessop. "He rang me at home this morning. I couldn't quite understand what it was all about."

"Oh, just a routine inquiry. A lot of your colleagues have been troubled in the same way." Haines glanced at some notes in front of him. "I'd just like to go over the ground again, if you don't mind. What time did you leave the office on that evening?"

Jessop felt a tremor of anxiety. "It was just before eleven," he said. "My usual time."

Haines nodded. "Just after the chess game, eh?"

"That's right," said Jessop, forcing a smile. How wise he'd been to take those precautions!—the police were more thorough than he'd supposed.

"And you went by car?"

"Yes," said Jessop. He could feel his heart pounding now. When Ogilvie had questioned him, he'd thought of saying that he'd gone by bus or train, but he wasn't familiar with the routes and timetables and in any case it would have been a simple matter for the police to check up on. It had seemed better to take the risk that he had taken. Now he was less sure about it.

"Did anyone actually see you leave?" asked Haines.

"I shouldn't think so," said Jessop, with a shock of relief as he realised that Haines wasn't trying to trip him after all—that he simply didn't know. "There wasn't anyone in the garage. Sarge might have seen me, but I can't really say. Anyhow, I'm telling you the truth. Why shouldn't I?"

Haines ignored that. "You didn't stop on the way, I supposed You didn't buy petrol, or get yourself a, hot dog, or anything?"

"Not at that hour, Inspector. I wanted to get home."

"You live by yourself, I believe?"

"Yes."

Haines sat back. "It would be a great help to us, Mr. Jessop, if you could produce someone who could confirm that you were actually in the house that night. You're not being accused of anything, you understand—it's really a case of eliminating you, and clearing the decks for others. We've already ascertained that your neighbours at Beckenham didn't hear the car come in, or see it go out the next day. That of course proves nothing . . ."

"Except that they mind their own business," said Jessop.

"Exactly." Haines got up. "Well, Mr. Jessop, I know it's very difficult for you in the circumstances, but if you do happen to remember any incident that would confirm your story, it would help us a great deal. And thank you for coming to me about the ZYKLON." He nodded. Jessop was dismissed.

Almost at once Cardew came in, with Ogilvie just behind him. He was pale, and if anything even more strained-looking than on the previous occasion. He ignored the chair that Haines offered him. "What is it this time, Inspector?"

"When you were last here, Mr. Cardew," said Haines quietly, "you mentioned as a point in your favour that you wouldn't have known where to get hold of cyanide."

"Oh, so that's it?"

"That's it. You've seen the ZYKLON notice?"

Cardew nodded. "I'm sorry, but I'd forgotten all about that stuff."

"It's strange that you should have done so, considering your special interest in it at the time."

"What special interest?"

"I'm told that on a day back in 1944 you were seen leaving this building with the tin of ZYKLON under your arm."

"I did nothing of the sort," said Cardew indignantly.

"I'm told that you had previously talked to the National War Museum on the telephone and arranged to take it to them."

Cardew stared in amazement. "The whole thing's a pack of lies from beginning to end," he said contemptuously. "I didn't touch the ZYKLON, and I certainly didn't talk to any museum."

"Did you, perhaps, pretend to?"

"No, I didn't. Who told you this rubbish?"

Haines pursed his lips. "I see no reason why you shouldn't know. Mr. Jessop told us."

"Jessop told you! *Jessop*!" Cardew threw back his head and laughed—a harsh, unnatural laugh. "Well, I must say that's pretty rich!"

"May I share the joke, Mr. Cardew?"

"You certainly may. For the past hour I've been sitting with that ZYKLON notice in front of me, trying to make up my mind whether I ought to come and tell you that it was Jessop who took the stuff away, and now I find he's got here first and accused *me* of doing so. The little swine!"

Haines's eyes narrowed. "Are you suggesting that he invented this story?"

"Yes, every word of it."

"Why should he do that?"

"I can only suppose it's because he hates me. He's jealous—he wanted the job I've been given, God knows why. He can have it as far as I'm concerned, and I hope he enjoys it." Cardew was still regarding Haines incredulously. "But, good God, what a thing to do to anyone!"

Haines. sighed. "This is getting very difficult," he said. "There seems to be a little game of tit-for-tat going on between you two, and unfortunately I don't know which of you is speaking the truth."

"For Heaven's sake, Inspector! I've nothing against Jessop—I don't owe him a grudge or anything. Why the devil should I tell you he took the stuff if he didn't?"

"To protect yourself, of course," said Haines dryly, "if *you* took it. I should have thought that was obvious. He makes a dangerous accusation against you. He's an independent witness whom I may believe. Your only course is to deny everything and make a counter-accusation and leave me to puzzle it out."

Cardew clutched his hair. "This is crazy. I saw Jessop leave with the tin. I didn't think of it until that notice went up, but directly I saw the word ZYKLON I remembered. He had wasps in his garden, and he said it was the very thing for them. For all I know, the tin's still at his home. He may even be the murderer—if he's crazy enough to invent wild charges against me, I should think he might well be. Why do you concentrate on me all the time? Why don't you search his house?"

"There happens to be a little formality of search warrants," said Haines. "And if I searched anyone's place, it would be yours. You had a motive for killing Mr. Ede, and Jessop hadn't, unless you think that being disappointed over a job is enough to make a man start throwing cyanide all over the place. Yes, Mr. Cardew, you had the motive, you had the opportunity, and now someone says you had the cyanide!"

Cardew was breathing hard. "What are you going to do—arrest me?"

Haines gave him a long, searching look. "No," he said at last. "Kindly oblige me by getting out. And don't start anything with Jessop, or you'll both be in trouble."

"You're making a big mistake, Inspector," Cardew cried. "I'm sure he did it . . ."

Ogilvie jerked his head peremptorily towards the door. Cardew looked from one to the other, saw the hopelessness of saying anything more, and turned to leave. The door slammed violently behind him.

Haines slumped in his chair, his head in his hands. Cardew, Jessop, Iredale? Jessop, Cardew, Iredale? Iredale, Cardew, Jessop? . . .

"Anyway," said Ogilvie, "the ice is breaking up nicely."

Chapter Twenty-Seven

The clock over the Sub-editors' table pointed to ten minutes to six. Jackson had left his own room and was sitting beside Price, the Night Editor, discussing the make-up of page one. Usually he found this an absorbing occupation, but concentration was difficult to-night and there was nothing in the news to stimulate interest.

Price ruefully scratched the side of his neck. "It doesn't look as though the customers are going to get much for their penny to-morrow," he said.

"If it's as hot as this," observed the Chief Sub, skilfully impaling a piece of copy on a metal spike without impaling himself, "the only use they'll have for the *Morning Call* will be to keep the sun off their heads."

"Still, passers-by might notice if the paper was blank," said Price. "Bad publicity!" He stared disgustedly at the sheet in front of him. "Damn it, we haven't even got a lead yet."

A chair leg squeaked and the Foreign Sub joined them. "There's something quite promising here," he said. "Just in from Belgrade. Only a 'flash' so far, but it looks as though it might be worked up into a lead."

Jackson took the piece of tape. Five Bulgarian communist leaders, according to the message, had fled across the frontier to avoid liquidation and been given sanctuary. The Assistant Editor pursed his lips. "It's a possible," he said, "if we can get something more on it. What do you think, Willie?"

Price shook his head sadly. "A foreign lead's all wrong for a holiday weekend."

The Foreign Sub, stood up for his story. "These are pretty high-powered chaps." he pointed out.

"By Balkan standards, chum! They'll mean a fat lot to bathing belles at Brighton!"

"Anyway," said Jackson, "we might as well get Cardew to do something on it. I believe I've heard him talk about this fellow Kolarov." He called out "Boy!"

A youth appeared with unusual celerity.

"Find Mr. Cardew, will you, and ask him to come and see me." Jackson gave the piece of copy back to the Foreign Sub. "We'd better ask our Belgrade man to send something, too. It might make a second-edition lead, anyway." He turned to Price. "Otherwise, what have we got?" The discussion was resumed.

In a few moments the youth re-appeared. "Mr. Cardew isn't in his room, sir."

Jackson frowned. "Doesn't Mr. Jessop know where he is?"

"No, sir. He says he hasn't seen him for a long time."

"Well, go and look for him," said Jackson testily. "He must be somewhere."

"Yes, sir," said the boy. He went cheerfully off on his errand, cuffing another boy as he left the room. Ten minutes later he returned, still without Cardew. He stood at Jackson's elbow, reluctant to report failure.

"Well?"

"I can't find him, sir."

"Blast the fellow!" said Jackson under his breath. He looked at Price. "I wonder if Haines has got him." He reached for the telephone and dialled the inspector's office. "This is Mr. Jackson," he said. "Have you by any chance got Mr. Cardew with you . . .? No, we can't find him. I suppose he must be around somewhere, though . . ." His forehead puckered. "Oh, very well—I'm in the Subs' room." He hung up with an exclamation of annoyance. "Now I've started something—Haines is coming up. Cardew really ought to know better than to go off without leaving any message. I wonder where the devil he's got to?"

Almost at once, Haines came into the room. He looked hot and far from benevolent. Jackson didn't want a lot of fuss and joined him at the door.

"I told Mr. Cardew he wasn't to go anywhere without letting me know," said Haines.

"Is that so?" Jackson suddenly looked grave. It was news to him that Cardew was in special trouble. "Well, let's ask the commissionaire. He may know something." The Assistant Editor dialled the front box. "Mr. Jackson here. You haven't seen Mr. Cardew go out, have you . . .? Oh, you *have*?" He glanced at the inspector.

"I'll go right down," said Haines, and rushed away. He found Sergeant Peach standing expectantly by the front box. "When did Mr. Cardew leave, Sarge?"

"About 'alf an hour ago, sir."

Haines swore softly. "He didn't happen to mention where he was going?"

"No, sir. 'E was in a great 'urry, and 'e was cursing like anything on account of 'is car."

"What about his car?"

"'E couldn't get it out of the garridge, not on 'is own. Miss Camden's car ain't workin' proper and it took two of us to shove it out of the way. Reg'lar job we 'ad, I can tell yer."

"What's his car like?"

"It's black, sir, with a long body. One o' them fast sporty models. I couldn't tell you the make, I'm afraid."

"It doesn't matter," said Haines. He rushed up to the second floor office and broke the news to Ogilvie. For the next ten minutes, both telephones were busy as the machinery of the Yard was set in motion.

Finally Haines sat back. "The damned young fool!" he said with great intensity. "Where does he suppose he's going to get to?"

"Scared stiff, if you ask me," said Ogilvie. "I thought he had a pretty wild look about him when he was down here. It seems as though he did it after all."

"He must know that he can't get away with this."

"I suppose he thought he had a good start. After all, if Jackson hadn't happened to want him he might have got a plane and been out of the country before we'd even realised he was missing."

"He'd have been picked up sooner or later," said Haines grimly. "He must be out of his mind. This was the one thing he couldn't afford to do."

Chapter Twenty-Eight

With his hands thrust deep into his pockets and a book tucked under his arm, Bill Iredale mouched into the Foreign Room. Since his return to the office after lunch he'd been up on the roof in a deck chair, trying to lose himself in a thriller, but smuts and anxiety had finally driven him down. He felt in a foul temper. He hated above all things to be tethered, and it seemed pretty clear that he wouldn't be allowed to leave London until the case was solved. And how could the police expect to solve the case if they wasted their time chasing him up a blind alley?

By now, he reflected grimly, everyone would have put two and two together and made five. They'd all have connected him with the ZYKLON, and they'd have pooled their information about his row with Munro, his row with Ede, his row with Hind. They would greet him warily—or, worse still, sympathetically. An unpleasant prospect. Not that he really gave a damn what they thought. At least . . .

He wondered about Katharine. She didn't know him very well and he'd given her plenty of cause for suspicion. Hardly a promising start to a beautiful friendship, to get tangled up in a murder case! Why, he'd even said something about breaking Hind's neck—Katharine wouldn't have forgotten that. *She* knew just how mad he'd been with Ede, too. It had been a bad week, he decided—one of those weeks he'd want to forget, for all its pleasant moments. He wished now that he hadn't made such an exhibition of himself over Sheila Brooks in the pub that night. He must have seemed an uncouth bear. He'd be going away soon, so it didn't really matter, perhaps, but . . . What was that idiotic song?—"I've got you under my skin."

He was just wondering whether to drop into the Reporters' Room and face the music when Jessop came in, obviously excited. "Heard the news, Bill? Cardew's bolted!"

"I don't believe it!"

"It's true." Jessop went to the tape-machine and tore off the accumulated copy. "The police are after him." He sat down at his desk and lit a cigarette. He could see now that his earlier misgivings had been quite unnecessary. The police were simpletons, and had believed his story. Cardew was finished; he had been scared into flight, and very soon he would be arrested. That would save Jessop trouble. He was conscious once again of an exhilarating sense of power. He strode this office battlefield like a Colossus, and on all sides his enemies were going down. Hind, Ede and now Cardew—and there might be more. In his unstable mind the enemy could change with kaleidoscopic suddenness. He had already ceased to feel animosity towards Ede. It was on Cardew that his present hatred focused. "They expect," he said, "to catch him before he leaves the country."

Iredale was staggered. His own anxieties now seemed trifling. "You surely don't believe that Cardew did it?" he said. "Why, he and Ede thought a lot of each other."

Jessop sniffed. "You can't always be sure who your friends are," he said. "People pretend they're on your side, and later on you find them out." He hadn't forgotten Iredale's attitude over his *opus*.

"It's not a question of being on anyone's side," said Iredale in a tone of exasperation. Really, Ed could be very childish sometimes. "Cardew liked Ede—I'll swear he did."

"On the surface, yes," said Jessop. "But what did he *really* think? Don't forget what I told you about him and Mrs. Ede."

"Even if you're right about that, which I doubt, Cardew wouldn't have killed Ede. I think the idea's fantastic."

"Well, why has he run away?" Jessop was beginning to resent Iredale's defence of Cardew.

"He's probably got fed up with all the bloody chatter in the office and gone for a swim. Sensible chap—I wish I'd gone with him."

A curtain came down over Jessop's face. "You and Cardew always did get on pretty well, didn't you?"

Iredale shrugged. "I hardly know the fellow, but I've certainly nothing against him. Damn it all, Ed, you're biased. He stepped in to take the job you wanted and it was bad luck for you, but you really can't blame him for seizing the opportunity—anybody would have done the same."

Jessop fiddled with a piece of copy, resentment surging up inside him. "You'll feel differently," he said, "when Cardew is hanged for murder."

Iredale paused in the act of lighting his pipe. "My God, Ed, you do hate him, don't you?" He puffed out a cloud of smoke. "Anyhow, I'll wait for the evidence. I'm fed up with flimsy accusations. Why, until he cleared off, people were probably thinking I'd done it. Look at all this ZYKLON business. And I reckon I had a darned sight more motive than he had."

"Yes, I suppose you had," said Jessop slowly. He'd been too busy organising the elimination of Cardew to think about Iredale's position until that moment.

"Well, there you are, then. But I didn't do it, so why should I believe that Cardew did? My guess is that the murderer is someone who hasn't come under suspicion at all, and I hope to God Haines soon finds him. This place is getting intolerable."

Jessop stared at the man who had once been his friend. It began to look as though Iredale were hand in glove with Haines. Iredale obviously didn't realise that Haines was employed by the forces of evil. He seemed to have dangerous sympathies, dangerous ideas—ideas that must be probed. Jessop said casually, "What do *you* think about the case, Bill? What do you imagine was the motive?"

"I don't see how there can be any rational motive," said Iredale. "The fellow's obviously a lunatic, chucking cyanide about all over the place. The sooner he's caught and put out of harm's way the better."

"He must have had his reasons," said Jessop.

"If he thinks he's got reasons, that proves he's a lunatic. What sane reason could there be for putting cyanide in olives that any one of five people might have eaten? Damn it all, Ed, if you hadn't kept me talking that day it might easily have been me instead of Hind. No, he's crazy, all right, and we shall none of us be safe until he's locked up."

Jessop's hands clenched till the nails pressed into his palms. So he was crazy, was he? Crazy!—when he alone had seen through the stupendous plot that had been woven, when he alone was fighting back against the ruthless men who wanted to destroy him and people like him. If Iredale thought him crazy, Iredale was an enemy too. He was probably in the plot himself. Iredale was ready to humiliate him and torture him and shut him up with lunatics. Yes, and hadn't Iredale wanted him to go to Malaya, where he'd have been shot and mutilated like Eversley? For the moment, Cardew seemed of secondary importance. As Jessop gazed towards the window where Iredale was standing, he no longer saw the face he knew. Hallucination gripped him. What he saw was diabolical, grotesque and hideous, with eyes that dripped blood. He knew he must destroy it, and gripped the steel spike which stood on his desk.

Before he could rise, the ghastly vision dissolved. He heard Iredale's voice, coming from far away. "Are you feeling all right, Ed?"

"Yes, I'm all right," said Jessop, his hand to his head. Iredale's face looked normal again now, but Jessop knew that it was just a mask. He had been vouchsafed a glimpse into the man's true nature. He was a traitor, a turncoat, a police stooge. Well, the revelation had come just in time—there was an obvious way of dealing with him. A safer way than physical assault. Jessop got up. "I think I'll take a turn along the corridor," he said. "This business is beginning to get me down. Will you keep an eye on the tape, Bill?"

"Sure," said Iredale good-naturedly.

"I won't be long. By the way, Jackson's interested in that Balkan escape story—there may be something coming through now."

"Okay." Iredale went into the tape room.

Jessop watched him go, and a crafty smile spread over his features. He had a wonderful plan—a plan that would make things bad for Iredale and worse for Cardew. A plan that would throw the police investigation into chaos. He stopped for a moment by the door, and then went out.

Chapter Twenty-Nine

Ogilvie had been going from room to room, making further inquiries about the ZYKLON in the hope that independent evidence might bear out either Cardew's or Jessop's story. He had had no success, however, and was returning to the second-floor office to make a report when the door opened with a crash and Haines, emerging at speed, almost knocked him down.

"What's up, Chief?" he asked breathlessly. "Have they got Cardew?"

"No, but he's not far away." Haines grasped his arm and plunged with him along the corridor to the stairs. "He's just been on the phone to me. He says Iredale's the murderer!"

Ogilvie gasped. "Well, I'll be . . ."

"He says Iredale keeps the cyanide in a tobacco tin in his jacket pocket. We'll check first and work it out afterwards."

"Sounds likely, I must say!" They clattered down the stairs. "Any chance of tracing the call?"

"No," Haines grunted. "Local—from a box."

"This is the screwiest case I ever had anything to do with," said Ogilvie. "What the hell does Cardew think he's playing at?"

Haines was rushing ahead. As they passed the Reporters' Room he flung open the door and looked in. No Iredale. Rogers said, "They've just taken the body away, Inspector."

"Let's try the Foreign Room," said Haines. Ogilvie was ahead now and threw the door wide as he reached it. Iredale was sitting on the edge of a desk, apparently engrossed in copy. He was alone. Ogilvie shut the door and stood with his back to it.

Iredale slid off the desk and confronted them. He could see that they meant business. “You know,” he said, eyeing each of them in turn, “if this weren’t England I’d say you’d come to beat me up. What is it?” He took a step towards them.

“Stay where you are, Mr. Iredale,” Haines snapped. He had a feeling that someone might do something desperate pretty soon, and without much warning. His glance travelled quickly round the room and came to rest on a tweed sports coat that hung on a peg by the door. “Is this your jacket?”

“It is,” said Iredale. “I wish you’d tell me what this is all about.”

“Any objection if I look in the pockets?”

Iredale shrugged. “Go ahead—help yourself.”

“Watch him,” Haines murmured to Ogilvie. His fingers explored the contours of the two side pockets and an “Ah!” escaped him.

“What exactly do you expect to find?” asked Iredale. “Perhaps I can help you.”

“A tobacco tin, Mr. Iredale,” said Haines. He wrapped a handkerchief round his fingers and felt carefully in the right hand pocket.

“You’ll find one,” said Iredale, frowning. “But I still don’t see . . .”

Haines drew out a flat, rectangular tin, shook it against his ear, and opened it with a snap. It was full of a strong flake tabacco. He put it back and felt in the other pocket.

“I’m a smoker,” said Iredale, “not an incinerator,” Suddenly he stiffened. He saw that Haines had produced a second tin exactly like the first.

The inspector shot him a quick glance, opened the tin, and sniffed at it cautiously. “Just come over here, Mr. Iredale,” he said, his face expressionless. Ogilvie was teetering on his toes, his hands in front of him, ready for instant action. Haines held out the tin in his handkerchief. “Does that smell remind you of anything?”

Iredale had gone pale under his sunburn. The tin was empty, but there were minute white crystals still adhering to it. He sniffed gingerly, and smelt tobacco and bitter almonds.

“What *is* this?” he demanded angrily. “A frame-up?”

"You saw me find it there," said Haines. "What do you know about it?"

"Nothing," said Iredale. "Nothing at all, except that it might be one of my old tins that somebody else has used. Good God, Inspector, you don't imagine I'd have left the stuff in my coat pocket if I'd been the murderer?"

"I'm assuming the murderer's crazy," said Haines. "He thinks he can get away with anything."

"Well, I'm not crazy. I wouldn't think so."

"How do I know that?"

Iredale felt a spasm of fear. It was bad enough to be suspected of something he knew nothing about, but if they were going to start doubting his sanity too . . .

He stared at the tin. "Who suggested you should come here and search my coat? Who put you up to this?"

"As a matter of fact," said Haines, his voice tinged with derision, "it was Mr. Cardew."

"*Cardew!*" Iredale was utterly at a loss. "Cardew did that . . .?" He looked incredulously from one policeman to the other. "But I thought he'd cleared out?"

"He just telephoned me," Haines told him. "He said that you were the murderer and that I should find the cyanide in your pocket. And I have."

Iredale's face was dark. "Well, of all the dirty . . .!" He broke off, baffled. "It's too monstrous."

"And you said you were on such good terms with him," said Haines. "You remember?—you made quite a point of it."

"It's true. I don't know what's happened—I'm completely at sea." Iredale made an effort to think calmly. "How would Cardew know about this tin, anyway?"

"I didn't have a chance to ask him," said Haines. "I *shall* ask him—as soon as I can lay my hands on him. Perhaps it was an inspired guess!"

"Inspired guess, my foot! Look here, Inspector, I don't pretend to understand what's going on, but I can tell you I know nothing whatever about this stuff. I haven't touched any cyanide and I didn't know the tin was there. I'm sorry to have to say it, but if Cardew knew that tin was in my pocket, he must have put it there himself!"

"Could he have done?"

Iredale looked bewildered. "I suppose he could. I've been up on the roof most of the afternoon, and he's been working here. God, it's unbelievable!"

Haines frowned. More tit-for-tat! He wrapped the tin carefully in his handkerchief. "Well, you're all very plausible. We shall have to hope for fingerprints." A new rhythm was beating in his head. Iredale, Cardew; Cardew, Iredale. Soon he would be driven in sheer desperation to arrest one of them. Perhaps he ought to arrest Iredale now. He stood still, trying to marshal the evidence.

Suddenly the door opened and Sergeant Miles looked in. "Ah, here you are, sir. I've got a bit of information that I think you ought to have."

"What is it, Sergeant?"

Miles bent to the inspector and his voice dropped to a confidential whisper. "Pringle's alibi has fallen down, sir. It seems he checked in at the hotel in Baldock, but he changed his mind and didn't stay there. He now says that he spent the night at his own home, but as all his family's on holiday we can't be certain of that either. Apparently he was trying to save the hotel bill and make a bit extra on his expenses. That's his explanation, anyway."

Haines groaned. "That fellow ought to be in a home for inveterates!" He looked dubiously at Iredale for a moment, then turned and left without another word.

Chapter Thirty

Cardew was driving his Riley through the southern suburbs at a speed well in excess of the legal limit. He was in a reckless mood, matching his purpose. No trouble he could get into now, he told himself, could be worse than the mess he was in already. He was in imminent danger of arrest for murder, with a mass of circumstantial evidence against him and no convincing answer to the charge. He could feel the net closing round him—motive, opportunity and means, all were there. Knowledge of innocence only made him more determined to prove it in the only way he could think of. Rosemary's attitude had been the last straw. He'd *had* to ring her up, to say how sorry he was about everything and to find out what she was thinking, and though she'd brushed aside as ridiculous the idea that he might have been concerned in the affair, the embarrassment in her voice had not been lost on him. Well, he couldn't blame her. The last words he had spoken to her during that humiliating scene they had had together came back to him now. "I'm so jealous of him. Why did it have to be him and not me?" And a few hours later, Nicholas had been nearly murdered. What could she be expected to think?

He crouched over the wheel, his young face drawn with the intensity of his emotions. He'd made a mess of things, but he could still struggle out of the mess if only he could prove his innocence. Jessop had done it, of course. Cardew was sure of that. Jessop must have done it, because he'd taken the ZYKLON away, and he couldn't possibly have forgotten that he'd taken it away, and yet he'd deliberately lied about it and accused Cardew. That added up to guilt. Cardew knew that his own memory hadn't betrayed him. He could perfectly recall the evening when it had happened. He had a clear picture in his mind of Jessop with the tin under his arm. And Jessop must have taken the stuff to his home, as he'd said he was going to. If he'd done anything else with it, it would hardly have been accessible after all this time. By now, of course, he might have taken fright and found a new hiding-place for the stuff, but it was only to-day that the ZYKLON had been mentioned, and Cardew didn't see how he could have had an opportunity. In any case, it was worth making the search. Anything was better than waiting to be arrested.

How Jessop must hate him! How he must hate everybody! A man with a chip on his shoulder. No—worse than that. He must be completely cracked, even though he hadn't shown any obvious signs of it. It was difficult to believe that a man you'd known and worked with for years was a murderer—an insane, indiscriminate slayer. Fantastic when one thought of Jessop's quiet manner, his unassuming diffidence. But why, otherwise, should he have told that monstrous lie?

As the car approached Beckenham, Cardew's thoughts became more practical. The first step had been easy—to find Jessop's home address in the telephone book—but he didn't know at all how he was going to set about the search. It was broad daylight, and there might be neighbours about. The house would be locked, and he was certain to make some noise getting in. Boldness seemed to offer the best hope. He must march up to the house as though he had a perfect right to be there, as though Jessop had authorised him to be there and to do what he was doing. That was the right mental approach, anyway. People were always slow to interfere if you gave an impression of self-confidence. If he were challenged, he would make up some yarn—anything. It didn't matter what he said if only he could get his hands on the cyanide, the one proof of Jessop's guilt that couldn't be explained away.

A couple of inquiries brought him to the road, and after a brief reconnaissance he found the house. It stood in a biggish garden, surrounded by well-covered trees and a hawthorn hedge, but it was semi-detached. That wasn't so good. He stopped the Riley with a scrunch at the gate—at least he had arrived in a most impressive car—and walked resolutely up the short drive. The problem was to know where to begin—and he mustn't hesitate. House, garage, shed? Where would Jessop be most likely to keep the stuff? It might even be buried in the garden. In spite of his resolve, Cardew couldn't help casting a nervous glance at the next-door upper windows. There was no one visible there, and he felt reassured. He saw that the garage doors, though closed, were not locked, and he pulled one of the doors open and went in. Here was temporary concealment, at least. He looked round and saw that this part of the search wouldn't take long. There was nothing much there—a couple of old oil drums, a hose for the garden, some lengths of timber, a bundle of pea sticks, and an ancient tarpaulin thrown over the beams—nothing promising. It was possible, of course, that Jessop had abstracted some of the ZYKLON from the original tin, put it in a small container, and disposed of the rest. It would take a long time to search every container on the premises. Still, that would have to be done.

He closed the garage door and walked quickly round to the back of the house. The curtain of green between himself and the adjoining house had a thin spot here, just near the garden shed. And the shed itself was locked. Cardew felt exposed, and decided to try the house first. There were french doors opening out from the sitting-room on to a crazy-paved terrace, screened by tall rose bushes. He'd have to take a chance on the noise. He picked up a thick piece of wood and tested its weight. With the right thrust, the glass should fall neatly on to the carpet. He could hear a car accelerating as it came up the hill. Just before it changed gear he thrust the wood through the pane of glass nearest the door handle. A hell of a row! He put the piece of wood against the wall, opened the door, and slipped in, his pulse racing. There was no turning back now! He stood listening for a moment, but all was quiet. Perhaps the people next door were away from home.

Encouraged, he began systematically to ransack the house. There was no need to worry about leaving traces. If he failed to find the stuff he was done for anyway. He'd never be able to conceal the fact that he'd been here. If he did find it, he'd be forgiven the escapade. He started with the pantry and kitchen, and they presented fewer problems than he'd expected. Jessop evidently did little more than sleep in this house. He opened every tin, every bottle, every receptacle that could possibly hold cyanide crystals, smelt each one and flung it aside. It took him a quarter of an hour to go through everything, and he drew a blank. He looked in the downstairs cloakroom, and in cupboards, bureau, sideboard and every article of furniture capable of holding anything at all. No luck! He went upstairs and tried the bathroom. More lids came off, but there was no hint of cyanide. He climbed a sliding ladder to the loft, switched on the light there, opened and searched a number of trunks. Nothing. He combed through the bedrooms with feverish speed, flinging back bedclothes and turning out wardrobes. Sweat poured off him, and very soon his hands and face were coated with grime. Still no sign. He looked desperately round at the havoc he had caused and for a moment stood aghast. He felt a bit crazy himself. It seemed incredible that *he* should be doing this. Incredible and yet exciting. Almost as exciting as going after Messerschmitts when you'd written yourself off for lost anyway.

He hadn't found what he was looking for, but it *must* be here somewhere. There was still, of course, the shed and the garden. He'd hoped he wouldn't have to tackle the shed. It was dangerously near the dividing fence, and it wouldn't be easy to break into. However, he couldn't stop now. He went out, pulling the french doors to behind him. He heard the voice of a child in the next house. So they weren't out! He walked quickly to the shed. It was secured with a heavy padlock, which he couldn't hope to smash, and its single window was too small to get through. Somehow, he would have to wrench one of the staples out of the wood. He looked around for a tool. Luck was with him—lying on the ground against the shed there was a small rusty handpick. He wedged the pointed end inside the staple and exerted leverage, his muscles straining. He felt it begin to give. He heaved with all his strength, and suddenly it came out of the wood with a dry, protesting shriek. He pulled the door open and slipped inside. The sight that met his eyes appalled him. There were tins everywhere. He found a screw-driver and began systematically to prise off lids. Through the thin weatherboarding he heard someone come out into the garden next door. He looked frantically up at the shelves, moved a row of empty jars. Nothing there. He shifted some old tins of paint and a big keg of washable distemper and . . . Holy Moses, there it was! He could have wept from exhaustion and relief. ZYKLON, bold as red letters could make it. The original container, and almost no effort at concealment. This was indeed the confidence of madness. He tucked the tin under his arm as though it were a rugby football and emerged from the sweltering shed, hot, dirty, but triumphant.

A voice came through the thin green hedge. "Is that you, Mr. Jessop?"

For a fraction of a second Cardew hesitated. Should he run, or should he bluff? It didn't very much matter now, except that he wanted to get back to the office without any delay. It might be simpler to bluff. "I'm a friend of Mr. Jessop's," he said, peering through the hedge. "He asked me to get something for him."

"Oh, I see," said the voice dubiously. Cardew could just make out a bald scalp shining through the leaves. "I heard a noise—I just wondered. Of course, if you're a friend . . ." The voice petered out. Cardew suddenly realised how little he must look like a friend of the neat, respectable Jessop. He must look more like a tramp, or the survivor of a bad street accident. He didn't stop to argue but went off quickly down the path, with difficulty preventing himself from breaking into a run. He flung the ZYKLON into the back of the car and dropped into the driving seat. As he started the engine he heard a front door open and glanced over his shoulder. The man with the bald head was looking out. Not so good! The chap was probably taking the number of the car. Still, Cardew had his proof. He let in the clutch with a slam and headed the Riley towards London.

Chapter Thirty-One

There was much less custom at the Crown than usual. The day men had left London in search of cooler spots, and the night men, sensing imminent drama, were standing by in the office for news of the missing Cardew. Bill Iredale was sitting alone at an empty stretch of bar with a copy of the *Standard* propped against a soda syphon, drinking iced whisky and water. When anyone came in he concentrated on the paper. He was in a morose mood.

He had just finished his first drink when Katharine Camden appeared, looking very attractive and cool in tussore silk. "Hallo, Bill," she said in a casual tone. She didn't want to give the impression that she had been looking for him.

"Hallo," he said, regarding her with mixed feelings. "What are you doing around at this time? Been on a late story?"

She nodded, puckering her nose. "Quads at Mile End."

"Salubrious spot."

"Horrible. I should hate to be a Mile End quad." She hesitated. The conversation seemed unpromisingly laconic. "Do you want to go on reading?"

He swivelled a stool round for her. "Not particularly, but I warn you, I'll be damn company."

"I can bear it." She slid in beside him.

"What'll you have?" he asked.

"Oh, I don't know. Gin and tonic." Her eyes searched his face. "What's the matter, Bill? You're not worrying about that notice, surely?"

"I'm afraid you're behind with the news," he said, prodding

tobacco into his pipe. He hated to tell her, but he'd have to some time. "This evening the police found cyanide in my jacket pocket."

She stared at him, her glass poised in the air. "Bill!"

He nodded grimly. "Traces, anyway. In a tobacco tin—exactly like this one. A thing like that doesn't make one feel very sociable."

She looked at the tin. "I don't understand. Somebody must have put it there."

"Thank you," he said gravely.

"What made the police think of looking?"

Iredale told her about Cardew's telephone call to the inspector and his own conversation with Haines.

"But, Bill—what a dreadful thing to do!" She looked appalled. "I know they were saying upstairs that Cardew was the man, but I couldn't believe it. Now it looks as though they were right."

"I can't believe it myself," said Iredale. "I don't mean he couldn't kill anybody, but I can't believe he'd try to swing it on to me. He's about the last man I'd expect to play a lousy trick like that." He rapped on the counter. "Let's have another drink."

"I suppose it *was* Cardew, and not someone else?"

He shrugged. "It was Cardew who telephoned—that makes it pretty conclusive."

Katharine sat in silence for a while. She too was trying to imagine Cardew framing a colleague for something he'd done himself, and she couldn't. Perhaps there was some other explanation—perhaps someone else had told him about the tin and he'd simply passed the information on to Haines. She twisted her glass to and fro. "I wonder . . ." she began, but didn't complete the sentence. "Of course, if the . . ." Her voice trailed off again. She was looking at Iredale but not seeing him.

He tapped her arm. "Of whom do you think when you talk to me?"

She jumped. "I'm sorry. I was thinking aloud."

"I feel privileged to be present."

"You are an ass," she said. "As a matter of fact. I was wondering about other people."

"Who?"

"Well, almost anyone. You say the jacket was hanging in the Foreign Room all afternoon. How about Jessop, for instance? He must have been around."

"Now don't *you* start that," said Iredale with a shade of exasperation in his voice. "The whole place is full of budding Sherlocks already. Why drag Ed in?"

"Why rule him out?"

"Ed? Why, he wouldn't hurt a fly."

"I've heard him say very bitter things about people."

"Oh, that's only talk. He's like an old sweat—full of grouses, but it doesn't mean a thing. He wouldn't shoot the sergeant-major!"

"You like him, don't you?"

"Sure—why not? We grew up in the business together." He had never really considered the matter before." I'd as soon suspect my own brother. Don't you like him?"

"He doesn't give me much of a chance. He always treats me as though I've no right to be in Fleet Street. Actually, I think I'm a bit sorry for him." She dropped the subject abruptly. "Any news of when you're going away, Bill?"

Iredale gave a rueful smile. "Better ask Haines. I'm still more or less on parole."

She looked surprised. "But if Cardew . . ." she began, and stopped. Of course, the inspector might believe Cardew's accusations. "Anyway," she said emphatically, "it's absurd to suspect you."

"I always said you didn't pay enough attention to the facts," he teased her.

"What do you mean?"

"It's nice to be believed in—especially by you, but I'm not out of the wood. That notice was put up for people like you. You ought to be watching your drink." He took the tin from his pocket again. "What is it—tobacco or cyanide? Just turn your head the other way."

"That isn't a bit amusing," said Katharine.

"Facts are facts. *I* quarrelled with everyone—you can't have forgotten. *I* brought the stuff to England. And now it's been found in *my* pocket."

"You're just being a masochist." Katharine was unperturbed by the catalogue. "I have a hunch about you and I prefer to stick to it. As a matter of fact you're just as unreasonable over hunches as I am. I can't believe you're a murderer—you can't believe Jessop is. Neither of us can really believe that Cardew is. Evidence is what proves that people we don't like are guilty."

"This week's great thought!" said Iredale. "Katharine, you do me good."

The door opened and a small group of people drifted in, Jessop among them. He detached himself and joined Iredale and Katharine. She gave him a friendly smile; if Bill liked him, she was prepared to make an effort. Iredale ordered a whisky. "Any more news, Ed?"

Jessop shook his head. "Cardew still hasn't turned up." He knew that the police had interviewed Iredale again, but he obviously couldn't mention the tin, and it didn't look as though Iredale were going to. Probably he wouldn't want Katharine to know about it. Jessop felt very cheerful. Everything was going well now. He was like a general who sees the enemy positions crumbling at all points, and senses a rout. Power—that was what he was enjoying at last. All the people who had despised and rejected him were now at his mercy. They were his puppets. His brilliant manoeuvres had confused the police and scattered his enemies. Hind dead, Ede disposed of, Cardew in flight, and Iredale scared. What a triumph! It was pleasant to watch Iredale, to gloat over him. The man who had called him a lunatic! He raised his glass. "Cheers, Bill."

"Cheers," responded Iredale. "Have you abandoned your post, Ed?"

"There's a boy there," said Jessop indifferently. "Anyway, who cares?"

"It's all right with me. I was only thinking that we might go on somewhere else. I feel like a pub crawl. What do you say, Katharine?"

She looked at him doubtfully. She didn't much care for his mood, and yet she was reluctant to see him go off alone. "If you're planning to get drunk," she said, "I don't know that I particularly want to be there."

"I won't. It's just that I can't stand this place any more—it's too near the office. Let's try the George—we can get some food there. How about you, Ed?"

"Good idea," said Jessop.

"All right," Katharine agreed suddenly. "I'll come."

Chapter Thirty-Two

Cardew was well out of Beckenham, his mind concentrated on the interview that lay ahead, when a peremptory blast on a horn jerked him from his automatic driving into an awareness of his immediate surroundings. What he saw in the mirror gave him a nasty shock. A police radio car was racing up behind him. It passed him at speed, cut in across his front wheels, and forced him to draw up at the kerb with a shriek of tyres on tarmac.

Two of its four occupants—a uniformed sergeant and a constable—got out and walked towards him with infuriating deliberation, as though they now had all the time in the world. The sergeant went round to the driving side and the constable made a slow, inquisitive circuit of the vehicle, as if he had never seen a car before.

"What's the trouble?" asked Cardew, with an effort at nonchalance that sounded unconvincing even to him. It had been all very well to tell himself that he didn't care what happened, now that he had the ZYKLON, but the roadside was hardly the place for explanations.

"This is not a racing track, sir," the sergeant said severely. "This is a public highway. You were doing forty-two miles an hour in a restricted area. Can I see your driving licence and insurance certificate, please?"

Cardew produced the documents with a sense of relief. What was a speeding charge to him? "I'm sorry, sergeant—I was in a hurry to get back to my office. Press, you know."

The policeman looked him up and down, noting his matted hair.

the black smudge across his cheek and collar, the grimy hands. "A dirty job!" he said ambiguously.

Cardew tried to smile. "I've been helping a colleague with some house decorations."

"You have, eh?" The sergeant handed back the documents. "He wouldn't be a man by the name of Jessop, would he?"

Cardew sank back in his seat. So the speeding was incidental. Jessop's neighbour *had* rung the police; these fellows had been watching out for him. He wondered just how much they knew.

"Look, officer . . ." he began.

"I think you'd better do your talking at the station," said the sergeant grimly.

The constable, who had been poking about in the back of the car, suddenly said, "What's in this tin?" He was trying to get the lid off.

"Careful!" cried Cardew. "It's cyanide—deadly poison."

"Cyanide, eh?" The sergeant looked even more grim.

"I can explain everything, though," said Cardew earnestly. "There's been a murder—you must have heard about it—at the *Morning Call*. That's my paper . . ."

"Yes, we know all about that," said the sergeant. "We have instructions to pick you up. Better come along."

Cardew's spirits sank. "Look, officer," he said desperately, "what you don't know is that I happened to find out who *did* the murder—only an hour ago. This cyanide is the stuff that was used, and I'm taking it along to Chief Inspector Haines. He's at the office, in charge of the case. I found it at Jessop's house. I'n not trying to get out of anything, but for God's sake if you're going to take me anywhere take me to Inspector Haines. I must see him at once. It may be a matter of life or death for someone, and I mean that."

The sergeant looked very hard at him. "You wait here," he said after a moment. He motioned to the constable to watch Cardew, and went back to the radio car at the same unhurried pace. Five long minutes passed while he sought instructions. Then he returned to the Riley.

"All right," he said, "you can tell your story to the inspector.

We'll come along with you." He climbed in beside Cardew and the constable got in at the back. The radio car went ahead; a traffic policeman on a motor cycle, who had attached himself to the convoy, brought up the rear.

Fifteen minutes later they drew up outside the *Morning Call* office. Cardew led the way in, avoiding the commissionaire's eye. The sergeant was close beside him; the constable carried the cyanide. They went up in the lift to the second floor and along to Haines's office. Haines was sitting at his desk, waiting. Ogilvie was standing with his back to the window, waiting. Sergeant Miles was beside him. They all looked as though they had gathered for the final curtain.

"Well!" said Haines, getting up and advancing across the carpet. "Here we are again, eh, Mr. Cardew?" He surveyed the dirty, dishevelled figure in front of him. "A little the worse for wear, too! I thought I told you not to leave the office without permission."

"I can explain everything . . ." began Cardew.

"Just a minute." Haines went to the table on which the constable had placed the tin of ZYKLON and prised off the lid. He looked at the grey crystals almost lovingly for a moment, and then slammed the lid back.

"All right, Mr. Cardew, let's hear what you have to say."

"I knew the cyanide was at Jessop's house," Cardew burst out. "I told you it was, but you wouldn't believe me. As you wouldn't make a search, I had to. I found it in the garden shed."

Haines nodded slowly. "Very pretty," he said, "very clever. So you found it in Jessop's shed." With a change of tone that electrified Cardew he rapped out, "How do I know you did?"

Cardew gasped. "*Now* what are you suggesting?"

"I'm suggesting that you picked up the cyanide from wherever you'd hidden it and that you took it to Jessop's house and ransacked the place to make it appear that you'd found it there."

"It's a damned lie!" Cardew cried. He was almost weeping with rage and frustration. "I found it in his shed."

"Why did you ring up and tell me that some of the stuff was in Iredale's pocket? What was the idea?"

Cardew ran his hands through his tangled hair. "I don't know what you're talking about," he said frantically.

It was Haines's turn to look bewildered. "Mr. Cardew, did you or did you not ring me up a couple of hours ago and tell me that Iredale was the murderer and that he had the cyanide in his pocket?"

"Of course I didn't," Cardew shouted. He was near breaking point. "Iredale has nothing to do with this. I tell you Jessop's the murderer. I didn't ring anybody. Why the devil should I say it was Iredale when I knew damn well it was Jessop? And would I have been planting this stuff in Jessop's house and accusing Iredale at the same time? You can't have it both ways."

"I answered the telephone myself," said Haines slowly. "It was your voice."

"It was not my voice, I tell you. Do you think I don't know whether I spoke to you or not? It must have been someone else . . ." He suddenly broke off as light flooded in. "It must have been Jessop. Yes, of *course* it was Jessop. He can mimic anybody."

"And why should Jessop pretend to be you, and tell me that Iredale was the murderer when he'd already told me that you were the man who took the cyanide from the office in the first place?"

"I don't know," said Cardew, "I just don't know."

"This case is going to drive us all crazy," said Haines in disgust. He stood in momentary reflection. "Well, Mr. Cardew, you've given us a hell of a lot of trouble, but as far as you're concerned this is the end. You won't get up to any more mischief. You're under arrest." Turning to the sergeant who had brought Cardew he said, "You can take him away, officer."

"Yes, sir." The sergeant looked puzzled. "What exactly is the charge, sir?"

"Housebreaking," said Haines.

Chapter Thirty-Three

The Inspector dealt swiftly with the new situation. The tin of cyanide was sent off to the Yard for fingerprinting and laboratory tests. Ogilvie was dispatched to Beckenham to see if he could get any confirmation of Cardew's story on the spot. Sergeant Miles was instructed to attach himself at once to Jessop and keep him under continuous observation until the inspector called for him. With this precaution taken, Haines relaxed. He felt immeasurably relieved. Whatever the final solution turned out to be, there should be no more deaths now. For the first time since he had been called in, he could reflect on the case free from the constant dread that the murderer might be a step ahead of him, and that he might at any moment find another body on his hands.

Cardew or Jessop—that was what it boiled down to now. If Cardew had really found the cyanide concealed in Jessop's shed, then Jessop was obviously the murderer. If Cardew had only pretended to find it there, then Cardew was obviously the murderer. Pringle was out, and Iredale was out, and endless other speculations were cut short by simple logic. Cardew or Jessop. So far, so good. But which?

Once again Haines mentally reviewed the evidence against Cardew. Access to the cyanide in the first place. Jessop's assertion that Cardew had taken it away with him. No alibi for the time the poison was placed in the shower room. A classic motive—desire for another man's wife. Guilty behaviour—an attempt to cast suspicion on someone else. There were loose ends in plenty, but as far as the attempt on Ede was concerned, there was undoubtedly a strong case. And Ogilvie might find a clinching piece of evidence.

If some independent witness could say definitely that Cardew had been carrying a large parcel when he entered Jessop's premises—the neighbour who had telephoned, for instance, or a postman, or a passer-by—that would settle it. Or, of course, that he had *not* been carrying anything—that would settle it, too. In the absence of such evidence, it was going to be very difficult to reach a decision about Cardew. The worst complication in his case was the death of Hind. That was still completely unexplained.

What of Jessop? Haines felt on even less secure ground where he was concerned. Almost the only evidence against him came from Cardew, and for the moment that couldn't be accepted without reservations. Jessop would obviously have to be questioned again very closely. Otherwise, what was there? No alibi for the murder of Hind, no alibi for the attempted murder of Ede. Nothing could be more negative than that. There was barely a trace of motive. There certainly wasn't enough evidence to justify Jessop's arrest. He was residual, that was all—one of the two suspects left over after all the sifting. A prosecution based on that alone would have no chance in court.

Some of Cardew's accusations against Jessop seemed pretty wild. There was the episode of the telephone call, for instance. It *might* have been Jessop—the telephone always distorted voices, and Cardew's public school accent was an easy one to imitate. Haines wasn't prepared to commit himself about it. But what on earth was Jessop supposed to have against Iredale, that he should have made such a call? It was Jessop, after all, who had delayed Iredale on the ocasion of that fatal lunch, and perhaps saved his life as a result. He'd hardly have done that if he'd had such a grudge against Iredale that later he was prepared to frame him for murder. It didn't make sense.

Of course, if the murderer were crazy, perhaps it made sense in some crazy way. Jessop showed no outward signs of unbalance, but that meant nothing. Haines remembered a woman he'd had to question at a mental hospital a few weeks earlier—a white-haired old lady, the respected wife of a clergyman, sweet as lavender and very gentle. She'd been so lucid and intelligent that after a quarter of an hour's conversation with her he'd begun seriously to wonder whether she ought to be there at all. And then, at the end, the startling request—would he stop the Medical Super-intendent coming into her room at night and trying to rape her? Paranoia, they'd called it.

Haines shook his head unhappily. He was a bit out of his depth with that sort of stuff. He had learned enough in a lifetime of police work to know that you couldn't hope to be a good detective unless you were prepared to probe people's minds, but insanity was something different. Better to concentrate on solid evidence and sound deduction, and leave it to the psychiatrists to find an explanation afterwards.

Where, he wondered, was Jessop at the time when the telephone call had been made? Haines was so deep in his reflections that he scarcely heard hurried footsteps in the corridor. Suddenly Sergeant Miles burst into the room, looking very worried. "I'm sorry, sir—Jessop seems to have given us the slip. He's not in the building."

"Hell and damnation!" cried Haines. So his relief had been premature! Jessop might be the murderer and in that case he might still have some cyanide, and if he thought the net was closing in on him he would be desperate. There was nothing he mightn't attempt. "We've got to find him, Sergeant—and quickly. Doesn't anyone know where he's gone?"

"Apparently not, sir. He left his room about half an hour ago without saying where he was off to."

"Is his car in the garage?"

"I don't know, sir. I thought I'd better report to you first."

"Okay, let's have a look."

They rushed downstairs, and once again Haines tackled Peach. "Do you know which is Mr. Jessop's car, Sarge?" he asked breathlessly.

"Yes, sir. It's the green Austin. I think it's still there—it was earlier on. I'll show you, if you like. Boy, look after the box." He led the way through the garage. "Yes, that's the one," he said, pointing. "That one over there's Miss Camden's, the one what me and Mr. Cardew 'ad to push. Proper old crock, it is. They didn't ought to allow cars to be left 'ere the way they do, if you ask me. Three days it's been there, to my knowledge, cluttering up the place, and Mr. Cardew 'ardly ever takes 'is out, 'cept for weekends."

Haines was turning away, his mind eased. "If Jessop hasn't taken his car," he said to Miles, "I don't suppose he's far away. We'd better find out what his haunts are." He began to move towards the door, then suddenly stopped abruptly. "What was that you said, Sarge?"

"About what, sir?"

"About cars being left here?"

Peach looked surprised. "I only said Miss Camden's car's been stuck 'ere three days, and Mr. Cardew's don't often go out."

"Do you know when it last went out?"

"It come in Monday morning and I'm pretty sure it ain't been out since—not till to-day, o' course."

Haines was conscious of a surge of excitement. He stood still and looked all round the garage. The floor sloped down from street level. Jessop's car was parked parallel to the wall at the bottom of the slope, with its rear wheels almost touching Katharine Camden's Morris. Ahead of it there was a space, just large enough to hold one car lengthways.

He found a pencil and a scrap of paper. "Look, Sarge," he said eagerly, "I want to know just how the three cars looked when you and Mr. Cardew were here. Do me a sketch, will you?"

"Okay, sir." Peach began to draw. "I ain't exactly an artist, you know," he said, licking the end of his pencil and standing back to survey his work. "Still, that's about it." He handed over the sketch. "We 'ad to push out Miss Camden's, shift Mr. Jessop's along, get Mr. Cardew's out, shove Mr. Jessop's back where it was before, and then let Miss Camden's run back into its old place."

Haines studied the diagram. "Well, just tell me this, Sarge. If Mr. Cardew's car has been here since Monday, and Miss Camden's has been here three days, and it took two of you to push Miss Camden's car out of the way before you could release Mr. Cardew's, how do you suppose Mr. Jessop got his car out the night before last?"

Peach scratched his head. "I don't reckon 'e could—not without

’e got someone to ’elp ’im. ’E couldn’t ’ave done it ’imself. Miss Camden’s car ain’t exactly ’eavy, but it’s a blinking steep slope, and don’t I know it!”

Haines’s thoughts went back to his talk with Jessop earlier that day. He had pressed Jessop to produce some evidence that he had actually gone home on the crucial night. If someone *had* helped him to push Katharine Camden’s car out of the way, he’d certainly have mentioned the fact to strengthen his alibi. He had lied. He hadn’t gone home by car. He hadn’t gone home at all!

The inspector turned to Miles. “We’ve got to get Jessop! By God, if I’ve left this too late, I’ll never forgive myself.”

Chapter Thirty-Four

Katharine was sitting on a stool near the wide-open door of the Green Man in Covent Garden—the third and, it would appear, the last pub they would visit that night, for closing time was at hand—listening with amused interest to the professional reminiscences of the two men and occasionally prompting them to fresh efforts. After a couple of hours of "shop" talk she could better understand the nature of the bond between Iredale and Jessop. They were like old campaigners recalling battles jointly fought, or ship-wrecked sailors who had survived a common ordeal in an open boat. There wasn't any special affinity, but their sense of comradeship was secure. So, at least, it now appeared to Katharine. In the light of their friendly exchanges her earlier fears seemed absurd, and she felt rather sorry that she had deliberately skipped several rounds in the interests of mental clarity. She might just as well have relaxed, for there was evidently nothing for her to be vigilant about.

A few drinks had made Jessop more voluble than usual, but up to now he had been neither self-revelatory nor aggressive. His pressing sense of persecution had been eased by the lance of action. In a glow of good fellowship, he had temporarily forgotten his grievances against the world. He had even forgotten that his original purpose in accompanying Iredale had been to revel in the man's discomfiture. For the moment—though the old bitterness might flare up at a word—Iredale was his friend again. Katharine, too, was acceptable. As Jessop talked he looked at her repeatedly for appreciation and approval, and from her expression he judged he was getting it. That warmed him. From time to time his fingers touched the tin in his jacket pocket, but without menace or intention.

Iredale, too, was in a much more tranquil frame of mind. Alcohol and pleasant conversation had dispersed his cares. It had been a good idea, this pub crawl *a'l trois*. Three were better than two when there was tension in the air—less effort was called for. Jessop's presence gave him a chance to study Katharine's profile for long moments without risk of embarrassment. Somehow he felt nearer to her with Jessop there than he had when they had been alone together.

The talk had traversed the world, lingering at the points of laughter. Iredale had been recalling some of his Russian experiences and was telling a story about an American air base in the Ukraine that he had visited during the war. "It was guarded by Russian sentries," he said, "simple peasant types but very much on their mettle and highly disciplined. Some of the G.I.s told them that the correct thing to do when an American officer went by was to spring smartly to attention and say, 'Hiya, bud!' And they did. It was damn funny while it lasted."

Jessop grinned and ordered a last round. Katharine said, "You two make me feel like one of those starry-eyed boys in the picture, listening to Sir Walter Raleigh talking about the undiscovered lands."

"Oh, I'm a stay-at-home, too," said Jessop. "But in my day it wasn't necessary to go abroad for excitement. Home reporting gave me all the thrills I needed Of course, reporting was a very different sort of job fifteen years ago, eh, Bill?"

Iredale took a reminiscent sip of whisky. "It certainly was," he said.

"I don't find it exactly dull now," said Katharine.

"That's because you've never known the real thing," Jessop told her condescendingly. "There's no space to print anything these days, and anyway all the news is streamlined and organised. Most of your stuff's handed to you on a plate. The readers are blasé, too—they simply don't get the kick out of good home stories that they used to do."

"It may only be nostalgia," said Iredale, "but there seemed to be far more really good stories in those days. Do you remember that fire at Wapping, Ed?—the rubber blaze. Now that was really something. It burned for more than a week, and we covered it in relays. The place was knee-deep in liquid rubber and water from the hoses. It's the only time I ever charged up thigh-boots on my expenses. Then there was the night the Crystal Palace burned down. What a story!" He smiled at Katharine. "I don't suppose you've ever seen what *we'd* call a real fire."

"I do happen to have seen practically the whole of London burning," she protested.

Jessop frowned. "That was wartime. Wars have ruined the newspaper business—they've made everything else seem flat." He shied away from the subject. "You know, Bill, one of the stories that made the biggest impression on me was a Mosley riot in the East End. I remember as if it were yesterday. There was a short street with half a dozen mounted police lined up at one end. In the street there was a seething mass of men, women and kids—Fascists and anti-Fascists and people who'd come to look on and people who lived there, all packed tight. Suddenly the police charged straight into the mass at full gallop, swinging their batons and hitting out wildly. You could hear the skulls cracking—it was brutal. They cut swathes, the murderous swine!"

"From what I remember of those riots," said Iredale, "the police couldn't do much else at that stage." He glanced mischievously at Katharine. "I suppose old Munro would have clapped his hands and said, 'Now, children . . .'"

"There's no need to bring that up again," she said.

"I still say they were swine," Jessop persisted. He had become rather flushed. "It was all the same to them whose heads they bashed; they probably enjoyed it. What did they care about the underdog? What does anyone care, for that matter? Look at the way people trample on you at the office."

"Oh, come off it," said Iredale gently. "You haven't done so badly, Ed, in spite of all your grousing."

"Small thanks to them!" The sudden venom in Jessop's tone startled Katharine, and her slumbering uneasiness revived. "What encouragement did I ever get? There was always some playboy around to take the plums while I did the dirty work." He plucked the cigarette end from his lips and ground it angrily under his heel. "That sort of thing should be stopped, and it could be. I'd like to get *my* hands on the place for a few days, I know that."

"I expect it all looks rather different when you're in charge," said Katharine. "It must be hard to keep everyone happy."

Jessop sneered. "Amateurs like Ede make a lot of fuss about running a newspaper, but it's not all that difficult. I could do it on my head."

"You mean you could do it on half a dozen whiskies," she teased.

"I could do it stone sober—Bill knows that." Jessop glared at her. "I'd make some changes."

"Heads would roll," said Iredale lightly. What a bore, he thought, that Ed had got on to this topic.

"They would," said Jessop. "A lot of people would get their deserts. Fleet Street stinks, the way it's run now. There's no sense of responsibility anywhere, no principles, no conscience. Everyone's climbing on somebody else's shoulders. It's just a bloody jungle."

"Is it worse than any other business?" asked Katharine. "I think you've got a bee in your bonnet about it—don't you agree, Bill?"

Iredale nodded. He was feeling pleasantly mellow. "You ought to have gone to Malaya, old son."

"Oh, no," said Jessop. "*Oh*, no! They're not getting *me* like that. I know they want me out of the way, but I'm not falling for that trick. I'm going to expose them, and I'm going to stay here till I've done it. They'll live to regret the way they've treated me."

Katharine was staring at him. "I do believe you mean it," she said.

"You bet I mean it."

"He's his own Royal Commission," said Iredale in a bored voice.

"I may be something more than that one of these days," said Jessop mysteriously.

Katharine wanted to ask him what he meant, but the barman called "Time" and the three of them finished their drinks and went out into the warm night. Jessop lurched a bit, steadying himself against Katharine's arm. She drew away and stood on the kerb, biting her lip. All the pleasure of the evening had faded. She felt more strongly than ever that Bill had a blind spot.

"Suppose we all go back to my place and brew some coffee," suggested Iredale. "It's early yet. What do you say, Katharine?"

"I'd like that," she said, but her eyes were fixed uneasily on Jessop. "Bill . . ." She broke off. She couldn't even hint at her fears with Jessop there. "All right, let's go," she finished abruptly.

"We'll take a cab," said Iredale. "It's too hot to walk."

They strolled into the Strand and he hailed a passing taxi. Katharine seated herself between the two men on the back seat. Jessop lolled in his corner.

"Are you all right, Ed?" asked Iredale. He knew that Jessop had a poor head for liquor, but the man really hadn't had very much.

"Of course I'm all right," Jessop muttered. He lay back with his eyes closed, and strange images floated in his brain.

"He *needs* coffee," said Katharine with a strained laugh. She stirred restlessly, and her hand touched Iredale's. He gathered it up.

"Don't," she said, releasing it quickly.

"Sorry." Iredale flushed in the darkness. He heard her bag snap, and a faint perfume filled the taxi. "Why do we all have to sit on this narrow seat?" she said, and moved to a collapsible one opposite. "That's better. Where *is* your place, Bill?"

"We're just coming to it now," he answered, peering out into the deserted canyon of Chancery Lane. "Wake up, Ed."

Jessop stumbled out as the taxi stopped. Katharine stayed by Iredale while he paid the driver. Then the three of them squeezed into the old lift and creaked their way past six unlighted office floors. Katharine gave an exaggerated shiver. "What an eerie place! Do you mean to say you live here alone?"

"I have a mistress, of course," Iredale said nonchalantly. The lift stopped with a shudder and they emerged on to a tiny landing with a single door opening out of it. "I know it isn't exactly palatial—it's really only an attic—but I'm here so seldom and for such short periods that there's no point in looking for anything better." He opened the door. "Go on in, folks."

Katharine looked curiously round the flat. There certainly wasn't much of it—a small bed-sitting room, a kitchen and a miniature bathroom, with the minimum of ancient, battered furniture. It was all rather cramped and angular and hot from the day's sun on the roof just above, but there was a fine view of the lights of London from the dormer window, and the place had unexploited potentialities. The sitting-room itself was littered with books, suitcases, sun helmets, ski sticks and a collection of curios from odd corners of the earth. There was a rack of tobacco pipes containing, it would seem, every known variety from corn-cob to hookah.

"It's more like a repository than a flat," she observed.

"I know," said Iredale, "but don't let that put you off. I promise you the coffee will be good."

Katharine ran a finger over the carving on a heavy wooden chest that stood just outside the kitchen door. "This is rather nice."

"Very fine, isn't it? I picked it up in Saigon."

She looked at the tip of her finger. "You should tell your mistress to dust, though."

Iredale smiled, and went into the kitchen to put the kettle on. Jessop had become very quiet and was stalking round the little room with his hands in his pockets. He seemed to have lost interest in the other two. His manner scared Katharine and she joined Iredale in the kitchen. "Bill. . ." she began again.

Before she could put her mounting fears into words the telephone rang shrilly. The strident bell was like an alarm and her nerves gave a convulsive leap. "I won't be a minute," said Iredale. "D'you mind getting the cups out—they're in the cupboard over there."

He went into the sitting-room, casting a quizzical glance at the sombre Jessop. "I bet they've discovered you've been playing truant, Ed."

Jessop said nothing, and Iredale bent over the phone. "This is Chancery 45321. Yes, Bill Iredale speaking . . . Oh, yes?" He had suddenly become wary, for it was Haines on the line. "Yes, I can hear you—go ahead." As he listened, his expression changed. Incredulity and horror froze his face. He gave one appalled look at Jessop. The knuckles that held the phone showed white, and the receiver felt moist against his cheek as he pressed it hard to keep the sound from the room. "Very well," he said at last. He saw that Jessop was making for the kitchen. "I must go now," he ended hurriedly, and threw the receiver back on its rest. Quickly and quietly he followed Jessop, fearful lest Katharine should come to harm.

She was at the sink, washing cups. When she saw. Iredale's strained, tense face she stood quite still, a mop poised in her hand. "Trouble?" she asked.

"Nothing much," said Iredale, making a supreme effort to sound unconcerned. He was watching Jessop out of the corner of his eye. "Rather bad news about someone I know, that's all."

"I'm sorry," said Katharine quietly. She went on with her cup-washing as though nothing had happened, but he saw that she knew.

"Now what about this coffee?" he said with feigned heartiness.

Jessop's mind was still on the telephone call. "Anyone I know?"

Iredale shook his head and wondered how long it would take Haines to arrive. Three or four minutes, perhaps. It should be possible to stall for that time. "It was my girl-friend, as a matter of fact."

"I didn't know you had one," said Jessop suspiciously.

Iredale put a hand on his thin shoulder. "What's it got to do with you anyway, you old busybody? Can't you see I'm trying to make Katharine jealous?"

"Was it the office?" Jessop persisted.

"It was not. I told you. Now why don't you go and take the weight off your feet, old man? Coffee won't be a minute."

Jessop's face had turned a blotchy grey. It had been a man's voice on the telephone, he knew. He felt certain the call had been about him. That suddenly concentrated manner of Iredale's, that quick glance across at him, had given everything away. Iredale was keeping something from him. Iredale's whole manner was peculiar. Peering at him, Jessop no longer saw the pleasant companion of the evening.

This was the man who had said he was crazy, the man who wanted to get rid of him by sending him to Malaya, the man who had inveigled him into coming to his flat. This was a trap. Jessop clutched the tin in his pocket. Well, he wouldn't stay in the trap.

"I think I'll be off," he muttered. "It's getting late."

"Oh, not yet," said Katharine. "The coffee's just ready."

Jessop gave a cunning smile. "I suppose you think I don't know what you're up to. You're wrong—I can see through you. I tell you, I'm getting out of here."

"Take it easy, Ed," said Iredale gently. There was a moment of dead silence in the room. The place felt horribly cut off. Iredale couldn't think what to do—he had never had to handle a homicidal lunatic before. Ought he to cajole and wheedle? Ought he to be firm? Ought he to seize Jessop and hold him until help came? The man's face was working; he looked as though he might lose control of himself at any moment. "Take it easy," Iredale said again, "there's a good fellow. Come and sit down. Nobody's going to hurt you."

"Nobody will have the chance," snarled Jessop, and turned to the door.

With a quick movement Iredale blocked the way. "You can't go, Ed, not now. You're not well. Stay here and we'll look after you."

"You bloody swine!" Jessop suddenly screamed. A stream of frightful obscenities burst from him. "You damned police spy! I've been watching you. You're all against me. You all want to kill me. You *fool,* Iredale. You can't kill me, but I can kill you. You're in my power. Everyone's in my power. I'll show you."

"No!" yelled Iredale, and leaped at the hand that held the tin. Jessop, twisting and contorting with maniac agility and strength, wriggled from his grasp and with a shout of triumph threw the tin into the wet sink, scattering its contents.

"God, it's the cyanide," cried Iredale, and grabbed Katharine. As he did so the kitchen door slammed behind Jessop and there was a sound of something heavy being dragged against it.

"Choke, you swine!" Jessop shouted. "Choke, both of you!" He gave a monstrous cackle and went on piling furniture against the door.

Chapter Thirty-Five

The police car raced up Chancery Lane and screeched to a standstill by the kerb. Four men tumbled out.

"Stay and watch the lift, constable." cried Haines to the uniformed policeman. He pounded up the stairs, with Ogilvie and Sergeant Miles just behind him. The pace was killing, but he kept going. Noises from above reverberated through the empty building. It sounded as though a dozen people must be rioting up there.

As they turned to take the last flight they could hear Jessop's voice. "I am the instrument of Providence," he was shouting, as though addressing a multitude. "All my enemies shall be swept away. The Augean stables shall be cleansed."

"Christ!" muttered Ogilvie. They reached the landing. There was a peal of maniacal laughter from the flat. Jessop was yelling and raving. Suddenly he began to sing "For I'm a jolly good fellow" in a high-pitched, unnatural voice.

Haines put his shoulder to the door. The racket stopped. He motioned to Miles and the two of them stepped back and flung their combined weight against the lock. It gave a little. They tried again, and the door burst open with a splintering crash.

The room looked as though a bomb had exploded in it. Battered and broken furniture had been piled up against the kitchen door. Jessop was sitting on top of it, giggling to himself. "They're dead," he said in a jubilant whisper, seeming not to notice the policemen, and giggled again.

The police advanced. From the inner room a voice suddenly called out, "Is that you, Inspector?"

"Yes, Mr. Iredale. Are you all right?"

"Yes, we're okay."

"Thank God for that."

Jessop gave a wild scream of rage as he realised that Katharine and Iredale were still alive and that these men had come for him. He struggled off the barricade and hurled himself at Ogilvie, biting and kicking like a child in a tantrum. It was a job to hold him, but in a few seconds he was overpowered.

"Take him downstairs," said Haines, wiping the sweat from his face. He set to work to dismantle the barricade. He could see now why Iredale had been unable to break out—a heavy chair was wedged firmly under the door handle. He worked it loose, moved the wooden chest and a divan, and pulled the door open.

"Thanks, Inspector." Iredale helped Katharine out and looked grimly round the shattered room. Jessop's frenzied cries were still faintly audible. "Where are they taking him?" he asked.

"Don't worry about him, Mr. Iredale—he'll be well looked after."

"Poor devil!" Iredale took a long breath. "My God, that was a darned near thing."

"It certainly was," said Haines. "I was afraid he'd use the cyanide."

"He tried to. Take a look in the sink."

Haines went into the kitchen. Under the tap there was a dirty mass of tobacco from which brown stains were spreading over the wet surface. He turned in astonishment. "What on earth . . .?"

"It's quite simple," said Katharine. She opened her handbag and took out a tobacco tin. "Here's the cyanide."

Haines looked inside and saw grey-white crystals. "I still don't see . . ."

"I switched the tins round," Katharine explained. "It was in the taxi on the way here—we were all three sitting close together and I happened to feel the tin in Jessop's pocket. I couldn't share Bill's faith in him—he wasn't *my* friend. So just as a precaution, I took it out and gave him the one from Bill's pocket instead."

"Well, I'm damned!" ejaculated Haines.

"And *I* thought you were being amorous," said Iredale.

Chapter Thirty-Six

Iredale slept little that night. The excitement of action, the interest of the story Haines had told them, relief that the suspense was over at last, pity for Jessop and warm, disturbing thoughts about Katharine, combined to keep him wakeful. The disturbing thoughts were still with him in the morning, and as soon as he decently could he rang her home number. He tried if several times, but failed to get any reply. It worried him a little, because he knew she was off duty that day.

At about eleven o'clock he strolled along to the office, hoping to pick up some news about her there. The place seemed unusually active for a holiday Saturday—the story of the night's events had evidently got around, and a lot of people had come in who weren't obliged to. One of the first he ran into was Lionel Cardew, looking a bit sheepish. Iredale impulsively gripped his hand. "So they let you out of the cooler? What was it like?"

Amusement flickered over Cardew's face. "I was comfortably accommodated—I've no complaints." The smile faded. "Shocking thing about Jessop, isn't it?"

Iredale nodded, and they walked along the corridor together. "By the way, Bill," said Cardew suddenly, "is your heart set on Malaya?"

"Not by any means," said Iredale in surprise. "Who said I was going there? As a matter of fact I rather wanted to stick around here for a few weeks. I've some unfinished business to attend to."

"Really?" Cardew seemed relieved. "Then I shall ask to go."

"Muscling in, eh? What's the trouble—claustrophobia?"

"Something like that. I thought I'd better ask you." Cardew nodded cheerfully and walked away with a light step.

Iredale gazed after him for a moment and then turned into the Reporters' Room. He looked at the duty list. Someone, he noticed, had scored Pringle's name through. As he had thought, Katharine was not down for duty.

Rogers, the skeleton staff, said "Hallo, Bill." He seemed unusually subdued. "I hear you had a busy night."

"Yes," said Iredale. "Wretched affair, isn't it?" He gazed disconsolately round the room. He didn't want to talk about Jessop, but he was at a loss what to do next.

"Looking for someone?" asked Rogers innocently.

"Not 'specially—why?"

"Well, she's touring the South Coast. She blew in about half an hour ago to collect a railway voucher—a special assignment. First stop, Bournemouth—the Grand Hotel. That'll be seven and six!"

"Thanks," said Iredale gratefully. He called in a loud voice, "Boy!" A youth appeared. "Bring me a timetable, will you?"

He began to fill his pipe, wondering if Katharine would think him a damned nuisance. She might have given him a ring, though, after all that had happened. He was looking up trains when the door opened and Jackson came in.

"Oh, hallo, Bill," he said warmly. "Well, it's all over, eh? How are you feeling?"

"Not so hot, as a matter of fact."

"I suppose not." Jackson gave a little cough. "What you need is work. I was wondering if you'd mind taking over the foreign desk to-morrow." He noticed the open timetable. "I don't want to upset any plans, of course, but we're in a bit of a spot, Cardew's got a long-standing engagement for tomorrow."

"Hell!" said Iredale. He tossed the timetable aside. "Oh, all right."

It didn't much matter, he reflected. Katharine obviously hadn't given him another thought, or she wouldn't have cleared off like that without a word. A job was a job, of course, but it wouldn't have taken her a moment to ring him . . .

He drifted disconsolately along to the Foreign Room and took up the bunch of newspapers that lay on Cardew's desk. There was a fat envelope beside them, addressed to himself. He opened it, and a new, very handsome tobacco pouch fell out. There was no other message.